DEDICATION

To Tristan and Nina, two characters who truly deserve a happily ever after, this is for you. Thanks for hanging out with this incurable romantic.

CONTENTS

ONE

Nina

Jordan waited for me at the end of the hallway, ready to head off to school. I was running late, so by the time I reached her, she was tapping her foot and giving me that raised eyebrow look she always did when she was well on her way to lashing out. I saw in her green eyes the anger simmering just below the surface this morning.

"I know this house is huge, but maybe you could remember I have an entire class of third graders and a principal who because of her lack of sex is literally the crankiest woman you'll ever meet. If Sister Fits Nice and Tight reams me out because poor old Jensen can't get me to school on time, you're going to see a whole new Jordan at dinner tonight."

"I'm sorry. I didn't mean to be late. I just got tied up with something," I said in my best "forgive me" voice.

Her face twisted into a scowl. "I bet if I checked your cell phone I'd see what was tying you up. You're still texting him every morning, aren't you?"

"And every night before I go to sleep in his bed as I stare at the painting I made just for him."

Jordan sighed, her shoulders sagging, and a frown settled into her beautiful features. "Oh, honey. It's been months since he answered you. He probably doesn't even have that phone anymore. I'm not saying he's not ever coming back or you shouldn't do that every day and night, but..."

Her words faded away as she stared at me with pity in her eyes. No matter. I didn't care if anyone believed what I believed. I knew in my heart he was receiving every text I sent. I didn't know why he didn't answer, but that didn't change the fact that I wanted him to know that I hadn't given up on us.

Picking up her bag, I handed it to her with a smile. "You're going to be late. Have a good day, and don't be too hard on those little darlings."

"You're not coming today?"

"No. I have a meeting with Daryl, so I can't head into the city today. Maybe tomorrow, though."

Grimacing, she spun on her heels and headed toward the front door. "Daryl? That guy who looks like a mountain man? I'll take the uptight nun and eight year olds, thank you."

"Have a good day, Jordan. What do you say to pizza tonight?"

She stopped and turned to face me. "Are you sure you can handle that?"

"You mean sauce and cheese on crust?" I joked, knowing she saw right through my facade.

"I'm serious, Nina. The last time we tried Tony's you were bummed for days."

"I'll be okay. I've been craving flat birch beer."

Jordan shook her head. "You rich people have weird tastes. I'm off to mold young minds. Later, gator."

I yelled after her, "After while, crocodile!"

As she opened the door, she looked back at me and smirked. "So uncool."

When I knew I was safely alone, I slipped my phone out of my pocket and scrolled through my messages to the one I'd sent Tristan just minutes earlier. My breath caught in my chest as I read the words and prayed for some kind of response.

Good morning. I dreamed about you last night. I miss you so much. Every night I convince myself that you're finally going to come back to me, but every morning I wake up alone. I love you. I haven't given up on us, Tristan.

I hadn't given up, even if Daryl had talked me out of going to look for him. I was sure he knew where Tristan was, but if he did, he wouldn't tell me. He was as close as I could get to the man I loved, though, so when he called and said he wanted to meet, I always agreed, every time hoping that day would be the one when he'd finally tell me what happened to Tristan and when he was coming home.

Scrolling through months of texts, I stood there in the entryway reading what remained of our relationship. Text after text showed the slow progression of my feelings over time from sadness to anger to acceptance. I'd lived through the loss of him from my life in those messages straight from my heart. Some days they'd been the only way I could get out of bed and face the world. Expressions of desperation and hopelessness, they gave me something no person or thing that remained in my life could.

They were a lifeline each morning and night connecting me to Tristan.

Jordan didn't understand why I continued to bother since he'd stopped answering my messages the day after he left. Some days I didn't understand either, but I couldn't stop myself. There was some small relief from my heartache in tapping out my feelings into words, regardless of where they went once I clicked Send.

Some nights I scrolled through every message, terrified that my phone had deleted some of the earlier ones. A sort of mania took over, and I'd have to count each one, reading every single text to make sure they all still existed, as if losing even one meant losing a part of him.

Over the months, I'd gotten better at pretending for everyone around me so they thought I was handling it all pretty well. Jordan knew more than the others, but even she had no idea how much I missed Tristan. Looking down at my phone, I read my newest message to him.

If you see these, you need to know that today's a hard day for me. It's never easy, but today's really hard. I miss you so much.

Send.

I stuffed the phone back into my jeans pocket because if I didn't, I'd stand there texting Tristan all day until Jordan got home. Daryl was scheduled to get there in just minutes, so at least I wouldn't have a lot of time to sit and think. That was the worst. It's why I went into the city most days. At least when I was thinking surrounded by millions of people I didn't feel so alone. The city did that for us lonely folks.

But even visiting art museums couldn't improve my spirits. Lately, I usually ended up at The Cloisters staring at images of death in the Middle Ages, and even in my funk I knew that wasn't a good sign.

A knock at the door told me Daryl was early, so I let him in and we sat in the same room we'd been in when he told me Tristan was gone and he didn't know when he'd return. It was like our ritual. Each time I'd sit on the couch where I'd sat that first night with Tristan, and Daryl would sit opposite me and begin talking about things I pretended to understand. Even now, months later, I had no clear idea about why Karl needed to have my father's notes, and I didn't think Daryl knew either, although he seemed to feel he understood better than I did.

I didn't care about any of that. Karl, my father's notes, and whatever Tristan's father had done meant nothing to me. I just wanted Tristan home and the two of us to live happily ever after. Or at least as much as that was possible with us.

Daryl was looking particularly mountain mannish, as if he'd decided trimming his rusty colored beard wasn't required as long as he wore a dress shirt. He had that chest hair peeking out look that I found gross, and his whole appearance made paying attention to him difficult, especially today.

"How are you doing out here? Any problems? Any security issues?" he asked in his best dad voice.

"West and Varo would have told you if there were any. I don't think they keep much to themselves when it comes to their job."

"True. Those boys do take their job seriously. I'm thinking Tristan must have found them at a military school or something. They're good for what we need them to be, though. I was talking more about Karl or anyone from the Stone Worldwide Board. Have they tried to contact you at all?"

I shook my head and frowned at even the mention of them. "No. Why would they contact me?"

"Because they likely think you know where he is."

"Well, as you well know, I don't, even though I think you do," I said in a voice that reflected my anger and frustration at the whole situation.

Daryl stared at me, and I waited for him to say either he knew or he didn't, but instead he simply continued his train of thought. "If Karl shows up here..."

I cut him off mid-sentence. "I know. Get West and Varo up here lickity split and have them rough him up for me."

"No. Nina, I need you to take this seriously."

"Roughing up Karl sounds pretty serious to me, Daryl."

"Nina, I'm responsible for making sure you're safe. I'm just trying to do my job here."

"Does your job include telling me where Tristan is?" I asked sharply, making the conversation come to a dead stop.

Daryl's expression lacked any emotion at all, and he stared at me, finally answering, "No, it doesn't."

Even his faded brown eyes gave no indication whether he knew where Tristan was or not, so as usual, I gave up and forced a smile. "Fine. What else do we have to talk about?"

"The Karl business is a real concern, Nina. He's gotten the Board to take over Stone Worldwide, but as long as Tristan is somewhere in this world, he can't truly take control of the company."

"I would think if he intended to pump me for information, he would have done it before. It's been four months, Daryl. Karl and the Board think he's never coming back."

My voice caught as I spoke those words. Never coming back. A knot twisted in my stomach as the words echoed in my head. Never coming back.

"We have to be careful," Daryl continued, likely not noticing that I didn't want to talk about this anymore. "Karl is going to be a danger as long as Tristan's gone."

I couldn't do this today. Jumping up from the couch, I threw my hands up. "Then maybe he shouldn't be gone! Maybe he should be here handling things instead of leaving everything up to me!"

Daryl stared up at me, his eyes wide for a moment until his expression calmed once again. I knew this whole situation wasn't his fault, and it wasn't right for me to shoot the messenger. It's just that it all was too much sometimes, and this morning I was really feeling down. I sat again, feeling guilty for my outburst. It wasn't even noon yet and I was exhausted.

"I'm sorry. I know you're just doing your job, Daryl."

"No problem. Everybody has to let off a little steam every so often. I understand."

"Just tell me what you need me to do and I'll do it," I said, resigned to the fact that today was yet another day that I wouldn't hear the words I so desperately wanted him to say.

"I need you to just stay strong. I can't tell you when he's coming back, but he will. You just have to believe."

Nodding, I plastered a smile on my face. "Got it. Believe. I'm on it."

"I also need you to make sure West and Varo know your every move."

I opened my mouth to protest, but he stopped me. "I know you don't like it, but this is the way Tristan wants it. Those two are just doing their jobs too, so how about you give them a break?"

"Got it. Give the big guys a break."

I wanted to scream that I wanted a break, but something about the way Daryl explained things made me feel like an ass for complaining. I lived a life most people would give their right arm for. I had a beautiful home, a cook who made my meals, a driver to take me wherever my heart desired, and bodyguards to ensure my safety. Tristan had made sure my bank account had swelled to a sum more than I could spend in ten years.

There wasn't a thing I couldn't buy. What on Earth did I have to complain about?

Tristan may have felt some bond with Daryl, but to me he was merely the bearer of bad tidings. Just once I wished he would show up with a smile on his hairy face and tell me that all this was over and Tristan was coming home.

Daryl took out his small notebook from his jacket and began to flip through the pages searching for some detail he believed I needed to know. I craned my neck in an effort to see what he'd written, but I couldn't read his handwriting upside down. He licked the pad of his thumb and flipped up one last page before he scanned what he'd written and nodded.

Raising his gaze to look at me, he said in a serious voice, "I knew I had one more thing to talk to you about. You're going to have to hire a gardener or caretaker for the grounds now that the weather is getting better."

"This is what you searched for in your little notebook? A gardener? I can't just have West or Varo do it?" Actually, since West was always so abrupt with me, I liked the idea of him stuck on a riding mower for hours a few times a month, but something told me that Jordan would be all about seeing Varo shirtless and weed whacking. She'd tried in vain to get his attention for weeks since she realized the gorgeous man she'd seen at the bar that night months ago lived just yards away from her.

Furrowing his brow, Daryl groaned. "No. They guard you. They don't prune hedges."

Daryl was no fun at all. "Fine. Then I'll get a gardener."

Finished with our meeting, he stood and looked down at me to ask the question he always asked right before he left. "Is there anything you need?"

I took a deep breath in and slowly let it out, letting my shoulders sag. Looking up at him, I said, "Please tell me if you've talked to him. Please."

His face was expressionless but finally he nodded. "I have. He asked about you, and I told him you were holding up."

"Is he okay? Is he hurt?"

A shadow crossed Daryl's face, and I knew his next words would be a lie. "He's fine."

Just the way his voice dropped when he said the word "fine" told me Tristan was anything but that. Fear raced through me at the thought of what condition he was actually in. My heart pounding against my chest, I asked, "Is he hurt? Tell me, please."

"Don't worry. If he's hurting, it's only because he isn't here with you."

Daryl moved to walk away, and I grabbed his arm to stop him. "Would you tell him something for me?"

"Sure."

"Tell him I'll be waiting right here."

I let go of Daryl's arm and he walked away without saying another word. I sat there for a long time thinking about the night Tristan and I had spent together after getting to know each other right there on that couch. God, that seemed like so long ago, even though it wasn't even a year that had passed. So much had changed between then and now.

"Nina, are you ready to go?" Jordan asked as she peeked her head into my room.

I swiped the lip gloss across my bottom lip and threw the case in my bag. One last check of my makeup and I was ready. "Pizza Heaven, here we come!"

Jensen was waiting for us, along with my two giant shadows who were never far behind. The five of us stood in the driveway in front of the garage, an awkward silence hanging around us as we eyed one another with curiosity like usual. Even though I lived with these people, for all intents and purposes, they were barely more than strangers to me, people I knew more by the way they dressed than their personalities. Jensen stood stiffly in his usual dark suit, while West and Varo looked more comfortable in jeans and button down shirts, as they always did. Leaning in next to me, Jordan whispered, "Tony's might be pizza heaven, but I think Varo would be the kind of heaven I want."

I looked at West and Varo, then turned to Jensen. "We're going for pizza. Do you guys want to join us? You're more than welcome."

Out of the corner of my eye, I saw Jordan's eyes grow wide. Maybe I should have told her about my new idea of being nice to my constant companions. It wasn't their fault that Tristan wasn't back yet, so it wasn't right that I took out my unhappiness on them. My change of heart, however, seemed to surprise them as much as it did Jordan, and while Jensen politely begged off, I thought I saw West's eyes light up at the mention of pizza. Varo, as always, stood silently with a smoldering glare that I was convinced was the way his eyes naturally looked.

When neither of them spoke, I shrugged and asked, "Any takers? You guys have to eat, don't you?"

"And we're a pretty good time," Jordan chimed in. "It would be nice to see you guys loosen up for once."

West appeared to rethink his earlier excitement at hearing we were having pizza and said in a low voice, "We're fine. We'll be nearby if you need us."

"Okay. If you change your mind, you know where we are."

Everyone looked around at each other at my statement of the obvious. Jordan chuckled nervously next to me, thankfully breaking the tension for a moment, and we all left for Tony's Pizza Heaven like some sad entourage.

I was glad to see that the waitress who'd been working the night Tristan asked me to marry him wasn't there. I wasn't up for answering questions about him tonight. A short, older woman took our order, and as I sat silently remembering how much this tiny, out-of-the-way restaurant meant to me, Jordan told me about her boss's mini-lecture she gave her for being three minutes late that morning.

Sheepishly, I apologized. "I'm sorry. If it makes you feel better, I had a pretty rotten day."

"Yes. Yes, that makes me feel much better." She rolled her eyes. "Now that I know you think I'm some kind of harpy, why don't you tell me why your day sucked?"

"Same old, same old. I'd rather hear about your class."

"And I'd rather talk about you wearing your engagement ring again. I'm happy to see that, but I'm wondering why now? Was there some news from Grizzly Adams today?"

Jordan's snarkiness always brought out a smile in me. Looking down at the diamond ring on my left hand, I shook my head. "No, no news. I just thought it was right."

She raised her hand to cover her eyes. "It's giving off a glare that's blinding. That man of yours sure does know how to give a gift."

I spread my fingers and moved my hand back and forth. "He does."

"I don't think my eyes can take what he'll be getting you after his little absence."

Now it was my turn to roll my eyes. "Funny. Just drink your flat soda."

"I want you to know that I'm going to miss us sharing a place again, Nina. It was like old times, except in a place ten times the size. With a pool. And a kitchen you could fit a small house in."

"You're just going to miss being so close to my hot bodyguard. Anyway, it's not like you're moving any time soon. Daryl didn't have any news about Tristan or if he'd be coming back," I admitted sadly.

Jordan reached over and covered my hand with hers. "When, honey. When."

Nodding, I smiled at her effort to cheer me up. "I know. When. When he's coming back."

"And as for Varo, I'm not going to deny it. I'll be all over him like white on rice the moment he gives me the chance."

After so much pizza my pants didn't feel like they fit right anymore, we found Jensen waiting outside for us and got in the car for our ride home. West and Varo didn't seem to be anywhere in sight, much to Jordan's disappointment, but I knew that meant nothing. As big as they were, they seemed to know how to blend in so they weren't seen. All the better. I rarely had anything to say to them, and even though I'd pretended all through dinner that Tony's didn't make me sad, the fact was that Jordan had been right.

I still wasn't ready to deal with all the memories.

Climbing into bed, I closed my eyes to remember when Tristan and I were together, happy and in love.

The warm summer air drifted in through the window, lightly billowing the deep green sheers and carrying the sweet scent of honeysuckle across the room to where we sat. Still dressed in his suit and tie, Tristan leaned against the back of the couch and closed his eyes.

I loved these moments together, just the two of us sitting quietly at the end of the day, not saying a thing to ruin the peaceful silence we shared. For me, this was a change. All my life, I'd filled in the gaps with words rather than experience an awkward silence, but with Tristan, I'd learned to appreciate that silence. Sliding my finger down his red silk tie, I watched a sly smile slowly spread across his lips.

"Did I ever tell you how much I love this after a long day?"

He opened his eyes, and I saw how much these moments meant to him. "Yes, but not yet today," I teased.

Tristan sighed and reached out to touch my hand. "All day I look forward to these moments. No more people wanting me for a thousand reasons. No more caring about hotels and the bottom line of the other Stone Worldwide businesses. Just quiet and you."

Even though we hadn't said the words "I love you" yet to each other, it was obvious in every other word and every action. We didn't need to say that to know we loved one another. It was the first time in my life that I truly knew how a man felt about me.

I rested my head on his chest and listened to the steady rhythm of his heartbeat next to my cheek. That steadiness made me feel secure like never before in my life. For all the strangeness that had been a part of our meeting, we'd settled into a sweet space that gave me a sense of stability I'd never known I wanted but now never wanted to be without.

Slowly, his fingers trailed up and down my back. "Tell me about your day," he whispered above me.

"You don't want to hear about my boring day full of art."

I knew how he felt about the artwork I chose for the suites and penthouses. He pretended to be interested, but the man was no art lover. That's what I was in his life for.

"I'd listen just to hear you speak."

Lifting my head, I looked up at him and saw that sexy look in his eyes. "Is that what you really want?" I teased.

"Want to know what I really want?"

I loved this Tristan, the playful, gentle soul who could be so open and sweet and who so infrequently showed himself. Charmed, I would have done anything he asked. He had that effect on me.

"I can guess," I said with a wink. "I thought you were tired, but I like the way you think."

He eased me off him, and standing up, held his hand out to me. "Come."

I joined him and expected to be led to the bedroom we now shared, but instead he smiled and whispered, "Don't move."

Walking over to the opposite side of the room, he dimmed the lights until the room glowed a soft amber color. I watched him do something in the corner before he returned and pulled me close. Kissing the top of my head, he whispered, "May I have this dance?"

I looked around and waited for music, but none came. "Tristan, what are we dancing to?"

"Give it a second."

Very slowly, he began swaying back and forth as he held me to him. At least ten seconds went by and then I heard the first sad notes of a song I hadn't heard in ages. I remembered it instantly.

Nothing Compares 2U by Sinead O'Connor.

While we danced there in the sitting room where we'd first kissed, Tristan whispered the words of the song to me, nearly breaking my heart. He sounded so sad. The song ended and another one I'd never heard began as we continued to slowly sway to the music. Quietly, he said, "When I was a little boy, I heard that song every day. My mother loved it and played it over and over."

Looking up at him, I said, "I never took you for a Sinead O'Connor fan. It's a pretty song, but not one I'd think of for you."

He smiled and shook his head. "I've never heard another song by her. All I know is that song."

"You know all the words."

"It's hard not to after hearing it hundreds of times."

We fell silent for a few moments as we held each other, and I listened to the song playing. "Do you know the words to this one?" I asked him while we danced.

He seemed lost in memory as he looked off in the distance, squeezing me tightly to him. "No. Just that first one."

"Is everything okay, Tristan? You seem a million miles away."

My question was met with a smile, and he looked down at me. "Just thinking. I never did understand why she listened to that song so often. Taylor hated it and would run out of the room every time she put it on. She'd just smile and begin singing the words."

I wanted to ask about his mother. Her beautiful face had stayed in my mind since that first time I'd seen her in their family portrait, but the way Tristan's mouth always turned down slightly whenever his family was mentioned stopped me every time.

"I think it's nice that it reminds you of her."

Tristan stopped dancing and kissed me softly on the lips. "It doesn't anymore. I heard it this afternoon in a store and realized it reminded me of you."

"Me? But isn't the song about how she feels after losing the one she loved?" I asked as a tiny lick of fear took hold of my heart. Was he breaking up with me?

He was silent for so long that I was sure the next words out of his mouth would be to tell me it was over. Bracing myself for the news, I held on to his forearms and waited, each second ticking by making my heart hurt.

I watched as his expression changed to one so serious that my breath caught in my throat, and then he said in a low voice, "No. It reminds me of you because that's how I'd feel if I lost you. Nothing and no one compares to you, Nina."

When he said things like that, my insides felt like molten lava. Never before had any man made me feel so wanted, so desired. His mouth covered mine in a kiss so deep and full of need that my legs buckled. Tristan caught me by the waist and pulled me hard against him, his stiff cock pressing against my body.

"See what you do to me? All the way home all I could think about was relaxing with you and now look. Obviously, my body knows something my brain doesn't."

"I did that, huh?" I asked with a grin as I ran my hand over the front of his suit pants, my body reacting to his excitement.

Leaning over, he nipped my earlobe and whispered, "Yeah, you did that. Turnabout's fair play too."

He lifted the little cotton skirt I wore and cupped my ass. Slipping his finger under my panties, he ran his fingertip up my already wet pussy, just grazing my throbbing clit. So skilled at knowing exactly how to tease me, he lingered there for just a moment before he moved away, making my body ache for his touch.

"Tristan, don't make me wait," I said with a moan as he stepped away from me to unknot his tie and slip it from around his neck.

"Don't move," he commanded, and I stood still watching him remove his black suit coat and begin to unbutton his white dress shirt.

I reached out to help him with the buttons, and he took another step back from me. "I told you not to move, Nina."

Filling my gaze with the sight of his perfectly sculpted body, I watched as he finished with the buttons and slid out of his shirt. "Why won't you let me help?" I asked, eager to feel his skin under my touch.

A look of unhappiness crossed his features for just a moment, like he didn't enjoy me wanting him so much, but before I could ask if anything was wrong, his expression changed and he was that same incredibly sexy Tristan I couldn't get enough of. He extended his hand, and I moved toward him, timidly touching the buckle of his belt as I stared up into his deep brown eyes.

"I so much want you to be happy, Nina," he said in a low voice as I began to undo his belt and pants, his eyes searching for an answer to some unspoken question or doubt he had about us. Did he think I wasn't happy?

His zipper slid open and all that stood between my hand and his cock was the cotton of his boxer briefs. Running my finger over the flat planes of his abdomen, I skimmed the tip of his cock. "I am happy, Tristan. Why wouldn't I be?"

He left my question unanswered and tugged my skirt over my hips, along with my panties as I stroked him from base to tip. Lifting my T-shirt up over my head, he moaned my name, telling me how much he wanted me.

I hurried out of my bra and followed him to the sofa, straddling him as he pulled me down on top of him. With one long thrust, he slid into me until there was nothing separating us. He held me still so he remained deep inside me, pushing on my hips as he kissed me hard. I wanted to move, to ride him until I came so hard my thighs shook, but I couldn't budge. I didn't think I could want him more, but somehow not being able to feel him moving in and out of my body made me almost desperate for him.

"Tristan, don't make me beg," I whispered into his ear. "You're driving me crazy."

"So impatient. If I move my hands, are you going to move?"

I looked into those eyes and saw he wanted me as much as I wanted him. I just couldn't understand why he didn't want to admit it then. "I'm going to ride your cock like it's never been ridden and fuck you like I know you want."

With anyone else, I would've been embarrassed to say those words, but with Tristan, I felt nothing but the desire to make him happy. Maybe that was why he always seemed to be so interested in my happiness—because he wanted to be happy too. I wanted to be the woman who gave him that.

Silently, he stared up at me and moved his hands from my hips, giving me the freedom to do just as I promised. With every tilt of my hips and every thrust of his cock, we raced toward that happiness we gave one another. His hands guided my movement, and mine clutched his broad shoulders until my body exploded into a million pieces, each one sublimely happy and fulfilled. Moments later, he plunged into me one last time and came almost violently, as if some demon inside of him released its control over him to me.

Smoothing the tiny beads of sweat from his forehead, I smiled down into that gorgeous face now so placid as he stared up at me. I loved him, even if I had never said the words, and I knew he loved me. We shared a need for each other that went far beyond what our bodies craved, and I cherished that vulnerable part deep inside him that he showed me in moments like this.

The memory of that night left me longing to hold him and tell him I missed him. Nothing compared to him for me. He was everything to me, and I was lost without him.

TWO

TRISTAN

Mid-afternoon was the hardest. I could deal with early morning. I felt like shit the moment I opened my eyes, but I could handle it. Nina's texts after I'd been up for hours doing nothing but thinking—that killed me. Every day I had to talk myself out of calling her and hearing her sweet voice tell me she missed me. I knew I shouldn't, but that didn't mean I didn't want to.

I scrolled through months of texts, feeling worse with each passing one. Telling myself what I was doing was for her benefit did little to make me feel like a hero in this. Four months had gone by, and other than feeling like I wanted to die most days because of what I was putting Nina through, I was no closer to finding out what Karl believed was in Joseph Edwards' notebook. I'd read it from cover to cover, dozens of times reliving the horror of what my father and Taylor had done, but still I couldn't find the slightest detail to explain why my possessing those notes meant anything to Karl or the Board.

Each day I spent hours emotionally crucifying myself, only to hear my phone vibrate in front of me with Nina's good morning text that never failed to rip my heart out. I imagined her waking up in our bed alone, all curled up like she always was in the morning, her hair all tousled and that sleepy look on her face.

Fucking hell! How long was I going to have to pay for what my father and brother did?

The first few months I barely remembered. Between the coke and the alcohol, I'd succeeded in losing days at a time, intent on finding some way of blunting my unhappiness. Easier than facing reality, all the self-abuse ended up achieving was making me feel worse.

Hidden in this secret place no one but Daryl knew about, I was more dead than alive, except for those moments when Nina's messages jolted me out of my own personal hell to the one I shared with her. I had all the money I could want in this world, but it was meaningless without her. I wanted for nothing but for the one thing my life with her had given me.

Love. With Nina, I finally understood what it meant to love and be loved. We'd endured her accident and even her learning the truth this time. I'd known by the end of that first day away that she'd forgive me, which made having to stay here even harder. Every ounce of my being wanted to return to her, but I had to find out what Karl was looking for first.

If you see these, you need to know that today's a hard day for me. It's never easy, but today's really hard. I miss you so much.

I wanted to text back and tell her I missed her too. How I would have given anything to hear her ask one of her questions, even the ones that put me on the spot and I didn't want to answer. How just the thought of sharing a pitcher of semi-flat birch beer and a tray of pizza at our favorite restaurant made me more homesick than I'd ever been in my life.

But I couldn't. I didn't want to risk putting her in danger any more than I already had.

Two hours later, my phone vibrated across the tabletop again, and I looked down to see not a message from Nina but one from Daryl. He only texted after he'd seen her or when he had something important about Karl to tell me, so I read his message with a knot forming in the pit of my stomach.

Coming to see you. We need to talk. See you tomorrow afternoon.

I looked around at the mess of my rooms in this place I'd visited first as a child with my mother. The old hotel she'd fallen in love with was now a building under construction, except for this part I'd taken over. Dirty clothes hung over the backs of chairs, unwashed dishes sat on the table and piled high in the kitchen sink, and newspapers lay strewn across the couch I sat on and the floor next to me. Too fucking bad if Daryl had a problem with the way things looked. He'd complained the last time he'd come to see me, not that I cared then either. I didn't need him to act like a parent. I needed him to act like a fucking detective and find out what I couldn't so I could get home to the woman I loved.

A knock at the door nearly fifteen hours later had me face to face with Daryl. Looking exactly like someone who'd flown business class for over half a day, he nearly fell into the recliner across from the couch.

"Remind me again why your damn plane couldn't fly me here?"

"Karl would know where I was if he found out the company jet was flown somewhere."

"I swear I'm going to end up killing that bastard myself after my return flight," Daryl groaned as he arched his back in pain. "Do you have any idea how terrible business class is from New York to Bucharest? Women in labor for days feel better than I do right now. Any chance you know a chiropractor here?"

"Are you here just to complain? You're supposed to be my detective, so please tell me you have something instead of whining about a bad flight."

"And you think I sound cranky? Is this what you get like when you're removed from power?"

I wasn't in the mood for Daryl's bullshit nonsense. It hadn't taken long for Karl and his friends on the Board to move on my position in my absence. I was still technically the CEO, but not for long. Every day I was forced to stay away was more justification for them to officially remove me and then replace me, likely with Karl or one of his handpicked lackeys.

"Just get to why you're here."

"Why aren't you staying at that five star hotel I read about on the plane? The Ambassador or something. I get why you aren't staying at one of your hotels, but why continue living here in this house? I mean, you can still afford it, so why aren't you living in style like usual?"

Looking around at the old building my mother had fallen in love with nearly twenty years ago, I said, "I like this place." Turning my attention back to him, I continued, "Enough with your bitching. Why are you here?"

"Your lady isn't holding up very well."

Leaning forward, I studied his face for any sign of what was going on with Nina. "What's wrong? Is Nina okay?"

"Physically, she's fine. The boys tell me she visits museums a lot. Pretty high brow stuff as far as they're concerned, but she's getting out. I think this whole thing is starting to take its toll on her, though. I'm wondering if you should consider another way of keeping her safe."

"I don't see any other way, Daryl. As long as Karl thinks what I have is a danger to him, I can't be around her. I don't know what he's concerned about. I'd be endangering her for nothing."

"You haven't figured out anything? It's been four months, Tristan. I know you spent the first couple out of your mind in more ways than one, but you've got nothing?"

Shaking my head, I admitted the sad truth. "Nothing. I've been through those notes over and over, and even those pages that are about other investigations. I've got nothing."

"Then maybe it's time to admit what he's afraid of isn't in that notebook. I think you're on the right track, though. Your assistant told me that your penthouse was ransacked twice in the past two months. Michelle said the police think it was an employee each time, but I don't think we're talking about some disgruntled maid or bellboy. Karl wants something he believes you have, so the penthouse would be a logical place to look for it, especially since he can't get at your house."

"West and Varo are still guarding Nina?"

"Of course. And the security system you installed is working fine. No one gets onto the property without them knowing."

"He's going to want to get into the house when he finally figures out that's the only place he hasn't been able to check."

Daryl nodded. "Have any other homes I'm not aware of?"

Chuckling, I shook my head. "No. I only kept the penthouse when I took over as CEO. Well, that's not entirely true. My father kept a place in LA, but I never go there. The house has been empty for years."

"Hmmm. I'll check into whether it's been broken into lately. Any chance what he's looking for is there?"

"I have no fucking idea what he's looking for, Daryl. If I did..." I ended my thought because I honestly couldn't say what I'd do if I had what Karl so desperately wanted. Maybe I wouldn't give it to him. If it just had to do with the terrible things my father and Taylor did to the Cashens and Nina's father, then he could have whatever it was. But was there something more my father had done that I didn't know about?

"I have to ask the question, Tristan. How far are you planning to go with this? Karl's a man who seems to have something important to hide. If we find out what it is, are you going to let it go or is this going to be some kind of crusade for you?"

Daryl's question wasn't an easy one. Karl had always been a dick to me since the day I took over Stone Worldwide, but I'd thought it was just the way he was. Now I had the sneaking suspicion it was something much more. Even worse, if he had his way, he'd have made sure Nina was dead by now. For that, I'd be willing to make it my personal crusade to make Karl's life a living hell.

"It depends on what he's trying to keep hidden. Karl's happiness isn't my concern. If he suffers, I won't be unhappy about that."

The conversation seemed to come to an abrupt halt with my thinly veiled threat, and we sat in silence as I fantasized about Karl Dreger suffering at my hands. My father's closest friend, he'd been in my life from the day I was born. I'd seen him around the table on holidays, a younger, more handsome man then making my mother smile with his jokes and always eager to take my father away immediately after he'd finished eating for private meetings in his study. Taylor had begun joining them in his last year of college, but I'd never been invited into their inner sanctum on holidays or any other time.

I remembered the first time I stood in my office looking at the space where I was supposed to now lead an international business I'd never given a damn about. As I studied my father's degree from Wharton School of Business and commendations from business associations worldwide that still hung on the walls, I felt small and inadequate. I'd never finished college, much less earned an M.B.A. like my father and Taylor.

I saw in Karl's face all I lacked as he stood leaning against the doorframe watching me. The son who'd never amounted to anything. The one who'd never been a part of their meetings. I'd eventually shown him I was more than that, but from the first moment, he'd been an enemy I always knew I'd have to keep an eye on.

"Well, maybe it's time for you to leave Shangri-la here and get back in the game," Daryl said as he looked around at the mess of my home away from home. "We need to find what Karl wants before he does."

"I'm not sure I want to join the world again." I wasn't. I wanted to be with Nina again more than anything else in the world, but the rest of it? I didn't give a damn about that.

"Yeah, well I guess I can see how wallowing in your own self-pity is quite the life, but you don't have the luxury of doing that. We need to get to the bottom of what Karl is looking for. The sooner we solve this, the sooner you and your lady are back together, and that means we need to get you back to the States."

I knew he was right, but I'd let myself enjoy the life of nothingness I'd created for so long that I wasn't sure I could do what I had to for Nina and me.

"And there's something else. It'd probably be better for Nina if it seemed like you weren't coming back for the time being. I'm thinking some kind of subterfuge would be best. You haven't been gone long enough to be declared dead, but I think a good show of her moving on might throw Karl off the scent for at least a little while, which might give us enough time to find out what the hell is going on."

"Declare me dead? What the fuck are you talking about, Daryl? I don't want Nina to think I'm never coming back. This is only temporary."

"Well, her looking like she's moving on will only be temporary too. We'll let the press see her with someone new and..."

Daryl stopped before he completed his thought and raised his hands to calm me as I leaned toward him, my face twisting as I thought about the words that would next come out of his mouth. The idea of someone new in Nina's life made me want to kill someone with my bare hands. Even the mention of it was more than I could deal with.

"I know you might not want to think about it, but it would help if she seemed to be starting a new life. It could take the focus off her. I'm worried it's only a matter of time before Karl turns his eye toward her. If she looks like she believes you're not coming back, he might leave her alone."

"You just said she wasn't holding up well. Now you want her to act like she's moving on?"

"Well, yeah. Just a few sightings of her with a new man would probably be enough."

Jesus Christ. Every word out of Daryl's mouth was like a punch to the heart. Even though I was more certain than I'd ever been in my life that I didn't want to hear the answer to my next question, I asked anyway. "Since you've obviously given this some thought, who's she moving on with?"

He got a sheepish look on his face, telling me he had thought about this. Quietly, as if saying the man's name in a normal voice might set me off, he said, "I think Varo could work."

Varo. Six foot four inches of brick shithouse Varo. Nina's bodyguard I hired and now lived just feet away from her while I remained here thousands of miles away Varo. If he had said West, I might have been able to handle it. At least I could believe Nina would never want him. But Varo wasn't as easily dismissed.

"No."

"Before you say no, hear me out. He's there already, so it wouldn't be much to just have him move into the house. Once or twice out for dinner for the press and I think that would do it."

"No."

Sitting back in his chair, he let out a frustrated sigh and made a clucking noise with his tongue. "You're not thinking clearly, Tristan. How do you plan to keep her safe? We've been lucky so far, but it's only a matter of time before Karl begins to focus on her. With Varo, we know we can trust him, he can keep her safe, and it could buy us some time to do our own research into what Karl wants."

"She'll never go for it," I mumbled, trying to convince myself as much as convince Daryl.

"She'll go for it if I tell her you need her to. Unless you have a better plan in mind, I say we do it."

I sat there unable to think of anything to replace Daryl's stupid idea. My brain was filled with the thought of Nina and Varo. Even their pretending to be a couple made my gut churn with jealousy.

"Only if we set some ground rules. He doesn't touch her, he remains in the carriage house, and they only pose for the press twice. No more."

Daryl shook his head. "That won't work. He has to move into the house with her if the deception is to be believable. He can stay in another room, but he has to be in the house."

I knew he was right. Karl would never believe Nina had moved on if her new supposed boyfriend still lived in the carriage house with West. Somehow the press would find out, and then the whole thing would be blown. It's just the idea of Varo living in my house, taking my place, acting like the man in her life now nearly drove me out of my mind.

"Tristan, don't you trust her? After all she's done to show you she's devoted to your life together, you can't believe she'll be loyal in this?"

My demons screamed "No!" inside me, threatening to take over my thoughts until I couldn't think straight. I'd never been the master of my jealous nature, and having another man living in my house filling my shoes when I should be there next to Nina wasn't something I was able to handle.

"It has nothing to do with that, Daryl. Can you imagine what it feels like to know that another man will be with the woman you love while you have to stay away from her side? As if it wasn't bad enough I can't go back to her, now I have to agree to being replaced?"

Standing, he looked down at me in sympathy and nodded. "I get it, but it's only for show and not for long. We just have to move fast to find out what there is at the heart of Karl's secrets so Nina's pretend relationship may only have to be those two dinner dates."

Relationship. Dates.

Fuck me.

"Fine. Tell her I think this is for the best," I bit out.

"Good, but that's probably not going to be enough. I think you're going to have to tell her. Oh, and no matter what she does—no matter how many times she calls you or texts you—I need you to keep your distance. This only works if she believes in this. Any sense of how much you hate this and she won't be able to do it."

"Fine, but how am I going to tell her?"

Daryl pointed to the notebook on the table. "Write her something. I'll take it to her."

I found a sheet of paper in an old desk and quickly wrote her a note telling her to pretend to be in love with someone else, my heart feeling like it was being squeezed in a vice the entire time. My notes to Nina always had been to show her how much she meant to me, and each word I wrote added to my betrayal of something I'd only done out of love before. Handing it to him, I silently prayed to God she wouldn't be able to do it. That we'd have to figure something else out that didn't involve her pretending to be another man's date, or worse, girlfriend. Something that didn't involve the woman I loved acting like I was dead.

"I'll be back. It's time you got the hell out of this place. We've got work to do." He headed toward the door as I began to spiral out of control and stopped as he opened it. "Hey, she wanted me to give you a message."

"What?" I asked, my heart pounding against my ribs.

"She said she'll be waiting. Don't worry, Tristan. Your life is waiting for you when you get back."

Daryl left me sitting alone with nothing but my demons to torment me. Each one in turn marched through my mind flying his fucked up flag and goading me to spin out of control until I was sure I couldn't go through with Daryl's plan. I couldn't go on knowing that Nina was with another man, even if it was only for show.

By the time night came, I'd drank enough scotch to drown my misery, but still I wasn't as numb as I needed to be to feel okay with what I had to make Nina do. I wanted to talk to her—I wanted to explain that this was the only way and I hated it more than I hated being away from her. It took everything in my power not to pick up my phone and call her just to hear her gentle voice tell me she missed me or even that she was furious with me for leaving. Anything would have been better than being alone.

I closed my eyes and thought back to the night I first met Nina. I'd barely recognize that man if I met him today. Surrounded by gorgeous, vapid women with little to offer other than their bodies, I'd walked into the Anderson Gallery oblivious to anything but my own desires, intent on finding Joseph Edwards' daughter and assuaging my guilt for my father's crimes. I'd scanned Nina's picture once or twice before leaving the penthouse and believed I knew what kind of person she was.

Simple. Nice. Not my type.

Not that any of that mattered. I wasn't looking for a girlfriend or fuckmate. I was looking to make myself feel better about being the son of the man who'd had her father killed. Maybe I could hand her some money or at least if I could somehow find a way to repay her for what she'd lost, I might have been able to sleep better at night.

The balls I had to think that my throwing money at her would ever be enough to make up for what she'd lost. Even now as I remembered the man I was then, I cringed at my fucking nerve.

"Tristan, what are we doing here? This gallery is filled with nobodies."

I ignored Kamara's comment along with her clinging hold on my bicep and scanned the room. A cluster of people stood oohing and ahhing over artwork that looked like shit, but what did I know? Art had never been my thing. I wasn't there to admire indecipherable pictures anyway.

The girls all grabbed glasses of champagne as the waitress passed by, emptying her tray. Traveling with six women in tow was a hassle on the best of nights, but having to deal with them drunk would likely hamper my efforts to meet Nina Edwards. I shot them all a nasty warning glance and saw they got the message loud and clear. Their job was to stand beside me, behave themselves, and look good, not cause me some bullshit hassle because they couldn't handle their alcohol.

They all chattered about whatever meant something to them as I continued to look for Nina. From behind a column on the far side of the room she peeked her head out as she straightened her waitress uniform. Long brown hair fell down over her shoulders, and she had a pretty look about her in person. I had to admit she looked even better up close than she had in her picture.

I had to play it cool, so I pretended to enjoy myself with the actresses, actually paying only the slightest bit of attention to them. Vanessa beamed up at me, happy to have her turn as the woman on my arm. Out of the corner of my eye, I saw Nina standing with a tray in her hands, waiting to serve the semi-wealthy and society wannabes who were right at home at Sheila Anderson's gallery. She took a step toward me and my entourage and stopped.

"Tristan, are you going to buy this picture?" Vanessa asked in her usual, cloying way. "I think it would look great hanging in one of your hotels."

I wasn't listening to her, though. I was too busy meeting Nina's gaze. She held my stare and didn't look away. She had a fearless vibe to her that impressed me. Standing there dressed like some cheap waitress, Nina looked too good for this place and her ridiculous costume. I wanted to know more about this person, but there was no way I could approach her with the gang surrounding me. I'd have to find another way.

There was a piece of art on the far wall, so I guided the actresses to that part of the room as Sheila Anderson busied herself with barking at Nina. After a few minutes of staring at another picture I didn't give a damn about, I led the girls to the car and instructed Jensen to take me to mine at the hotel and drop the women off wherever they wanted to go. They'd done their job for the night, and I had no further use for them.

A half-hour later I was parked behind the Anderson Gallery unsure of what the hell I was doing there but sure I wanted to meet Nina in person and not only to make amends for what had happened to her father. I hadn't planned on being interested in her. All I wanted to do was see if I could find a way to help her, but something in the way she held her head high as she did the dirty work dumped on her at the gallery impressed me.

I wanted to know more about this woman, and that was something pretty rare for me, so I stood there waiting in that alley next to the Dumpster hoping she'd be the person forced to take out the garbage and not one of the other two women serving drinks and cocktail wieners that night. When the door opened, I saw luck was on my side.

"Nice show, huh?" I asked, willing to lie if it got the ball rolling.

She spun around, obviously frightened, and I realized that a strange man standing in a dark alley waiting for a woman probably wasn't the best move. I was no rapist, but it still didn't look good. I remained cool, standing against the Jag with my arms folded, hoping to give off a non-attacking vibe. I didn't need to begin whatever this was with her screaming for the cops.

Regaining her cool, she answered, "Yeah, it was great. The artist is quite talented."

I didn't know her, but I knew bullshit when I heard it. Whether or not the artwork was as bad as I thought it was, she hadn't liked it. That was clear.

"It was shit and you know it. Nice outfit, though."

I don't know why I took the cheap shot at her clothes. It wasn't like they were anything anyone would willingly wear if they didn't have to. Sometimes I was a real asshole. Instantly, I felt shitty as a frown settled onto her mouth and she snapped at me. I deserved it and tried to fix the damage my stupid comment had already caused to the situation.

I couldn't help but smile at the memory of Nina putting me in my place within a minute of meeting me. She was strong even then, standing there alone with a strange man in an alley way and telling him to basically go fuck himself when he stepped out of line. Looking back, I guessed I should have been happy she even agreed to get into the car with me after my stupid comment.

She'd taken a chance on me that night and trusted me not to be some ax murderer. Now I had to trust her. Whether I liked it or not, I had to give up control of us and hope to God I didn't lose her to someone who could give her the one thing all my money couldn't buy.

A stable life.

THREE

Nina

For the second time in a week, Daryl wanted to speak to me. Just hearing his voice on my phone made my stomach flip with nerves. I still hadn't given up on the idea that one day he'd call and tell me that Tristan was finally coming home. So as I waited for Daryl to arrive, I busied myself with fantasies of Tristan's homecoming and the beginning of our life together as husband and wife. It seemed like we'd been fighting for that life for so long that it was hard to remember when we were just us—Tristan and Nina, happy and in love.

I heard a noise behind me and turned in anticipation to find Jordan standing in the dining room doorway. My disappointment was surely clear in my face, and I saw her react to it with pity. I hated the pity.

"Oh, I thought you might be Daryl," I weakly explained.

"I need to invest in some better makeup if people are beginning to confuse me with that guy," she joked.

I knew she was trying to keep my spirits up and appreciated the effort. "No, he called to let me know he needs to speak to me, so I thought it might be him when I heard footsteps."

Jordan laughed. "I better get back to my Pilates then. Want some company until he arrives?"

Nodding, I smiled at her joke. "Yeah."

Throwing her bag on the table, she sat down and reached out to give me the "sympathetic hand touch" she did when she thought I was sad or depressed. Not that she was wrong. I was feeling bad.

Giving my hand a gentle squeeze, she asked, "Anything I can do to cheer you up? Maybe the tragic story of how I've resorted to doing the most idiotic things to get Varo's attention might bring a real smile out of you."

I'd seen Jordan's attempts to get Varo to notice her and wondered why he never seemed to even give her a second glance. She was knockout pretty with beautiful green eyes and long blond hair. She had a much better body than I'd ever had, probably since she actually exercised regularly and took care of herself. On top of all the outside goodness, she was funny and vivacious. What was there not to like?

Just the day before I'd watched from the sitting room window as she took her daily stroll around the grounds and intentional turn toward the carriage house to try to speak to him. He just stood there leaning against the car, barely smiling in response to whatever she was saying. I knew Jordan well enough to know what she sounded like when she was flirting, and never before had I seen any man just stand there with a stony face like Varo did. It was almost like he was deliberately trying not to like her. West appeared more interested in what she'd been saying and even stood there to talk to her after Varo walked away.

"I think that man must be nuts, but don't feel bad. I can barely get a word from him, and he's supposed to actually work for me," I said in an attempt to make her feel better.

Jordan shrugged. "It's no big deal. I mean, what would I do with someone like that anyway? He's as big as a house. Probably on steroids, and you know what they say about those guys." Measuring out an inch between her thumb and forefinger, she snickered. "Hung like a chipmunk."

I laughed out loud at the thought of such a huge man with such a tiny penis. Leave it to Jordan to make me laugh at her misery and lessen my own at the same time. "You're so bad!"

"His loss. I could have rocked his world, even if he is Needledick the Bug Fucker."

Her words made me choke on my morning coffee, and liquid nearly came shooting out of my nose. Coughing, I croaked out, "Jordan, I'll never be able to look at him the same way again! Jesus, I have to deal with him."

"You're not supposed to deal with his junk. Just his silent as a statue routine. I'm sure you'll forget what I said before you see him again," she said with a wink.

"I doubt I'll ever forget it. Needledick the Bug Fucker is something that sticks with you."

From behind us came the sound of someone clearing their throat, and I slowly turned to see who'd heard us slandering my bodyguard's penis size, hoping that it wasn't Varo himself. Thankfully, it was just Daryl, although the look on his face was pure confusion.

"That's my cue to leave," Jordan said cheerfully as she grabbed her bag. "Call me later, Nina. I'll be in prep time right after lunch."

"Okay. Have a good one filling those kids' minds with knowledge."

As Jordan passed Daryl on her way out, her gaze slipped to below his waist and she chuckled. If he had any idea what she was doing, he didn't show it. Taking the seat she'd just left, he reached into his coat pocket to pull out his little notepad and began flipping through the pages as I sat there stifling my own chuckle.

"We have a few things to deal with today," he pronounced ominously without looking up from his notes.

"Okay. Hit me with them."

He continued to flip through the pages of his pad until he reached one covered in scribbles. I was in no mood to try to decipher what he'd written, so I sat back and watched his lips move as he read over his notes.

Daryl stopped reading and looked up at me. Taking a deep breath, he let the air leave his lungs in a slow sigh. "We think Karl is going to start focusing on you. He's looking for something and we think he's eventually going to run out of places to look other than this house."

"Look for what? What could possibly be here that he wants? I thought the problem was the notebook Tristan has."

"He's looked through that tablet of your father's over and over and can't find anything. If what Karl is looking for is somewhere else, it's not in Tristan's penthouse. It's been ransacked twice already."

"What?" The word ransacked sent shivers down my spine. That Karl and his goons had turned to breaking into Tristan's penthouse scared the hell out of me. It also made me feel violated. While the penthouse wasn't exactly anywhere I'd ever called home, it bothered me that strangers may have gone through our clothes looking for whatever they wanted or trashed the picture I'd picked out for the bedroom.

"It's okay. They didn't do too much damage, but it's obvious that they were looking for something and didn't find it."

"So you think Karl and his people are going to come looking here?"

Daryl gave me one of his rare smiles and shook his head. "Don't worry. The security system Tristan had installed is first rate, and Varo and West are always nearby to make sure you're safe."

"Then why are we talking about this, Daryl? I don't understand what the problem is if I'm safe." He hesitated, making me nervous. "What? You just said Varo and West keep me safe. I'm not?"

"You are. We just think that might not be enough. Tristan thinks you need to make it seem like you're, uh, living your life."

"We think? Tristan thinks? What are you talking about, Daryl? You're freaking me out."

He looked away and then turned back to face me. "Tristan thinks it would be best if you made it seem like you've moved on."

Daryl's words hit my brain and suddenly it felt like the room was swimming around me. Moved on? My hands began to shake at the very thought of moving on without Tristan.

"What the hell does moved on mean?" I asked in a scared voice. "Are you saying Tristan isn't coming back?"

"No, no, no. Nothing like that. Just that you need to pretend that you're with someone else now so Karl can think that Tristan's dead."

My jaw fell open as I stared at Daryl, who acted like he'd just said something entirely reasonable. Was he saying Tristan wanted me to pretend to date another man? Had I heard him correctly?

"I can see by your face that I might have said that wrong. It's just that Tristan doesn't want you to be in danger and if Karl believes you've moved on..."

I didn't let Daryl finish his sentence before I blew up. "I'm not doing it. I don't care what you and Tristan think is best. I'm not pretending to be with someone else. It's just ridiculous! I don't want to be with anyone else, and even if I agreed with this, where would I find someone willing to playact with me? No way. You'll have to tell him I'm not going to do it."

Reaching into his coat pocket again, he mumbled, "I thought you'd say something like that." He handed me an envelope. "This is from Tristan."

I looked down at the first letter I'd received from Tristan since he'd left and felt the tears well up in my eyes. The first time he'd bothered to write anything to me and it was to tell me to be with someone else. My stomach clenched at the thought.

"I'll give you some time to read it and be back in a bit," Daryl said as he stood to leave.

I didn't want to read it. All I wanted all these months was to hear from Tristan, and now that I had, it was just to tell me to show the world that I'd moved on. The envelope had nothing written on the outside, and when I turned it over, I saw the flap was just tucked in, not sealed. It was like nothing of him was there.

Slipping the letter out, I unfolded it and began to read, prepared to remain angry and unwilling to go with his plan. Just two sentences in and any hopes of that disappeared.

Dear Nina,

By now, Daryl has told you what I need you to do. I know you don't want to and God knows I hate the idea of you acting like you care about another man almost as much as I hate being away from you, but I need you to do this for us. I know it won't be easy, but my biggest fear is that it won't be hard for you since I've left you alone for so long. Please know that if there was any other way, I would have done things differently.

Every letter you wrote me, every text you send means more to me than you'll ever know. They're my lifelines—the things that keep me going when I feel like I have nothing of any worth left anymore. I can handle losing everything else but not you. Knowing you're waiting for me is the one thing that makes me go on.

Nina, it tears me up inside to ask you to pretend you've moved on to another. Do this for us and at least I can believe you'll be safe. Think about me and know that I never stop thinking about you. I promise that someday when all of this is over we'll get to live that life we both dream of. Never doubt that we can make it through this.

I love you and wish we were together. Your love is what I live for. Until we're together again, keep me in your heart. What we are is worth fighting for, and trust me, I'm fighting with everything I have.

Love,
Tristan

Just when I was ready to be stubborn, Tristan accomplished what no other man could—instead of being angry at him for what he was asking, I felt sorry for what I had to do. I sensed his heartache in every word he'd written, and it broke my heart.

"Everything okay in here?"

Daryl looked uncomfortable as I wiped a tear away from under my eye. He took his seat again and waited for me to speak, but I could tell he was still feeling uneasy about how emotional Tristan's letter had made me.

Resigned to doing as Tristan asked, I said quietly, "I'm fine, Daryl. Just tell me what you need me to do."

"You won't have to do anything but appear to be with him. Just a few times in public to make the press think you're on a couple dates. He will have to live here with you, though."

"Who? Who is this poor soul you're going to force to pretend to be my new boyfriend?"

"Varo."

"Varo? My bodyguard? No offense to him, but why would I fall for one of my bodyguards?"

Daryl shrugged and smiled meekly. "You know. You were thrown together after Tristan disappeared and one thing lead to another and...well, we can let the press take it from there."

I rolled my eyes at such a ridiculous story. "Nice. So I was able to easily forget Tristan Stone and turned to the comforting arms of a man who barely speaks to me and has never once shown even the slightest interest in me. Yeah, that sounds like a real romance."

More shrugging. "The outside world doesn't know that. All they know is what we show them, and you two will look like true lovebirds when the cameras are flashing."

"I'm a little confused why you think the press would care at all. I'm nobody. They only came out when I was with Tristan."

"They'll care because you're all that's left of Tristan Stone. They can't have him, so they'll take you. Haven't you noticed the press milling about at the end of the driveway?"

I hadn't noticed, but that was because I was too involved in being depressed. The few times I'd left the house recently I'd gone straight to the city, and there I was followed by West and Varo, so they had made sure nobody got close to me.

"So they'll take our picture as we go on our dates and that will make it look like I've left Tristan behind? Isn't that going to make me seem like a heartless bitch? He hasn't even been gone for six months."

"That's another reason why they'll be interested. The press loves showing the worst in people. They'll eat it up."

I already hated this.

"So I get to look like the world's biggest bitch, Varo looks like some kind of gold digger since I'm living in Tristan's house with him, and this helps keep me safe. Is that about right?"

"Yeah. Oh, one more thing. You can't tell anyone about this being a fake. That means your giggly friend there with the fixation on penis size."

I crossed my arms defiantly. "I'm not going to lie to my best friend, Daryl. We tell each other everything. I've never lied to her before, and I'm not starting now."

Daryl stood from the table and leaned down toward me until his furry face was just inches away from mine. "Then you better figure out a way to not tell her and not lie because if you tell her and someone gets to her, all of this will have been for nothing. Remember, your safety is the reason you're doing all of this. Tristan is going to be busy finding out what Karl is up to and he needs to know you're not in danger."

"Does Varo know about this yet? I can't imagine acting like my boyfriend was in the bodyguard work description he agreed to when he was hired."

"Don't worry about him. I'll take care of that. We'll have him moved in here tonight."

Terrific. I suddenly had a new man and somehow I had to find a way to explain to my best friend that he was none other than the one she'd tried to seduce to no avail. Fucking fabulous.

"By the way, how is the gardener search going?" Daryl asked, ripping me from my thoughts.

Confused by the change of topic, I shook my head. "You're all over the place today, aren't you? I hired one yesterday. West and Varo were supposed to check him out today and let me know."

"Good. I'll ask them about it when I talk to him. In the meantime, I'd suggest making plans for where Varo will be staying while he's here. Perhaps the room next to yours? That way he can be close."

"Why does he have to be close? The press can't get onto the property, so why would we have to pretend to that extent?"

"You can never be too careful, Nina."

What the hell did that mean? Was he implying that Jensen, West, or any of the other people who worked for Tristan couldn't be trusted? Did he mean that Jordan couldn't be?

Craning my neck, I turned to look at Daryl as he walked from the room. "Is there something I should know? You and Tristan seem to think that Varo is okay, but everyone else can't be trusted?"

He stopped and seemed to think about my question for a moment. "Varo is okay, but we can't be sure about anyone else. We'd like to think they're safe, but for now, we can't know."

Before I could comment on how much I hated all of this, he was gone and I was left to think about what I had to do. Daryl acted like it would be a piece of cake to just pretend to care for someone else and act like Tristan was never coming back. Nothing was further from the truth. Just the thought of never seeing him again made me feel like curling up into a ball and never getting out of bed again.

I so just wanted all of this to be over. How wrong I'd been all those times I'd wished for a more exciting life. If I'd have known that it would involve all of this, I would have been happy with my boring life of sitting at home and watching TV alone every night.

But then I wouldn't have Tristan. He was worth every bit of craziness our lives were now, although I couldn't lie. A little less crazy would be even better.

FOUR
Nina

Unable to figure out a way of telling Jordan what I had to do, I retreated to my room and wished the world would just fix itself by the time I decided to come out. I knew it wouldn't, but that didn't mean I didn't wish for it.

Even though I now knew Tristan received all my texts, I didn't send him a message right away. What was there to say? *Hey, I got your letter and I'm all cool with pretending I'm doing someone else?* Or maybe something like *I miss you. I love you. And now I'm going to be acting like I've forgotten you and moved on just as you said to.*

Over and over, I typed in so many words, only to backspace through them until there was nothing. Finally, I let my fingers spell out what was in my heart, no matter how much it hurt.

I hate what I have to do. I don't want to pretend I care about someone else. I could never just move on like that.

As usual, there was no reply. At least I knew he received it, though.

Where was he? I imagined him sitting on a beach somewhere, his feet in the sand as he sipped some frothy umbrella drink in the sunshine. No, that wasn't right. He was likely somewhere in a hotel fully dressed in a suit and tie with a glass of scotch on the table in front of him. Was he in Venice enjoying the beautiful sunset each night—the same sunset that had been the perfect backdrop to our time together there?

Two light knocks on my door shook me from my daydreaming, and I opened it to see Varo standing there looking distinctly uncomfortable. In fact, I didn't think I'd ever seen him look like that. Instead of looking me directly in the eyes, as he always did, his gaze was fixed on the floor and his hands were hidden behind his back.

"Hi, Varo. What's up?" I wanted to be cool, but my words came out stupid sounding, like I didn't know what was happening.

His gaze met mine, and I saw just how uncomfortable he was. Those dark blue eyes that had reminded me of a snake's more than once seemed bigger, like they were filled with uncertainty and searching for an answer in mine.

"I thought we should talk before we begin doing whatever we're supposed to be doing."

"Okay. Give me a minute and I'll meet you in the living room."

As soon as I walked into that room I knew I couldn't sit there with another man like I had with Tristan. There were just too many memories. It would be wrong. Daryl was one thing, but Varo? No. I couldn't sit there and talk about us being a couple, even if it was all an act. Stopping dead two feet in, I shook my head. "Let's go somewhere else. I could use a drink or something to eat. How about the kitchen?"

Varo had no idea what the problem was and merely nodded as he rose from the couch. I wasn't lying about needing a drink. Even though it wasn't yet dinnertime, I had the strongest urge for anything that would dull my senses and make all this easier to deal with.

He followed me into the kitchen and stood silently near the doorway, as if he was preparing for a quick getaway. I knew how he felt. This whole facade we had to put on made me want to run away too.

As I considered what to say, I truly looked at Gage Varo, possibly for the first time. I'd seen him before, of course, but I had never really looked at him. He was the bodyguard or the guy Jordan liked, but now that he was standing there in my kitchen waiting to talk about how we were going to pretend to be a couple, I felt like I was seeing him in a brand new way.

His dark blue eyes still scared me a little, but I had no fear that he wanted to hurt me. They were just so unlike Tristan's with their warm chocolate color. Varo's were cold in comparison, and they gave me no real sense of what he was feeling.

"So I guess we should talk," I said awkwardly as I stood with my back pressed against the counter, unable to put any more space between us. "Maybe if we got to know each other this might not seem so bizarre."

"This isn't the first time I've done this."

His statement was like an unexploded bomb dropped into the middle of the room. It just sort of sat there for a moment while my brain processed what he'd said. Did he mean he'd been a bodyguard before or that he'd had to pretend to be someone's boyfriend before?

"What?"

"I've done this before. You know, the whole fake boyfriend thing. It's not as hard as you'd think. It's just a matter of acting like you're happy. Once you get that down, it's a breeze."

"Oh, okay," I muttered, still surprised that Varo had committed this same fraud before. "Do you mind me asking who you did this with the last time?"

Shaking his head, he said, "Angela Macaran. She's an actress."

I'd never heard of her, but the fact that he'd been her fake boyfriend made me want to know more about her. "Why did she need you to pretend to be her boyfriend?"

"I have no idea. They never told me, like all I know is what Daryl told me about this. You need me to act like we're together, so that's what I'll do."

This wasn't making it any less weird.

"Did you sleep with her because you won't be doing that with me. We don't have to do that. In fact, I don't think Jordan would ever forgive me if we did, not to mention the fact that I'm in love with Tristan and when he comes back we plan to get married. So there will definitely be no sleeping together." I stopped talking as I realized I was rambling and took a deep breath before I began again. "I'm sorry. I must sound crazy. It's just that this isn't something I have any experience with."

Varo gave me the first smile I may have ever seen from him. It was genuine and lit up his face, making him look so much friendlier than he'd ever been toward me. "It's okay. I know my part. I assume Tristan knew my background when he hired me."

"Oh. Is there anything I should be doing that I'm not?" I asked, feeling supremely stupid at that moment. "I mean, how did that Angela person act?"

Varo's smile grew wider. "She acted like we were sleeping together because we were. I guess that doesn't help, does it?"

"No, not at all. But thanks."

He took a step into the room and then another until he stood next to the huge island in the center of the kitchen. "I think all we have to do is look like we like each other. Hopefully, by the time Daryl parades us out in front of the world, we can pull that off."

"It's not that I don't like you, Varo," I said apologetically.

"Gage. It might be more convincing if you called me by my first name instead of what my Chief Petty Officer used to call me."

"Okay. It's not that I don't like you, Gage. It's just that you've never really been very friendly toward me."

Nodding, he seemed to consider what I'd said. "I'll give you that. It wasn't part of my job, as far as I was concerned. Now that it is, I promise to be friendlier."

I liked this Varo a lot more than the one I was used to. For the first time, I could see what Jordan saw in him. Since I had the chance, I decided I could do some girlfriend recon for her.

"So are you single, Gage?"

"I am. There's not much opportunity to settle down with this job since I have to live in the carriage house with West."

I moved toward the island to grab a handful of grapes from the fruit bowl. Popping one in my mouth, I said, "Well, that's true, but you might have a girlfriend. It's not like you have to work twenty-four-seven."

"Nope. No girlfriend."

"That's good. I mean, you having a girlfriend might make what we have to do a little harder."

In truth, it was good because that meant Jordan had a chance. I was happy to hear that he was single and couldn't wait to tell her all the details about him.

"Are you from around here?"

"No. I grew up in Wyoming, the Cowboy State. That's the nickname for Wyoming."

"You don't look like a cowboy," I said with a smile, hoping he recognized that I wasn't trying to be insulting.

He reached across the island and picked a few grapes off the bunch. "I'm not. I got out of there as soon as I could. Spent some time in the Navy and then spent a few years bouncing around the country before I got into this line of work."

I subtly scanned his muscular frame, imagining him in Navy whites. Jordan was going to melt when she heard he was former Navy. That May we got to experience Fleet Week had made quite an impression on her, and she'd said for months afterward that she'd love to have a sailor. Hell, she might melt when I told her he was from somewhere they call the Cowboy State.

"Ever been married?" I probed.

He smiled broadly. "No. No ex-wife and no kids either."

Check. Single and unfettered. He was looking better and better by the minute. I filed these facts away and popped another grape in my mouth. "Don't you want to know anything about me?"

Varo folded his arms across his chest and shook his head. "Since I'm not scoping you out for a friend, I figured I'd just let you tell me about yourself when you felt comfortable."

Caught red-handed! Damn.

I felt my cheeks grow hot as a blush of embarrassment spread over me. "I...it's just...Jordan's a great..." I stammered out, not having much success in getting my point across.

"It's okay. I'm flattered, even if I can't ask her out."

"Why? She's fantastic. She's a teacher, a wonderful person, and she's a great time. I think you'd like her."

"I already do, but it doesn't change the fact that we can't get together while I'm on this job. It just wouldn't work out."

My shoulders sagged under my disappointment at his words. "Oh. Are you sure?"

"I don't think it's a good idea as long as I'm guarding you. Conflict of interest. Plus, I don't think my boss would like it."

All of a sudden there seemed to be a light at the end of the tunnel. "Then it's all good because I know your boss and he'd be fine with it," I said grinning with satisfaction.

Varo stood silently for a moment and nodded. "You make a convincing argument. Maybe when all this is over I might try to see if we can get together."

A might was better than a no, so I clapped my hands together in triumph. "That's great! I'm not going to say anything to her, though, so I don't ruin it. I don't want to meddle."

"I think they call that matchmaking instead of meddling."

Shrugging, I explained, "I just like to see everyone as happy as Tristan and I are."

Varo looked at me oddly, as if he couldn't believe what I'd just said. I could understand that. It's not like Tristan was anywhere nearby for months now, but I still had hope. "I know that sounds strange, but we are happy. It's just that we're not together now. Soon, though. I have to keep believing it'll be soon."

"I'm all for being happy, but as far as I can tell, very few get that blessing."

Hmmm, the bodyguard is a little jaded.

"Well, as Jordan always says, good things happen to good people. She says that to me, and I'm saying that to you. They do."

"I'll have to take your word on that, Nina. I haven't seen that to be true yet."

"Just you wait and see, Gage. Trust me. I know about these things," I said as I grabbed another handful of grapes and headed out of the kitchen. "Now let's get your stuff moved into your room."

By the time Jordan got home after work, Gage had moved all of his things into his new room next to mine. Not that he had a lot of belongings to his name. A large garbage bag would have held every item he owned. The man certainly traveled light. Even though I'd been uncomfortable about Tristan's idea to make the world think he was never coming back, the part that involved Gage wasn't so bad, after all. I still hated the idea that anyone would believe I'd be able to move on so easily and replace Tristan, but at least I'd found out my partner in the deception was a decent guy. I'd be happy when he and Jordan finally got together.

I met her at the door, thrilled to tell her the small part I could about him moving into the house. Since Daryl had warned me against keeping her in the loop, I had to come up with a story that sounded somewhat believable.

"Hey, you! How was your day with the little darlings?"

She looked up from putting her keys in her purse and frowned. "Awful. Two of my students got into a fight, and now I have to go back at six tonight to meet with the parents. The worst part is that my principal thinks this happened because I can't handle my classroom."

"I'm sorry you had such a bad day. Come into the kitchen and sit down with me so we can talk and eat a little dinner before you have to go back to the city."

Jordan shook her head. "I can't. I'm just going to grab a quick shower and get ready. I hope you don't mind me asking Jensen if he'd take me back."

I took her bag and walked with her down the hallway to her room. "Of course. It's not like you're going to take a bus there. I can come with you, if you like. I didn't get out today, so I can get dressed and be ready to go in no time."

Pushing her bedroom door open, she took the bag from my hand and threw it on the bed. "No, that's okay, Nina. I better do this alone. When I get home, hopefully I'll be in a better mood."

"Okay. Just remember how great a teacher you are. Those kids are lucky to have you, and your principal needs to remember that."

She took a deep breath and forced a smile. "I know. I promise we'll talk when I get back."

"Good because we need an old-fashioned girls' night in, complete with our favorite movies and buckets of popcorn, and tonight looks like the perfect night for that."

Jordan's expression softened. Nodding, she said quietly, "It's a date. I'll see you when I get back."

At a little after seven, she texted me to say everything had worked out and her principal had even apologized for jumping to conclusions before she had all the facts about the fight. I was thrilled and texted back that I was heading to the kitchen to make the popcorn. Girls' night in was on!

We both needed this kind of night. I was feeling a little better since finding out Tristan had been receiving all of my texts, but I couldn't say it wasn't frustrating that he never responded. I was sure Daryl would have some valid reason why he couldn't if I bothered to ask, but it was still aggravating. And with Jordan's job woes, she was dealing with her own frustrations. A few great chick flicks and too much popcorn were definitely what the doctor ordered.

Two Jiffy Pop pans into my popcorn popping, I heard a knock and turned around to see Gage standing there. "Hey, want some popcorn?"

"No. I just wasn't sure who was in here making all that racket," he said with a smile.

"Yeah, it's just me. You have to shake this stuff or it burns," I said as I turned back toward the stove.

He walked in and stood next to me. "Wouldn't microwave popcorn be easier?"

"No way! That stuff is bad for you. Something in the chemicals they use and the heat of the microwave, or something like that. It's Jiffy Pop all the way."

"Health nut, huh?"

I looked up at him and laughed. "Not exactly. I think there's like two hundred grams of fat and carbs in all this popcorn."

He looked down at the giant bowl half filled with Jiffy Pop that sat on the countertop and scooped out a handful for himself. Throwing a piece up in the air, he leaned his head back and caught it in his mouth. "Mmmm....not bad. A little buttery, but not bad."

"Don't tell me you're one of those popcorn eaters who doesn't like butter?" I asked as I continued shaking the pan on the stovetop.

Throwing another piece up above his head, he caught the second one in his mouth and smiled. "Butter's okay, but I don't like my food swimming in it."

I grabbed a kernel and threw it up in the air, but it came nowhere close to my mouth and fell on the floor next to me. I'd never been good at that kind of thing.

Chuckling, Gage looked down at the floor and back up at me. "Looks like you need some practice at that trick. Watch." He stepped behind me and leaned in close so his head was next to mine. "I'll throw it up in the air and just position yourself underneath it."

He tossed the popcorn in the air and moved back away from me so I could catch it. Leaning my head back, I watched as the kernel dropped right toward my face. All I had to do was keep my mouth open and it fell right in. Excited, I stopped shaking the pan of popcorn and turned around to face him.

"I did it! Now with just a little practice, I'll be able to do it without your help."

"Glad to be of assistance. Any time," he said with a smile.

I caught a glimpse of someone standing in the doorway and looked around Gage to see Jordan standing there with a hurt look on her face. Before I could say a word, she turned on her heels and disappeared. Taking the pan of popcorn off the burner, I set it down and asked, "Can you pour this into the bowl when it cools down? I'll be right back."

Jordan had gone to her room, and by the time I got to her, hurt had turned to anger. I knocked on her door only to hear her yell, "Go away!" and knew she misunderstood what she saw in the kitchen between Gage and me. I knocked again and waited a minute for her to let me in, taking her silence as the okay for me to enter.

The look on her face was one of complete betrayal. It stopped me dead in my tracks as I closed the door behind me. "Jordan, I think I know what's wrong, but you're mistaken."

"I don't think I am. What was going on in there, Nina?"

"Nothing. Nothing at all. Gage was just keeping me company while I was making our popcorn, and then he was teaching me how to do that throwing it up and catching it in my mouth trick. That's it."

"Gage? When did he become Gage? What happened to calling him Varo, like you always have? Since when did you two become such close buddies?"

I took another step toward her, but she moved away, her anger coming off her in waves. "He's still Varo. It's just that he told me his name today and I was just trying to be nice."

"You've changed, Nina. I can see it clear as day now as you're standing there. You're different. Maybe it's the money or maybe you're just lonely since Tristan doesn't seem to ever be coming back."

Her words hit me like a fist to my chest. "That's not fair, Jordan. I'm no different than I've ever been. I can't believe you'd bring up Tristan never coming back like that."

"Isn't that what the whole Gage thing is about? You knew I liked him, and still you're acting like that with him? Why would you do that?"

Defensiveness raged inside me, and I lashed out. "That whole Gage thing, as you call it, is just me being the same old Nina I've always been. That I'd never been really nice to him or West wasn't because I didn't think I should be but because I was feeling depressed all these weeks. So now I feel a little better and I get accused of being someone else and not myself? That's bullshit and I don't deserve it."

Tears welled up in her eyes, and she screamed, "You have everything here! Why do you have to go after him too? Isn't it enough to have all the money you've ever wanted? Now you want another guy in addition to Tristan? What happened to waiting for him and being so madly in love?"

Jordan had never yelled at me like that and I stepped back in astonishment for a moment, but I wasn't stunned for long. I barked back, releasing all the months of unhappiness on her. "I have nothing here! What do I care about money when the man I love is absent all this time? You think I stay in my room curled up in a ball so much because I'm fucking happy? I stay there because it's all I have left of him. It's the only place that truly feels like he's there with me. I'm not doing anything with Varo, and if you think I would do that to Tristan or you, the two people I love more than anyone else in this world, then maybe you're the one who's changed, not me."

She looked stunned by my outburst, but I saw the hurt in her eyes too. As I turned to leave, I heard her mumble about West and something he'd said, but I didn't care. I stormed out of her room across the house to my own room, devastated that my best friend had just accused me of trying to steal the man she wanted. Burying my face in the pillow, I let the tears flow from all the frustration and hurt bottled up inside me. How could she think I would ever do that to her?

I wanted to believe she'd lashed out at me because of her problems at work, but her words had hurt. All the money in the world meant nothing without Tristan, and she knew that. She knew how much I loved him, so why would she think I'd ever go after Gage? And that she thought I'd ever break the girlfriend code and chase after someone my best friend wanted, even if there was no Tristan in the picture, was crazy. Since that first day in college, we'd been like sisters. My own sister had never rejoiced in anything that made me happy, but Jordan did. From the moment we met, I'd been able to tell her whatever was in my heart and she supported me, and I'd always been there to do the same for her. I'd never betray her, and it hurt like hell that she could even entertain the idea that I would.

I needed to clear the air with her. No matter what else was going on, she was my best friend. Hurt or not,

I had to make her understand there was nothing between Varo and me. How I'd ever explain the two of us being seen as a couple in public was beyond me at that moment, but I'd cross that bridge when I came to it.

Just as I sat up to go back to her room, my phone vibrated with a text. Looking down, I saw the first words scroll across the top of my phone.

I think it might be better if I move

I quickly swiped the phone and read her entire message. *I think it might be better if I move back to the city for a while. Maybe we just need some time apart. I know you'll be safe here with all these people to take care of you.*

My heart sank as her words sat there staring up at me in orange on the screen. What hurt more were the ones she hadn't typed in. That somehow I'd changed and didn't need her anymore. By the time I reached her room, she was gone. She'd cleaned out her dresser and much of her closet, but most of everything she owned was still there. I ran to the garage to catch her, getting there just in time to see Jensen drive through the gate at the bottom of the driveway.

I typed out *I don't want to lose another person in my life* and clicked Send. All I wanted to do was curl up in a ball and close my eyes. I already missed her. When she didn't text back, I walked back to my room and climbed into bed, the smell of buttered popcorn still hanging in the air. It wasn't even nine o'clock at night, but it didn't matter.

Grabbing my phone from the nightstand, I typed out my last message for the day, as I always did before

I went to sleep, but unlike usual, it wasn't a profession of love. Losing my best friend had put me in a mood that was anything but loving.

Jordan moved out because she thinks I'm with Varo now and she liked him. I hope this whole plan of yours is worth it. Now it's just me, Varo, West, and Jensen. Maybe it would be better if you got rid of West and Jensen so the world really could see Varo and me as the loving couple we are. Just a thought.

FIVE

TRISTAN

As I lay in bed awake just staring at the ceiling, I heard the phone vibrate on the night table next to me. It was the one Nina messaged me on. Picking it up, I read her text so full of anger—at me, at the entire situation we found ourselves in—and I couldn't blame her. That didn't mean her mention of her and Varo as a loving couple didn't make my insides churn from jealousy. Just the thought of it made me want to race back to the house and remind her how much I loved her.

Except I couldn't. Doing that would put her in as much danger as I was in, and the last thing I wanted to do was get her hurt in all this.

Fuck. I hated this. I'd intentionally avoided the whole business thing with my brother and father for this very reason. All this cloak and dagger shit was what they'd always reveled in. I didn't care. If it weren't for Nina, I would have handed Karl the damn notebook at the beginning of all this and walked away to live on a secluded island somewhere. The problem was that whatever he was looking for didn't seem to be in that notebook.

I'd combed through those pages until I knew their contents by heart. How my brother and father were the monsters I'd never imagined they could be. How the

Cashen family had paid more than any should for my family's greed and callousness. Some days, I sat with the tablet in my hands, unable to open the cover because I didn't want to face the ugliness inside. On those days, I hated the name Stone more than I ever thought possible. I wasn't like them, no matter what lies I'd told in my life, but the real fear that what they were wasn't something I could choose but something innate in me terrified me to the bone.

Other days, I did nothing but read those lines over and over, needing for some masochistic reason to be reminded of my family's crimes and the terrible consequences that had resulted. Not that I would ever forget what they'd done. The memory of Taylor's treatment of that young girl and her tragic death, along with Judge Cashen's murder and the killing of all those innocent men, women, and children all for the sake of saving my father from losing some sexual harassment lawsuit would forever be imprinted on my mind and my soul.

I'd be stained by their guilt for the rest of my life.

But what about my mother? Had she known what my father and brother had done? There was no mention of her in any of Joseph Edwards' notes about Amanda Cashen's suicide and her father's murder, but the thought of what she may have known loomed as an unanswered question in my mind every time I thought about what Nina's father had uncovered.

Sleep wouldn't come if my mind continued to race with all these thoughts, but I couldn't stop them. They spun in my brain like some tormented top, slamming into good memories and corrupting even them. Of all my family, my mother had always been an island of kindness in a sea of ruthless behavior, a quiet presence I now understood I never appreciated enough. While my father and brother had worked to rearrange the world to suit their twisted desires, my mother had been the often silent, gentle force behind our family.

Nearly invisible to even me, she'd been an angel among devils who looked on her with distaste and an indulgent son who ignored her in favor of satisfying his hedonistic soul. But as she watched the three men in her life do as they liked with little regard for those they hurt, had she known or even had the tiniest hint of what they truly were?

I slid out of bed and made my way to the living room, lured by Joseph Edwards' notebook like sailors to the sirens' calling. Tonight was one of those nights I couldn't fight the need to read those words once again, filling myself with a loathing for my family and by extension, myself.

My eyes glided over the pages, taking in the words I knew as well as my name. The details never changed, as much as I wished they would. Was it madness to hope that just once that tablet wouldn't contain the horrible truth of who I came from?

I told myself that I continued to read through every page to find that one detail I'd missed so I'd finally know what Karl was looking for, but that wasn't the entire truth. I read these notes written by a man my father had murdered because I couldn't help myself. It was like some kind of penance I felt I needed to pay. Somehow, if I read them just one more time, I'd be able to reconcile who I was with who my father and brother were.

So far, it hadn't turned out that way.

As always, I reached the end of Joseph Edwards' notes on my father and brother's crimes and felt revulsion at every word. My usual next move was to skim over what remained of the notebook and throw it off to the side, discarding it as if it was the reason my life had gone to fucking hell. My first instinct was to do exactly that tonight, but I stopped myself and forced my eyes to focus on the remaining pages in his tablet.

It's not that I hadn't read them before. Separated from the notes about Amanda and Albert Cashen and my family by just one page, there was information about some drug I suspected Edwards had researched concerning another suicide—some drug for heart disease I'd never heard of. It appeared, from what he'd found, that it had received FDA approval but had become a killer drug for those that needed it most. His notes on this only took up a page and ended with the letters TR and a question mark.

I had no idea what that could mean, but as far as I knew, it had nothing to do with the ugliness between the Stone and Cashen families. The next page read like some kind of foreign crossword puzzle, full of clues I couldn't decipher. Edwards had written a series of words repeatedly, the order never changing.

-Cordovex—death?—TR—October

Again, TR. Who or what was TR? Had they committed suicide? Had my family been implicated in their death? TS would make sense because it could refer to Taylor, but TR just sat there on the page meaning nothing to me. Was TR supposed to indicate a name? Someone's initials? Thursday? I had no idea.

A knock on the front door yanked me out of my thoughts, and I cautiously walked over to look through the peep hole to see Daryl standing on the other side. I opened the door, and he pushed past me before I had a chance to welcome him into my temporary home.

"Shit's getting interesting, to say the least, my friend," he said ominously as he plopped down into the chair across from my seat on the couch. "Karl obviously knew about the LA house since it's been turned over three times already."

I sat back down and considered what Daryl had just said. "Not a coincidence since that house hasn't been touched since my father died. What the fuck is he looking for?"

Daryl shook his head, all the while stroking his beard that seemed to grow bushier every time I saw him. "I don't know. I can't decide if he's looking for you or that tablet you have there."

"There's nothing in it. I've looked. Other than the ugly details about my family and the Cashen family, all Edwards seemed to be interested in was some prescription drug for heart disease. Seems it was anything but helpful for some people."

"The girl Taylor was doing died. Any chance she didn't hang herself but instead took the drug?"

I shrugged and shook my head. "No. It wouldn't matter anyway, would it? The problem my father would want to cover up was that she killed herself because of Taylor, not the way she did it."

Daryl silently agreed. He took a deep breath and closed his eyes. "We're missing something here. I say we have to look at the obvious first. Your places are being ransacked for something, but what? Karl's looking for evidence, and he wants that tablet enough to make the copies he got from Nina's sister not good enough."

Leaning forward, I rested my elbows on my thighs. "You're missing the big question. We have no idea if Karl knows what's in this notebook. Maybe he just thinks what Kim gave him wasn't the entire book."

Daryl stared at me with a look of confusion. "But why would he think that?"

"I don't know. I can tell you that he doesn't have everything. I don't know why, but Kim didn't have copies of the pages about the drug investigation her father was pursuing. When Karl showed me what he had, there was nothing about Cordovex or anything like it. He only has the pages about Amanda's and her father's deaths."

Daryl leaned forward toward me, his eyes wide. "Then that's it. Karl worries there's more, and he knows what it's about. What do we know about this Cordovex?"

"Nothing. I've never heard of it. All Edwards says over and over is that he associates it with death."

"Let me see that notebook," he said, reaching out his hand. "I want to see what he's talking about with this Cordovex."

I handed him Joseph Edwards' notebook opened to the page where he had detailed the information he'd uncovered. Daryl's brows knitted as he read it over before he flipped to the last page of the tablet. Running his finger down over the metal coils holding the pages together, he made that clucking nose with his tongue he often did when he was thinking.

Looking up at me, he held the notebook up in front of him. "There's a page missing here. Did you tear any out?"

"No. That's how I found it in Edwards' safe deposit box."

"What about Nina's sister? Any chance she took out a page?"

I shook my head. "No. I saw the copies she had and none were about anything but Taylor and my father."

"Damnit! Why did she give those goddamn copies to Karl in the first place?"

"Because I told her to."

"Why?"

"I didn't want her or her family to get hurt. I knew if Karl found out Joseph Edwards had kept any notes from his investigation of Stone Worldwide, he'd go after her and Nina. I could protect Nina, but not Kim. So I told her to give him everything he asked for. Then I got her and her family to safety as soon as Karl left. If I didn't, they'd probably be dead right now."

Daryl looked unimpressed. "I guess, but she's made this much easier for Karl."

"She did what I told her to do. Not that she didn't fight me tooth and nail. I could barely get her to speak to me at first. It was only when I told her what I'd found out about what Taylor and my father had done that she agreed to even talk to me about all of this. I guess I don't blame her. She probably thought if two Stone men were heartless fucks, why wouldn't the third be?"

I sat back on the couch, tired from trying to convince myself that I wasn't just like them. Kim hadn't made it easy, and by the time I explained everything to her, I still didn't think she believed I wasn't just what she'd always thought I was.

A bad man who shouldn't be anywhere near her sister.

Even when I promised to keep her and her family safe on the island where Nina and I were to be married, protected by guards and catered to twenty-four hours a day, she still looked at me like I was some criminal.

"Well, speaking of that, the last time I checked, they were fine. The guards tell me that they're enjoying a wonderful vacation on St. Vince and the girls love it."

"Good. Speaking of being happy, I'm to understand Nina isn't, if her text is any clue to how she's feeling," I said, leveling my gaze on the one who'd convinced me the whole Nina and Varo plan was a good idea.

"Nah, she seemed fine the last time I saw her. She didn't take to the Varo idea easily, but she seemed okay with it by the time I left. Not that I gave her much of a choice."

"Well, between the time you left and the time I received her last text, things obviously changed. She's anything but okay now."

"Why? What's up? She can't pretend to like Varo? I guess we could have chosen West, but he's got a weird vibe to him."

"It's not the Varo part so much as the problem between her and Jordan. I guess Jordan liked Varo and Nina's charade may have been a little too convincing. She moved out."

Daryl rolled his eyes and sighed. "So? I wasn't feeling great about her friend there anyway. Too many players in the game makes this whole thing more difficult to manage."

I thought about how angry Nina's text sounded. I'd asked a lot of her, but losing her friend was too much to expect. "Jordan's like a sister to Nina. She's upset about her leaving the house. I didn't want that to happen. Maybe you could remember how hard this is on her."

"Tristan, I do understand the hardship of losing her friend, but losing her life or you would be infinitely worse, don't you think? She and her friend can make up when all this is over. They can go shopping or do whatever women do when they make nice."

It wasn't up to Daryl or anyone else to make up for all this. I knew that. I was the one who'd have to make amends for the mess of all this.

"How did Varo take his new assignment?" I asked, trying to mask the jealousy that lingered inside me.

Chuckling, Daryl stroked his beard. "Considering how it's a step up from his regular job, he wisely smiled and happily moved his things into the house. It's not like it's a chore, really. He's just adding devoted suitor to protector. He'll be fine."

Devoted suitor and protector. I hated the way Daryl described Varo with those words. I was supposed to be that for Nina, not some bodyguard I'd only hired because of his size.

"He shouldn't get too comfortable in his new surroundings. I intend on being back in my own house as soon as possible."

My jealousy came through loud and clear, and Daryl knew it. He looked at me as if I were some lovesick puppy to be pitied. I didn't care. He was just some cynical curmudgeon who thought little of love. So be it. I didn't need his approval anyway. All I needed was his help to get back to the woman I loved and the life I'd left behind.

"Not to worry. Varo's not Nina's type. I suspect, if those muscles aren't all from nature, he's not her friend's type either," he said with a chuckle.

"What?" I asked, feeling the smallest relief from his words.

"Nothing. We have more important things to do than gossip about lovesick girls like hens. It's time you returned to the land of the living. Get your stuff, but don't bother shaving." He looked me up and down and added, "You look like you've been sleeping with your head in manure. That's good, though. The longer hair works for what we need."

I hadn't touched a razor to my face more than three times in the past months, even after I'd decided to quit losing myself in coke and alcohol. After the initial itchiness, I'd gotten used to the beard and seen it as yet another thing I didn't have to bother with every day. Not that I had a lot to deal with other than cultivating my self-loathing and missing Nina.

The hair, on the other hand, drove me crazy. I'd kept my hair short since I became CEO of Stone Worldwide, and having it hang in my eyes was a pain in the ass.

"I look almost as bad as you," I joked as I began to gather my things into a duffel bag.

"You wish you looked that good in a beard. You kids today don't appreciate the fine art of the beard," he said proudly as he continued to stroke the shaggy hair around his chin.

"Are you planning to tell me where we're going or do I just get to be in the dark about my immediate future?"

"Sure. We'll be flying coach back to the States so you get to experience the pain and suffering I've had to endure all these times back and forth to visit you here and from there we'll be getting you settled into your new place where you'll have to stay for a while. I've made sure it's close enough for you to keep an eye on the house but far enough away to make sure you're not seen."

I stopped stuffing clothes into the bag and turned to face him standing next to me. "So I get to spy on my own house and Nina is what you're saying."

"Spy is such an ugly word in this case. I just think it would help to have another pair of eyes watching when we can. I don't plan to live out in the middle of nowhere, no offense, so you can."

I thought about all the time I'd spent out at the country house and smiled at Daryl's description of it. After all this time away, it was the only place in the world I thought of as home. Far away from the hustle and bustle of the city, the house was where Nina and I had fallen in love. How many hours had we spent just lying in each other's arms at that house, every second of our time together the most wonderful moments of my life? There was nowhere else I wanted to be, but if all I could have was somewhere close to Nina, then I'd take it and do whatever I had to in order to get back to my life with her.

"Ready to get your life back?"

"I am, and Karl better hope to God he doesn't get in my way. I have too much to fight for to let him get what he wants."

I took one last look around the rooms where I'd spent months hiding out from the rest of the world. I'd lost part of myself in this place, the one part that I couldn't live without. Even though Nina had never given up on me all the while I'd been here, I'd given up. Now it was time to take the chance again to have the life I knew I wanted more than anything else.

SIX

Nina

Jordan's leaving sent me into an emotional tailspin, and for days I didn't get out of bed. Nothing made me feel better, even texting Tristan. How could it? I felt like I was constantly sending out messages in bottles and although I knew he received them, since he never answered it was a one-sided conversation, at best. As the days dragged by, my unhappiness morphed into anger at everything and everyone.

I wanted answers. I wanted Tristan to finally send a message back, even if it just said that he received my texts. I wanted him to hear what my words were saying and come back, even if it wasn't safe for him or me. I didn't care for excuses. I wanted him back.

Our bed became the only place I wanted to be because it reminded me of him. No matter how many times the sheets had been washed, they still held his scent. Not of his cologne but *him*. Closing my eyes, I imagined him next to me, silent as a statue as I chattered on about something. Like he always did, he smiled when I looked up to see if he was paying attention, muttering, "I'm listening" when I gave him that questioning look because he'd said nothing for so long.

God, I missed him.

My phone still held months of messages to him, so I spent my time scrolling through them reading my feelings for him as the time passed. Some were sad, while others made me smile. Each one marked a moment in time without him.

By the third day, it was all I could do to drag my body to the shower and wash my miserable self. While I didn't feel like I had when my father died and when Cal cheated on me, in some ways I felt worse. Those had both been horrible times, but they'd been endings I had to handle. Learning to accept the loss of someone was like having your heart torn out every day, but this was different. Tristan wasn't gone forever. He was just gone.

There was nothing I was allowed to mourn about this situation. Instead, I was supposed to stay in this house haunted with memories of him and act like everything was hunky dory. Well, it wasn't. After months of waiting every day for him to return, all my hunky dories had disappeared, and all I was carrying around was frustration and resentment at what our life had become.

And now Jordan was gone but not gone too. I didn't know how to feel about that. Something had come between us in the time she'd lived here. I really didn't think I'd changed, but had I? Had the world Tristan showed me made me so different that even my best friend didn't recognize me anymore? Even if I had changed, I still didn't know why she'd jumped to all the wrong conclusions with Gage. That wasn't like her at all.

It wasn't like her to not want to talk to me either. I'd tried calling and texting her, but she'd never answered or texted back. I'd apologized for something I really didn't mean to do, if I had done it at all, but still nothing. We'd disagreed before, but never had there been a rift like this between us.

As I stood in the shower remembering all the good times we'd had, I realized for the first time in my life, I was alone. Nobody I'd relied on was there for me anymore. Not my father, Jordan, or Tristan.

Dressed in the clothes that had become my usual outfit for hanging out at the house—yoga pants and a comfy shirt—I made my way to the kitchen, hoping I didn't see a soul since my face didn't have a stitch of makeup on it, my hair was a damp, stringy mess, and I wasn't even wearing a bra.

Maybe I had changed. Or maybe I was just depressed. Whichever it was, I wasn't in any shape to be seeing anyone.

For the first time in days, Maria had brewed the French Roast I loved, like she'd known this morning was the day I'd finally drag my butt out of bed. The only other female with me in the house now, she cooked for me, Jensen, and my giant shadows. She and I rarely spoke since her English was broken on the best of days and my knowledge of Portuguese was non-existent. Maybe if I'd taken Spanish in high school and college I could muddle through a conversation with her, but my three years of German was useless in comprehending what she was saying. Maria was kind, though, with hooded dark eyes that had a motherly feeling to them when she looked at me, and unlike every other person Tristan had working for him here, she seemed to have no interest in what I did with my time. For that reason alone, I liked her.

The coffee was exactly what the doctor ordered, and slowly my body began to come back to life. My spirit was still disheartened, but coffee wasn't going to fix that. The only cure for that wasn't to be found anywhere close, though.

I heard a sound behind me and turned to see Gage standing in the doorway. I couldn't be sure, but I had the sense that a look of surprise crossed his features for a moment. I probably deserved that since I looked like the walking dead.

"Hey, what's up?" I asked in my best pretend chipper voice.

"Daryl called me. It looks like we're doing the dinner thing tonight."

Swell. Daryl had wonderful timing. The day I emerged from my cave of depression looking like shit warmed over was the perfect day for me to pretend I was moving on with my life with my bodyguard. Yeah, this was fantastic.

I put my coffee mug down on the counter and folded my arms across my chest. "I bet right now you're wishing you hadn't agreed to this. I'll see what I can do to look less like a hot mess."

A slow smile spread across Gage's mouth. "No worries. How does six sound?"

"As good a time as any, right? So what does Daryl have planned for us? Casual or black tie formal?"

"He didn't say, but he said I should wear a suit. That's my task today, unless you're planning to leave the house. It seems my usual suits aren't good enough."

I looked down my body and back up at him. "Uh, no, I have no plans, but if you want a woman's help with your shopping, I'd be happy to join you. Sort of kill two birds with one stone."

He thought about my offer and nodded. "It couldn't hurt. Maybe we'll even get some people to see us together shopping. I'm sure Daryl would love that."

"Okay. Give me half an hour and I'll whip my head into shape. Wouldn't want to take out your brand new girlfriend with her looking like a train wreck. What would people think?" I joked.

Thankfully, he said nothing since telling me I looked great in any way would have made him sound like a true boyfriend and simply being supportive would have made him like a girlfriend. Either way, it would have been weird.

"I'll let Jensen know. Daryl was quite clear about that. For some reason, he seems to think that any man who's supposed to be dating you wouldn't drive."

I had to laugh. Daryl had everything planned down to the car we'd be seen in. He was nothing if not thorough. "I'll meet you at the garage in thirty then. I have to tell you, though, that I don't know where Tristan buys his suits. He has a shopper do that for him, so I don't know where to tell Jensen to take us."

"No worries there either. Daryl already told me. You up for Gerard's?"

I'd seen the store mentioned in magazines before, but I'd never been there. "I'm sure they have very nice men's suits there. I wonder why Daryl chose that store? How much do you want to bet he's already arranged for all eyes to be on you today?"

Gage chuckled. "I'd bet on it. No pressure, though, right? All we have to do is convince the entire world that you'd move on from someone like Tristan Stone to someone like me."

I stopped in front of him, struck by how his voice dropped when he basically said that he wasn't the kind of man someone like me would ever be with. Nothing could be further from the truth. In fact, the reality was that Gage was very much the kind of guy someone like me would go with. Tristan was the kind of man girls like me never ended up with.

Well, almost never.

"Don't worry. Just promise me you won't leave me standing in Gerard's while you go off with some salesgirl who doesn't look like a trainwreck."

His mouth turned down in a frown, and I quickly realized I'd offended him by implying he wasn't going to do his job. Touching his sleeve, I lightly squeezed his forearm. "I didn't mean you would really do that. I know you take your job very seriously. I was just trying to say that it's totally believable that the two of us would be together. I mean, you're a good looking guy and I'm sure lots of women are attracted to you."

I was rambling, but I didn't want to chase yet another person away, even if my insult had been entirely unintentional.

He looked down at me, and I saw in those dark blue eyes that I hadn't ruined everything. "It's okay, Nina. No need to apologize. Thanks for the compliment."

"I'm just glad you're not mad. I'll see you in thirty and we'll head out."

Gage stepped out of the dressing room in a dark grey suit and black dress shirt. I'd picked out a few combinations for him and this was by far the nicest looking. Much bigger than Tristan, he still wore a suit well, even if there was a lot more of him to fit inside one.

Standing stoically in front of the tri-fold mirror, he didn't seem to know what to do with his hands suddenly, stuffing them into his pockets and then pulling them out to let them hang at his sides before he fiddled with his shirt collar. The salesperson, a silver-haired older man with a long face who'd introduced himself as Phillip and had an interesting way of slowly buzzing around the periphery while Gage stood admiring himself, made a cooing sound of appreciation behind me. I had to agree. The suit looked good on him.

"Well, how's it feel?" I asked as Phillip swooped in to begin his job.

"It looks fantastic on you," he beamed as he gently tugged on the sleeves near Gage's shoulders. "Fits perfectly."

Gage looked back at me in the mirror with a look of discomfort that made me laugh. Nearly twice the size of the salesman, he looked like he was under attack but didn't know how to fend off the older man.

"Do you like it?"

He looked back at me and nodded. "It's a nice suit."

Phillip looked appalled at Gage's tepid reaction to what was definitely more than a nice suit. Nice suits cost a couple hundred dollars. The one he wore at that moment came in at over a grand. A little more than just nice.

"I can tell by the look on your lady's face that she likes it," Phillip said in a singsong voice. "Whatever the occasion, this suit will be the right one."

That same look of discomfort crossed Gage's face at the salesman's mention of me as his girlfriend. I merely smiled and played my part in Tristan's charade, convincing enough it seemed for Phillip, who interpreted my smile as approval for the suit and scurried away mumbling about picking out the perfect tie for the occasion. That he didn't know a thing about the so-called occasion didn't seem to matter.

I took my place next to Gage in the mirror and whispered words of support. "The first test wasn't so bad, was it? He seemed to believe we could be a couple."

"He did. If he was paying attention to my face instead of the suit, he might not have, though. I need to work on that."

"I thought you were experienced in this. Looks like you need to work on your gazing longingly technique."

My joke made him laugh, easing the tension, thankfully. Phillip returned a moment later with a stunning black and turquoise swirl pattern tie that truly was the perfect tie for the suit. Placing it in my hand, he watched as I held it up against Gage's chest, all the while staring into the mirror in an attempt to let him know now was the time to practice that gazing skill.

"Doesn't it look great, dear?" I teased. "Perfect indeed."

"Wonderful!" Extending his arm, Phillip pointed toward the register. "I'll take you over here when you're ready. Take your time."

As he walked away, Gage looked at me in the mirror. "Laying it on a little thick there, weren't you?"

"I was just practicing my doting girlfriend bit. Think I should dial it back a little?"

"Yeah. I think if we can find some happy medium between you and me, we might pull this off."

"I don't doubt it for a minute. Go get changed and I'll deal with Phillip."

Gage walked back into the dressing room while I paid for his new look, careful to drop heavy handed hints about how happy we were as a couple as the very nosy salesman hung on every word. Handing me back my credit card, he winked and leaned toward me. "You make a lovely couple."

"Thank you. My fiancé thinks so too."

Assuming I meant Gage was the man I planned to marry, he began to chatter on about how lucky he was to have me as his intended. I smiled, more at my cloaked reference than Phillip's compliments. I had to find the bright spot in all this somehow.

With his new suit in hand, Gage escorted me to the front door of the store, stopping just before we stepped outside. Leaning down, he whispered, "Plans have changed. Daryl's made sure we're seen. He wants us to go to Malone's a few blocks away for lunch instead of dinner. I'm assuming the men standing around outside are here for us, so be ready."

I looked out the glass doors and saw the small crowd of men I recognized as photographers waiting for us. Daryl sure did know how to put on a show. Taking a deep breath, I walked past Gage as he held the door, very much like the boyfriend he was playacting but leaving me wide open for the throng of press to surge toward me. Instantly overwhelmed, I was surrounded by a sea of eager faces pushing toward me as their cameras flashed. I frantically looked around for Gage as I scrambled to make my way to the car, totally unprepared for how close they got to me. From all sides, they yelled for me to look their way, wanting to know how I was holding up with Tristan gone and presumed dead and how long I'd been with my bodyguard. The insinuation was clear—I was a heartless bitch who could forget one man easily and replace him with another even easier.

Something deep inside pushed me to answer that I still loved Tristan, but when I opened my mouth to speak, Gage inserted himself in between me and the men, shielding me from them and quickly getting the two of us into the car. "Jensen, we need to get to

Malone's. The quicker the better too," he said calmly as I struggled to stop my hands from shaking.

Turning toward me, he frowned. "Are you okay? I'm sorry about that. I was so wrapped up in acting like a boyfriend that I didn't do my job as your bodyguard. That's always got to be my first concern, no matter what Daryl wants. I need to remember that."

I heard in his voice the anger he was feeling. Trying to help, I rested my palm on his forearm. "It's okay. Nothing bad happened. We're good. I'm Jezebel and the press is eating it up like it's candy."

"Nina, although I'm not entirely clear on what danger you may be in, I do know a slip up like that could let someone close enough to really hurt you. My job is to make sure that never happens. We may be pretending to play house, but Tristan Stone expects me to keep you safe from every kind of danger, even one that only looks like a nuisance like those photographers."

I hung my head, not caring about whatever danger there was around me. Those photographers had gotten to me, their words echoing in my mind. *Who's the new man, Nina? How long have you been together? What do you plan to do if Tristan Stone ever returns?*

The mere thought of Tristan's return as an *if* instead of a *when* hurt. I'd thought with Gage's help I could do this pretending thing, but I didn't realize it would be so hard. I didn't want to be with anyone else, and making people think I did felt wrong.

"You okay?"

I looked over at Gage and forced a smile. "I'm fine. I just wasn't ready for that."

"They're vipers, but that's their job. If you think about it that way, it might be easier."

Looking down at my left hand as it rested on top of my other one in my lap, I regretted ever agreeing to this. The finger where my engagement ring should have been looked like I felt. Empty.

"I guess. I want to go home."

"We need to eat at Malone's before we get to head home," he said, sounding almost apologetic.

"Fine. We'll do that, but then I want to go home."

SEVEN
Nina

Malone's was exactly the kind of place I dreaded and exactly the kind of place I knew Daryl would send us to. Small and intimate, it was dark even in the daylight and screamed romantic rendezvous. God, I wished Daryl wasn't so good at this.

The hostess escorted us to a table near a window looking directly out to the street. I quietly protested, but Gage simply showed me his phone and a text from Daryl indicating this was exactly where he'd arranged for us to be seen.

Fucking fabulous.

I held the menu up in front of my face as a small group of photographers began to gather outside. Nothing on it sounded even remotely appetizing, but I tried to convince myself that as long as the bar could whip up a chocolate martini or two, I might make it through our latest performance.

"Nina, I understand you're not happy, but hiding behind the menu isn't really what Daryl wants, I'm guessing."

"I don't care what he wants," I said from behind my menu.

The waiter arrived to take our order, entirely too chipper for my mood. I listened as Gage ordered his meal of a steak cooked medium and roasted red bliss potatoes with steamed asparagus dressed in parmesan. Ordinarily, that would have sounded good, but at that moment, just the thought of it nearly made me sick.

"What will Miss be having?" the waiter asked as he turned and looked down at me.

"Chocolate martini. Make sure the glass is sugared."

He tugged on my menu, forcing it from my hand, and smiled fakely before turning away. I looked across the table at Gage and saw a look of pity on his face. I hated his pity. Self-pity I was all about, but pity from someone who barely knew me just felt wrong.

"Liquid lunch?"

"Yeah."

We sat in silence as the waiter brought Gage's soda and my martini, the crowd outside growing the whole time. What the fuck had Daryl told them? Did they think they would catch us having sex right there in the window of Malone's?

Gage slid his hand across the table to touch mine. "Nina, I know this is hard, but we have to try."

"I don't want to try. I want to drink. I want to forget that I'm sitting here with people watching our every move and waiting for us to act like we care about each other."

"Maybe if I tell you something about me and Angela that might help?"

"Sure," I mumbled as I focused on the taste of my martini as it sat on my tongue, all chocolately goodness.

He didn't move his hand away, keeping it on top of mine and giving the photographers something to snap away at, which they did. Every part of me wanted to take my hand back, but I kept it there as he began to tell the tale of the woman he'd loved.

"I remember the first time we knew we thought more of each other than just bodyguard and client. She was on location in Spain. We'd been pretending to be a couple for months, but one night, it all just came together."

"Was it love at first sight?" I asked as I took a healthy gulp of my drink, enjoying the warming sensation it left in its wake as I swallowed.

Gage shook his head. "No. She was like a spoiled child when I first began guarding her. I don't think we spoke our first words to one another for weeks after I was hired. Well, that's not true. She snapped at me constantly in those weeks. When we finally began talking, I could see she wasn't that diva I'd thought she was."

"Sounds like that Whitney Houston movie, The Bodyguard."

"Not exactly. She wasn't that bad."

I held up my glass to let the waiter know I needed a refill. "Well, it's nice to know there was a happy ending," I said as I looked around the restaurant for the missing waiter.

"Not really. She married someone else last March."

Turning to look at him, for first time I saw emotion in his eyes. God, I was such a bitch! I placed my glass down on the table and rested my other hand on top of his. "I'm sorry. I didn't mean to be so flippant about everything. You obviously cared about her."

"Yeah, well, that whole good things happening to good people thing doesn't always happen to everyone. Sometimes things are bad and that's all there is."

The waiter brought Gage's food and another martini for me, and we sat in silence as he ate and I attempted to drown both our troubles. The press milling about outside had taken lots of pictures when I touched his hand, so I hoped we'd done our job well enough for Daryl to be happy. I didn't want to think Tristan would be happy. I wanted to believe he'd be as jealous as I'd be if I saw him holding hands with another woman.

By the time I'd drunk three martinis, Gage was finished with lunch. In addition to tasting great, my chocolate martinis had the wonderful effect of making me hate the facade we had to keep up a little less, at least for the moment. I was also feeling more talkative.

"It was love at first sight for me with Tristan," I announced as Gage finished the last of his steak and wiped his mouth.

"That's cool. I didn't realize that even existed in real life."

"Well, maybe not first sight, but the first time he kissed me, it was definitely something like love."

"Those drinks sure have an effect on you," Gage joked. "Even your body language has eased up. You look like you did that night at ETA."

"You were there with us that night?" I asked, surprised to know he'd seen Tristan and me then.

Gage nodded. "West and I have been in the shadows with you since you returned home from the hospital, especially when you're alone without Tristan."

He knew that I'd gone to see Cal that time and probably knew I'd secretly met with him those other times. I didn't know why, but I needed to explain that I hadn't cheated on Tristan.

"Then you know about me meeting with Cal Johnson. I didn't do anything wrong, you know. It was all on the up-and-up."

"I know. If you had done anything, we would have had to tell Tristan. I know it's not my place to say so, Nina, but your ex-boyfriend is a scammer."

"I found that out. I guess it's nice to know that you guys were around to make sure nothing bad happened."

"And Jensen too," he said with a smile. "I was surprised he jumped in that night at that bar. You must have made quite an impression on the guy."

Gage's phone dinged, and he lifted it to show me it was Daryl texting him. I didn't have to see the entire text to know what he wanted. All it took was one word I saw scrolling across the top of his phone.

Kiss

His text was longer than that, including where and when to kiss me, and as Gage read it to me, I felt the intense need for another drink. Maybe being entirely hammered would make it possible for me to kiss another man for the cameras.

I lifted my glass, but Gage pushed my wrist down so the glass sat back on the table. "I think we need to go."

"I think I want another drink. You just read the decree from Daryl that I have to kiss you, and what that means is that the man I love told him he's okay with that. I need another fucking drink."

"Let's get you home and then whatever you're feeling you can let out all you want. I just don't want to see you unravel in front of these people."

Turning to look out the window, I saw the photographers and suddenly hated them. I hated this whole thing. I didn't want to do this anymore. As I stared out at them, my phone vibrated and I swiped the face to see Daryl had sent me a text too.

But it was even worse than the one he sent to Gage because this one wasn't from him. It was from Tristan.

Daryl says you won't do what he asked. I know this is hard, but we need the world to think you've moved on. It's just for a short time, princess. Remember that and we'll be okay.

Princess. It was Tristan, after all. All those texts and this was the one he decided was worth responding to? Crushed, I let my fingers fly over the keyboard on my phone. *What happened to the man who was so jealous that I couldn't even have drinks with my ex? Now you're okay with me kissing Gage, the guy the world knows as my incredibly sexy bodyguard who's doing so much more than just guarding my body these days? Thanks for bothering to clear this up for me.*

I waited for another text from Tristan from Daryl's number, but it never came. Whatever he felt about me kissing another man, he couldn't even bother to reply.

The Kiss happened just as Daryl dictated—or maybe it was how Tristan dictated—right outside the restaurant as we walked to Jensen and our waiting car. It meant nothing to me physically, but emotionally, I was devastated that Tristan had actually wanted it to happen. All those months alone and what did I have to show for it? The man I loved and prayed every day and night to see again telling me that I had to kiss another man.

We rode back to the house in silence, my misery stewing inside me as I listened almost hypnotized to the sound of the tires rolling over highway, and I beat a path for my room the moment the car jerked to a stop in the garage. All I wanted was to be alone. No more pretending with Gage. No more orders from Daryl. No more anything. Just me curled up in bed.

Before I did that, though, I had to text Tristan. Even if he didn't answer back, which he never did, I needed to say some things. Slowly, I spelled out how much I hated all of this, ending with the one question I couldn't push out of my mind.

Do you even care about me anymore?

Closing my eyes, I let the tears burning my eyelids slide down my cheeks and prayed to God I could at least suffer in solitude.

Unfortunately, I couldn't even have that. Just minutes after pulling the covers up over my head, I'd barely closed my eyes before I heard a knock on my door. I hadn't told Gage I didn't want to be bothered, assuming he understood that by my behavior all the way home from the city, so I padded over to the door and opened it to find not him but Daryl standing there. His bushy red beard looked like he'd been tugging on it all day, and he looked about as bad as I felt.

"Can we talk?"

"Now? I'm a little busy trying to sleep, Daryl. Come back later."

"Why are you sleeping in the middle of the afternoon?" he pried, irritating me.

"Because I'm goddamned exhausted after my little shopping trip with Gage and the subsequent show you made us put on. So if you don't mind, I'd like to be alone. Why don't you talk to him? Maybe you have some more things you want us to do together. A make out session on Broadway? Or maybe a live sex show right outside the gate so the press can get their pictures and their rocks off? Sort of a kill two birds with one stone kind of thing."

"I can see you're upset, but we need to talk. Tristan wanted me to tell you..."

I pushed my hand in front of his face to cut him off. "Don't. I don't want to hear another thing about what Tristan wants. I know what he wants, so thank you for that. Now leave me alone."

Before I could slam the door in his face, he pushed it back and stuck his hairy face toward me. "We really need to talk."

All the sadness at realizing Tristan was with Daryl but couldn't even contact me, except to tell me to kiss another man, came flowing out of me, and I released the door. I didn't care if my crying made Daryl uncomfortable. I didn't care what he thought at that moment. I was sick and tired of his edicts or Tristan's edicts, or whatever the hell they were.

I just wanted my life with Tristan back.

"Nina, I know this is hard, but it's important."

"I don't care anymore! The only goddamned time Tristan bothers to text me back is to inform me that he wants me to kiss Gage? Are you kidding? I'm supposed to be okay with all of this? Well, I'm not!"

Daryl stepped back as my voice grew louder and louder until it was nothing less than a shrill scream. All the better. After all this time, I wanted to scream. I wanted to hit my fists against something, or better, someone.

"And you can tell my dear fiancé that he should be nervous. I mean, Jordan already thinks that I snuck behind her back to snag Gage from her. Maybe I am. Maybe I'm sick of waiting for Tristan and living here all alone. You had Gage move into the room right next to mine. He's pretty good looking, Daryl. Maybe I'm ready to move on, even though I know Tristan isn't dead. Maybe you should tell Tristan all of that and see how he feels. Tell him I'm all for fucking my hot bodyguard, you know, just to make sure the press really believes our story. Maybe then he'll understand how awful I feel."

I'd never seen Daryl surprised before. He usually wore a mainly bland expression with me, but at that moment, I saw that he knew I was serious. Maybe he even believed I did want Gage. Good. Then maybe he'd go back to Tristan and let him know that their stupid plan was tearing me apart.

"Nina, I don't think Tristan meant to upset you."

Rubbing the mascara from underneath my eyes, I snapped, "Well, he did! Let him know that too."

He reached into his coat pocket and pulled out an envelope with my name on it. I recognized the writing instantly. Tristan's. Daryl held out his hand for me to take it, quietly saying, "Maybe this will help you feel better."

This time one of Tristan's love letters wasn't going to do it. In fact, it only served to make me angrier. Shaking my head, I folded my arms across my chest. "Nope. You can take that back to him, wherever he is, and tell him that whatever he wants to say to me he can say in person. And since I'm getting closer and closer to Gage every day, tell him he doesn't have to worry about me being in danger."

I knew my words were harsh, but the ones I left unspoken were even worse. And I knew Daryl. He had no sense of romance whatsoever and little tact, so he'd tell Tristan exactly what I'd said. When he did, Tristan would read into my words, like always, and hear everything I'd said and what I'd left unsaid.

Backing away, Daryl still wore a look of shock on his face as he stood with Tristan's letter in his hand watching the door close in front of him. I walked back to my bed and slipped under the covers again, swearing that I wouldn't come out again until Tristan was the one knocking on my door.

That pledge didn't pan out either, though. As I lay there hearing someone knock on my door once again, I found it stunning that in a house where I was surrounded by mostly men I couldn't be left alone. It was like being in the middle of every woman's dream of having men who wanted to talk. To me, it was more like a nightmare.

I shuffled over to the door, fully prepared to read Daryl the riot act this time. This was my house, and he had it coming. Flinging it open, I saw Gage standing there looking down at me. Reaming someone out would have to wait.

"I just wanted to check to make sure you're okay."

"I'm fine."

"If you want to talk..."

Gage's voice faded to silence, as if he instantly regretted his offer. In truth, I didn't want to talk. I wanted to scream.

"What do you want to talk about? How my fiancé thinks making me kiss other men is a good idea? How I'm devastated over knowing that he's obviously with Daryl and can't be bothered to even fucking text me to tell me he misses me?"

With each syllable, my voice grew louder until by the end, I was yelling at my poor bodyguard-turned-fake boyfriend. At that moment, I didn't care if I was hurting anyone else's feelings. I was just sick of what I was feeling.

I turned away from Gage and walked back to my bed, suddenly exhausted from the weight of my emotions. He cautiously followed me, taking a seat next to me on the bed as I began to sob, and put his arm around my shoulders as they heaved from my crying.

"It's okay, Nina. I know it seems like everything's crazy now, but sometimes that's how it has to be," he said softly as I buried my face in his chest.

"I can't do crazy anymore. This is too hard."

For the first time since that night Tristan and I first made love, the thought that I couldn't handle Tristan's world settled into my mind. I still loved him, but I just didn't know if I was the right person to deal with all that came with him.

Gage let me have a good, long cry, and I sat back from him to wipe the tears from under my eyes. Shaking my head, I apologized for being such a fucked up mess. "I'm sorry you have to see this. I bet right now you're wishing you never said yes to pretending to be my boyfriend, although I'm guessing Daryl didn't give you much choice, did he?"

A gentle smile lit up his face. "Not really, but it's okay. This isn't so bad. I'm used to crying females. I had three sisters all within five years of me, so high school was an almost constant stream of crying and screaming."

"Three sisters so close together? The bathroom arrangement alone must have been a nightmare."

Chuckling, he said, "I don't remember seeing the bathroom much in high school. Thankfully, we had a half bath in the basement or my father and I would have been in real trouble."

"Your family sounds nice."

"My family sounds like a bunch of crazy people. It's okay. You don't have to lie. I know."

Sniffling back the last of my tears, I said, "I don't know what it's like to have a family like that. My mother died when I was little, and my sister's six years older than me. By the time I was old enough to want to hang around with her, she wasn't interested in hanging around with me."

He nodded. "Yeah, siblings can be like that. I never had a brother, but I had three younger sisters, and I can tell you I never wanted to hang with them back then. People change as they get older, so maybe you and your sister could hang out now."

I shook my head, all too sure that would never be the case with Kim. "I doubt it. My sister and I are just two very different people. Do you know that even before she met Tristan she accused him of being a murderer? A murderer! She hadn't even laid eyes on him or ever talked to him for a minute and she was sure he was some ax murderer or something. That's who she is. I just don't think she ever wanted me to be happy."

"I'm hoping he's not an ax murderer because I'm not in the mood to defend myself right now since if he saw us sitting together like this he might want to kill me," Gage said with a smile.

Turning to face him, I folded my legs underneath me and hung my head. "I doubt it. He seemed perfectly fine with me kissing you, so I doubt you sitting here with me would bother him even a little."

Gage shook his head. "I think you're wrong there. Men don't appreciate other men sitting on the same bed with their girlfriends. Sorry, fiancée. I know I wouldn't."

"I would think those men might not order their girlfriends or fiancées to kiss other men then."

Smiling, he shook his head again. "He thinks you're in danger and is trying to keep you safe, Nina."

"Then he should be here taking care of that himself instead of making you and me play house."

"Powerful men have enemies. Dangerous enemies. I don't know Tristan at all, to be honest, but from what I've seen, he cares about you."

I knew Gage was right, but that didn't mean I was feeling any better about Tristan and Daryl's plan. "Sometimes I wonder."

Without any warning, I broke down in tears again. God, I was a mess! Burying my face in my hands, I sobbed at the reality that I wasn't sure if Tristan even cared anymore. Months of wondering where he was and if he was okay had turned into wondering if he still loved me at all.

The bed shifted, and I felt Gage move closer to hug me again. I guess I shouldn't have let him, but being held felt so good. After so long, I didn't feel alone. "It's okay, Nina. Let it out."

Lifting my head to say thank you for him being so understanding, I looked up and time seemed to change into slow motion. Those dark blue eyes gazed down at me so full of concern that for a moment I felt like I should comfort him and let him know I'd be okay. Instead, I just stared up into his face and then it happened.

I didn't know if he kissed me or I kissed him, but we kissed. I hadn't been kissed in months, and for a split second I let myself enjoy the sensation of his soft lips on mine. It was the nicest, most innocent kiss I'd ever had, and instantly, I felt guiltier than ever before in my life.

When time resumed its normal motion, I abruptly pulled away and shook my head over and over. From behind my hand covering my guilty mouth, I mumbled, "I'm so sorry. I don't know why I did that. That should have never happened."

The expression on his face was a mixture of the guilt he shared with me and surprise, which made me believe I'd kissed him. Maybe I had. I didn't know. It all just happened so unexpectedly.

"I better go. I'm just glad you feel better."

He left without another word, and as I sat there with my hand still covering my mouth, all I knew was that I'd never felt so awful in my life.

EIGHT

TRISTAN

While I waited for Daryl to return, I took a look around the apartment he'd rented for me on the edge of the town closest to the house. He'd done a good job getting me as close as possible to Nina. On foot, I was probably only a few minutes away across a field that butted up against the property. All of three rooms and a bathroom, the apartment wasn't even big enough to measure up to the rooms Nina stayed in when she'd first come to live with me, but I didn't plan to stay here long.

I sat on the full sized bed that took up most of the space in the tiny, white bedroom and stared into the mirror across from me. I barely recognized myself. Months of exile had whittled away at my body so I was much leaner. Hair longer than I'd worn in years fell into my eyes, and my beard was practically as long and bushy as Daryl's. Only my eyes still told others I was Tristan Stone, assuming anyone could see them through the hair.

It felt good to be back home, or at least close to home. Soon I'd find out what Karl was up to and finally get to return to Nina and our life together. Until then, I had to hope she'd understand what I had to do to safeguard that life.

A knock on the door told me Daryl was back, and I answered it to find him looking shell-shocked. He pushed past me and walked into the apartment's narrow galley kitchen to rummage through the cabinets.

"I know I stored a bottle up here somewhere. You couldn't have drank it all already, did you?"

I leaned against the doorframe and pointed toward the cabinet on the far end of the wall. "I didn't have any yet, but I'm not sure how I feel about you drinking my Lagavulin. Get your own bottle."

Daryl poured himself a glass neat, never asking me if I wanted one, and sagged against the Formica countertop as he gulped down my expensive scotch. "You owe me, buddy. After what I just went through, I deserve the entire bottle."

Fear that something had happened to Nina raced through my body, settling into my heart. "What happened? Is Nina hurt?"

Downing another mouthful of scotch, he shook his head. "No. The only person injured is me."

I looked him up and down and saw the same old Daryl. "What are you talking about? You look fine enough to drink all my scotch."

He took the envelope I'd given him for Nina out of his coat pocket and threw it on the counter. "She went nuts when I tried to give her this. Told me she didn't want your letter and that you can say what you want to say to her in person. And when I say told, I mean screamed her bloody head off."

Nina had always loved my notes and letters. The fear that I was losing her had haunted me since I'd left and suddenly became very real. Picking up the envelope, I ran my fingers over her name, unsure of what I needed to do.

"That was after she literally balled me out. Her exact words were 'You can tell my dear fiancé that he should be nervous. Maybe I'm sick of waiting for Tristan and living here all alone. Gage is right next door in the room next to me. He's pretty good looking. Maybe I'm ready to move on, even though I know Tristan isn't dead. Maybe you should tell Tristan all of that and see how he feels.' And all of that was done screaming at me!"

"Did you tell her this is only for a short time?"

He mumbled, "Then she mentioned something about fucking her hot bodyguard before she slammed the door in my face."

As he finished his drink and poured himself another glass, I began to spin out of control. I'd expected too much from her. Leaving her alone for months and believing that she'd be fine with it was wrong. Even worse, I'd put another man right in front of her—a man she very well might be attracted to.

"I can't stay away any longer, Daryl. I need to go home."

His eyes bugged out of his head as he threw his hands up in the air in disgust. "Jesus Christ! You can't go home. If Karl knows you're there, you'll put Nina in danger too. You need to just sit tight while we find out what that fucker's up to."

"You figure that out. I need to get back home. I've expected Nina to deal with too much."

"She's fine. Don't worry about her. I'm sure it was just a bad day for her. She's tough. She can handle it."

"I can't handle it."

Unable to admit to Daryl that Nina's hopefully empty threat had made me more jealous than I thought I could be, I just stood there as my mind spiraled trying to figure out how I could go home without putting her in any more danger.

"I know what you're worried about, Tristan, but you can trust her and Varo. He's a good guy."

That made what I was feeling even worse. A good guy sleeping in the room right next to her after they pretended to be in love all day. Fucking perfect. No, I had to go home. Somehow, I had to be able to be near her.

"I don't care. I need to go back. Now. So help me figure it out."

"You're killing me here, Tristan. The two of you lovebirds are just killing me." Stroking his beard to a long point below his chin, he pursed his lips as he thought. "I have an idea, but I need to know. Can you can speak any languages other than English?"

"You mean like French or Spanish? No."

He sighed. "Well, that doesn't help."

"I know sign language, though."

Daryl narrowed his eyes to slits, as if he was considering what I'd just said. "You mean for deaf people?"

"Yeah. I had no interest in learning any language in high school, so they said I could take American Sign Language. I'm still pretty good at it."

I began to fingerspell, quickly remembering the alphabet and some common signs like I'm sorry and thank you.

"Can you do that with gloves on?"

I closed my fist and moved it up and down to sign yes. "As long as my fingers are free, I can sign. Why? What are you thinking?"

Downing the last of his drink, he smiled for the first time since he arrived. "I'm thinking I'm a genius. Hang on."

He took his phone out and tapped in a number before putting it to his ear. In seconds, I understood his plan. "Nina, it's Daryl. You need to fire the gardener. I'll have a new one there tomorrow."

Nina's voice came through the phone loud and clear. "Why? There's nothing wrong with Chip. West and Gage cleared him and he's fine."

"I found out something that makes it appear he might be connected to Karl. I can fire him, if you like."

"Fine, you do it. I don't want to fire him. He's been nothing but nice."

"I'll be right over to take care of it."

Daryl put his phone away and turned toward me with a broad smile. "Okay, now that that's taken care of, you can be the gardener. I'll say you're deaf and dumb and only communicate through signing. We need to get you some sunglasses to hide your eyes, but other than that, you barely look like you after all these months."

"One problem. I can't keep sunglasses on every moment I'm at the house, and one look at my eyes and she'll know it's me in a heartbeat."

Walking past me into the living room, he shook his head. "I'm one step ahead of you. Come with me. It's time to head to Wal-Mart to change those big brown eyes to something even your lady won't recognize."

I followed him, thrilled to know that I'd be close to Nina again and taking pleasure in his amusement at all of this. "You seem almost happy, Daryl. Enjoying yourself?"

"I'll enjoy myself when all this is over and you and Nina are back together so she doesn't ream me out anymore. Ever been to Wally World?"

I followed behind Daryl as he walked the stone path toward the gardens behind the house. Our Wal-Mart trip had been a success, but my color changing contacts wouldn't be in for up to a week, so I questioned whether his whole grand plan was going to fall apart the minute I was introduced to Nina.

Slowing down to walk next to me, he whispered, "No matter what she says, do not take off those glasses. Just let me handle everything. Remember, you're deaf and dumb."

I made the OK sign with my hands, which were hidden inside gloves. That I was already wearing gloves before I began the job seemed even odder than the sunglasses, but I was afraid she'd suspect something if she saw my hands.

"Is that supposed to be something I know?" he asked, staring at my fingers.

"It means OK," I whispered out of the side of my mouth.

"No talking. You want to be able to see her every day or not?"

He knew the answer to that. Just being on the grounds again filled me with anticipation. My stomach flipped when I thought about finally seeing her after all these months. Even if she didn't know who I was, I'd finally be able to be close to her.

Then I saw her. In the distance, she appeared angry as she stormed down the pathway toward us, and I recognized that look of unhappiness on her face. All at once, I knew the story Daryl had told me about her reaming him out was no exaggeration, but even angry she looked beautiful. She wore her long hair up in a ponytail and had no makeup on. But it didn't matter. She was still the most beautiful woman I'd ever seen.

"Nina, how are you today?" Daryl asked as we all met at a bend in the path.

"I'm fine, Daryl. I don't really know why you needed me out here for this, but I'm fine," she said sourly.

"I felt you should meet the new gardener since I had to fire the old one."

"I liked Chip, Daryl. He was a nice guy. I feel bad that you fired him. To be honest, I can't imagine he'd be involved with anyone bad."

"Not to worry. This is Ethan and he's going to be fine."

Nina looked me up and down and then looked back at Daryl. "Ethan?"

"Yeah. He doesn't speak because he's deaf and dumb, but he knows his way around a shrub."

She looked me up and down once more and turned her back toward me to speak to Daryl. "Are you two brothers at the Water Buffalo Lodge or something and you owe him a favor? He looks oddly like you. And deaf and mute? How is he going to do this?"

"He's got a disability, but we can't hold that against him. As for the beard, it's not as nice as mine, but you have to give him points for trying. Don't worry. He's perfect for this."

She turned around, and I saw her expression soften. After studying me for a few moments, she extended her hand. "It's nice to meet you, Ethan. I hope you'll be happy here." I shook her hand, wishing I wasn't wearing gloves so I could feel her skin against mine. I wanted to take her in my arms and fill my nose with the familiar scent of lavender her shampoo left in her hair. I wanted to hold her against me and tell her I was there with her.

Turning toward Daryl, she continued, "I think Chip was working on fixing up the garden so it would be ready for the summer. I'd told him I wanted to plant some vegetables, so have Ethan pick up where Chip left off."

"Got it."

"Anything else, Daryl?"

Smiling, he shook his head. "No. I'm glad to see you're in a better mood today."

"You can thank Gage for that," she said with a chuckle before she turned on her heels and walked away.

In that second, my chest felt like someone hit it with a sledgehammer. I'd never been so jealous in my life and unable to do a thing about it. All I could do was stand there pretending like I hadn't heard her just imply she'd slept with her bodyguard.

Daryl's hand clamped down on my forearm and he whispered, "Relax. She didn't mean anything by it. Remember, they're pretending to be together. I've got an idea on Cordovex to check out, so get to trimming the hedges or whatever and I'll check in with you tonight back at your place."

I barely heard him over the sound of my heartbeat pounding in my ears.

By the time I got back to the apartment that night, I'd nearly gone out of my mind with jealousy. From where I was standing as I raked and hoed to prepare the space Nina wanted to use for her vegetable garden, I was able to watch the inside of the lower level of the house. Varo looked quite at home as he swam in my pool in the middle of the day, joined by Nina at one point who didn't swim but sat and watched for a few minutes as he did.

Sat and watched as his ridiculously muscular body swam back and forth in front of her while she kept her eyes fixed on him.

I spent a half hour filling in the hole I accidentally dug with the spade as I watched the two of them together. He was lucky I was committed to this plan of Daryl's because if I wasn't, I would have used that spade for another far more satisfying purpose that would have required me to dig a much deeper hole.

While one of the bodyguards I hired to protect Nina was busy taking his job far too literally, the other seemed intently interested in me. West watched me pantomime gardening for nearly an hour before he approached me, tapping me on the shoulder none too lightly after I ignored his efforts to say hello three times. When I said nothing in return even after acknowledging his presence, he left frustrated and spent the next hour spying on me, his enormous frame obvious from his hiding spots behind trees and bushes.

Maybe I wasn't fooling anyone. He didn't even make an effort to be sly as he watched me muddle through cleaning out twigs and weeds from the garden area. By the time I finished, I'd decided that once I was back West was gone. If he was this clumsy watching me, I couldn't imagine how bad he was at protecting Nina. Of course, that meant I had to be thankful for Varo's presence around her, which was the last thing I wanted to admit.

I needed a drink.

Sitting down in front of the TV Daryl had been nice enough to include in my new place, I tried to get lost in some sitcom and scotch with little success. There I was, sitting in some hole in the wall apartment while Nina and Varo were enjoying my house, probably my liquor, and...

I couldn't bring myself to think about them enjoying my bed, but somewhere in the back of my mind a tiny, insidious voice whispered again and again, *"They're together."* I'd never been good at handling jealousy, and my paranoia about Nina sleeping with Varo quickly mushroomed in my brain, leaving me with the choice of blowing Daryl's plan by storming over to the house to reunite with the woman I loved and in the process putting her in danger or getting stone drunk.

The half-inch of scotch left in the bottle sitting on the coffee table in front of me made my choice next to impossible. If I was going to get through that night, a trip to the liquor store was in order. All the better. I was already feeling trapped in my new place and looked forward to the half mile or so walk to get more of the only thing that was going to help me forget, at least for a few hours.

I set out on my quest for alcohol and met few people on my way, all of them shying away from me by refusing to make eye contact and one even crossing the street to get away from me. For a moment, I couldn't figure out why until I remembered I didn't look like Tristan Stone with my scruffy hair and overgrown beard. Never before in my life had I experienced people avoiding me because of my appearance. The tiny village of Millbrook, New York must have been used to a better class of person. I used to be that class, but as the gardener Ethan, I definitely stuck out like a sore thumb among Manhattanites visiting their country homes. It was eye-opening, to say the least.

The greasy-haired liquor store clerk gave me a similar reception when I walked into his store, watching me intently as I passed him on my way to the scotch aisle. I stood staring at the various bottles, my mind preoccupied with how differently I was treated looking like I did now. A little longer hair and a bad beard and suddenly I was persona non grata.

I felt a tug on my sleeve and turned to see Nina standing there staring up at me. Immediately, I realized I wasn't wearing my sunglasses. My hair hung in my eyes, so I squinted at her, hoping to hide my eye color.

She smiled and waved at me, obviously remembering that I couldn't hear or speak. I smiled a closed mouth smile back, afraid if I acted too much like myself that she'd figure out my ruse. She made a motion with her hands that looked like she was trying to ask if I drank, and I nodded. Hoping to deflect her attention from me, I signed *Are you here to buy alcohol?* She had no idea what I was asking and shaking her head, said sweetly, "I'm sorry. I don't know what you mean."

I pointed at the bottles and then pointed at her as I repeated my question with my hands. My distraction seemed to work because she walked away, and for a moment I thought I was safe, but she returned a few seconds later with a bottle of hazelnut liqueur in one hand and a bottle of cheap vodka in the other. I recognized the liqueur bottle instantly as the same one the bartender at ETA had used that night when he made her the chocolate martini.

"I fell in love with this chocolate cake martini a while back and really wanted one tonight," she explained as I smiled down at her and pretended not to understand what she meant, all the while loving the sound of her sweet voice again.

She sensed I didn't understand and put the two bottles she was holding on the shelf next to her so she could take out a pen and paper. She scribbled a few words and held it up so I could read it.

Do you like scotch? My fiancé likes it too. I can't drink it, though. Too hard. :(

God, she was sweet. How much I wanted to hold that beautiful face in my hands and tell her it was me standing in front of her instead of some guy who worked on her garden all day, seething with jealousy as he watched her be friendly to another man.

Thinking it might seem too obvious if Ethan liked scotch too, I shook my head and pointed at the American whiskey further down the aisle away from where I was standing. Then I took the pen from her hand and wrote *I like whiskey instead,* forgetting that I didn't have gloves on. She could clearly see my hands and knew my handwriting from all my notes and letters.

Fearful I'd ruined Daryl's plan, I dropped the pen onto the paper she held in her hand and stuffed my hands into my pockets. Thankfully, she was too busy reading what I'd written to notice that I was hiding my hands. She wrote something else and smiled up at me as I read her message.

It was nice seeing you here. Have a great night!

Before I could nod and hope she understood I wished her the same, I saw Varo come through the front door and march up behind her, his expression filled with protective concern.

"Nina, is everything okay?" he asked.

"I'm fine. I was just talking to Ethan. He's the new gardener."

Varo sized me up and quickly moved to guide Nina out of the store, but I was thrilled to see her fight him. A tiny flicker of joy crept into my heart as she pushed him away to be nice to someone she'd just met that day. She was still my Nina, the same old gentle soul she'd always been.

"Let's go," he insisted, again trying to direct her toward the register.

"Okay, let me say goodbye," Nina answered in a tone I recognized immediately as her impatient voice.

Waving to me as she backed away, she smiled and nearly melted my heart. "See you."

I nodded, remembering not to take my hands out of my pockets and to keep my eyes squinted, watching her walk away with the makings for her chocolate martini and Varo. Even after I couldn't see her anymore, I stood there waiting to hear the jingle of bells on the door when she left, grabbing her note she'd placed on the shelf and a bottle of Lagavulin when the coast was clear and confusing the clerk when I paid with a couple fifties.

By the time I got back to what I was now calling home, I was sick of being judged by everyone I met and in need of a good stiff drink. Two glasses of scotch later, I sat back against my cheap couch and replayed my meeting with Nina at the liquor store, loving that of all the people I'd encountered that day, only she'd been truly kind to me.

As I nodded off to sleep, all I could hope for was that my time away from her wouldn't last much longer. I didn't want to be a stranger anymore.

NINE

TRISTAN

Over the next week, my contacts came in but I saw little of Nina. I tried to get a glimpse of her whenever I was close to the house, but she never seemed to be in any of the rooms I could see into. I saw Varo quite often, usually walking back to the carriage house or hanging out with West on the grounds near where he used to live. He paid little attention to me, which could have been attributed to either Daryl telling him about my real identity or his lack of interest in me since I was just a mute gardener.

I didn't care which it was since a ball of hate for him inside me grew larger by the second. It was irrational and it didn't matter. I hated him for being able to come and go in Nina's life as he pleased while I stood there pretending to care about the shape of the fucking hedges on my property or how long the damn grass should be.

One sunny morning, eight days after our chance meeting at the liquor store, she came walking down the pathway to where I stood cleaning up weeds against the fence on the property line. I didn't remember her ever coming out this way when we were together, but I was thrilled all the same. Any time I got to spend with her was better than any without her.

As I watched her make her way toward me, she waved and smiled broadly, looking truly happy to see me. I loved it, but then the fear that she'd found me out raced through my mind, and I stood frozen on the spot waiting to hear what she had to say.

She stopped in front of me and waved again as she said, "Hi!"

I smiled and waved back, putting down the weed whacker.

Then she spoke the sweetest words I'd heard in months. "I don't know much sign language, but I've been reading up on it to learn some." That she coupled that one sentence with an attempt to sign what she meant made me happier than I thought I could be still separated from her.

Even if I wanted to, I couldn't have stopped myself from smiling. Knowing I had to contain my joy at her kindness, I signed back *Thank you* and then finger spelled *M-i-s-s E-d-w-a-r-d-s*.

Her eyes focused on my right hand as I spelled out her name, and she looked up at me with a quizzical look. Shaking her head, she said, "You're too fast. What did you spell?"

I spelled out Miss Edwards slower this time, and she nodded her understanding. "Can you read lips?" she asked staring up at me with a look of hope in her eyes.

Wobbling my right hand to indicate I could read them a little, she finger spelled O-K with two letters, obviously thrilled that she knew how to do at least that correctly. She was too cute, but I still put up the OK sign nearly everyone in the world knew, making her blush at her mistake.

"Oh. I guess I should have known that."

All I could do was smile at how adorable she was. But why did she bother to come all the way out here and why had she taken the time to learn some sign language?

We stood there looking at one another until I signed, *Why did you come here to see me?*

She recognized the why and the see me parts and an uneasy look crossed her face as she shifted her weight from one foot to the other. Signing the words with effort, she answered, *I wanted to say I'm sorry for how I acted that day I met you.*

I touched the tips of my fingers to the center of my forehead and pulled my hand forward and down into the letter Y to sign the question *Why?* as I shook my head to let her know she didn't have to apologize.

Opening her mouth to speak, she shrugged instead. Looking back toward the house, she signed, *How do you get here every day?*

I pointed to my legs and smiled. In truth, I hadn't walked as much in years as I did now. Not that I liked it. I'd have taken the Jag over my feet any day.

Signing, she asked, *Do you live near here?*

Again, I didn't sign but pointed, this time toward the village that sat less than a mile from where we stood.

"Do you live in Millbrook? Have you ever had Tony's pizza?" she asked, forgetting to sign in her excitement.

I pretended not to know what she'd just said, secretly thrilled that the idea of Millbrook immediately made her think of where she'd agreed to marry me. She finger spelled the name of our favorite restaurant and looked up at me in anticipation.

Nodding, I smiled and signed, *Good.*

I love their pizza! she signed with excitement, getting the finger spelling for pizza wrong, but it didn't matter. I was in heaven just listening to her speak.

Unfortunately, Varo made his appearance right at that moment, interrupting what had been the best fifteen minutes in a long time. Just as he had at the liquor store, he marched up behind her, his brows knitted and his expression looking almost too protective as he informed her it was time to go. I enjoyed watching her brush him off with a quick "Okay" and loved that she didn't make any effort to follow him, as he obviously wanted her to.

Needing to know how she felt about him, I probed with the question, *Is that your fiancé?*

She looked back in the direction of Varo and then focused on me. I watched as her eyes welled up with tears, and then she finger spelled, *N-o. M-y f-i-a-n-c-é i-s T-r-i-s-t-a-n.* She stopped signing and looked away to wipe a tear from her cheek, but quietly said, "I hope you get to meet him soon."

I promise it won't be long, Nina. I promise.

Obviously, Daryl hadn't explained to her that she needed to pretend Varo was her man even at home. That she didn't pretend here made me feel better. I still didn't like Daryl's plan, but Nina's willingness to share the identity of her fiancé with me, someone she barely knew and merely worked for her, told me my fears about her with anyone else were based in my stupid jealousy and nothing more.

She looked past me again toward the house and smiled. "This is a lot of property for just one gardener. Do you think I should hire someone to help you?"

As I shook my head to let her know I didn't understand what she'd said, she stared up at me, as if she was studying my face for the real answer. Something told me she wasn't sure about the man she'd hired to handle her gardening.

"Ethan, I just realized other than knowing you're Ethan Cole, I don't know anything else about you."

Her tone possessed a sharp edge, but she didn't sign her words. She was trying to catch me lying. Always my Nina, she hid a great brain behind those innocent blue eyes and gentle smile.

I shook my head and signed *I don't know what you're saying* to indicate I hadn't been able to lip read her words, stifling my smile at her cleverness.

With great effort, she signed what she'd just said, and I signed in return, *Ask me anything.*

She signed *How old are you?* and looked more like Daryl tugging on his beard as he thought about some great question than making the sign to ask how old I was.

Before I could think about my answer, I signed the number 29 and my eyes grew wide at my slip up. I really should have been better at lying by now, but just being around her made all my defenses melt away. My age being the same as her fiancé's didn't seem to register with her, though, and she simply smiled.

Do you like gardening? she asked, fumbling over the sign for gardening and making it look more like a dog scratching for fleas than her fingers raking over her left palm.

I nodded, which was a complete lie. To be honest, I couldn't wait for the moment I wasn't Ethan Cole, mute and deaf gardener. Every night I waited for Daryl to call and let me know that he'd finally figured out the secret of what Karl wanted so I could finally return to my life as Tristan Stone and the woman I loved.

You're doing a nice job, she continued, this time doing much better with her signing.

Thanking her, I added, *And thank you for learning to sign. You're very thoughtful.*

In front of me, Varo stood about twenty yards away impatiently yelling Nina's name. She didn't even bother to turn around to answer him, preferring to stay facing me.

"Time for me to take the stage," she said without signing.

Shaking my head, I shrugged to let her know I didn't understand.

Smiling, she signed, *It's nothing. Just my pretend life.* Nina turned to leave and stopped short to sign one more thing. *Have a good day, E-t-h-a-n.*

It wasn't what she signed but that I got to hear her speak those sweet words, even if her voice was tinged with unhappiness. I hated knowing what I'd convinced her to do was making her miserable, but I had to tell myself that it was what had to be done.

That didn't make it any better, though.

She walked away, her pace a little slower than when she'd approached me, I thought. My mind immediately began to spin out of control thinking about where they were going, what they'd be doing, and how I'd be standing there raking. Taking a deep breath, I told myself I couldn't let that affect me. This was the way it had to be, and that was that.

By six o'clock, I hadn't seen Nina or either of her bodyguards return home, so I left, needing a hot shower and something in my stomach. I had a newfound appreciation for the people who'd worked on my family's properties. I'd always been so spoiled that I never once considered what their lives were like. Where did they live? Where did they eat lunch? What did they do when they weren't landscaping the gardens or cleaning up after my family and me? My stint as Ethan the gardener had made all those people who'd been invisible to me for all those years suddenly come into sharp focus. To say that I didn't like what I saw was an understatement.

It's not that Nina or anyone at the house mistreated me. Quite the opposite, in fact. Nina was welcoming, and although Varo and West weren't altogether friendly, they weren't nasty or rude. I was, however, invisible there, for all practical purposes. Unlike in my life as Tristan Stone, no one wanted to spend time with me for meals or clamored to hear what I had to say about anything.

The change in my status was enlightening, to say the least.

Standing in the shower, I let the water sluice over me, loving the feel of its stinging heat on my skin. Working as a gardener was much harder work than I'd ever believed, and my body already showed the signs of its effects. Muscles that had atrophied for months when I was in exile now grew again, the result of hours of manual labor. I hadn't seen a gym in nearly half a year, but I couldn't remember my body being in better shape. Those muscles didn't come easily, though, and the hot water only did so much to ease the ache of my day job.

Scotch did the rest.

I relaxed on the couch and put my feet up on the coffee table, groaning as I stretched the tired muscles in my legs. A slice of Tony's pizza filled my stomach, and I washed it down with a gulp of scotch. Not exactly the right pairing, but I'd forgotten to ask for soda when I placed the order. It wouldn't have been the same, anyway. Tony's was great not because it was the best pizza in the world but because it symbolized something far better I shared only with Nina.

My phone vibrated across the top of the table, signaling I had a message. It was the one Nina used, and my heart leaped in my chest at the thought of what she might say. Scooping the phone up, I read her message and instantly felt like someone had my heart in a vice, turning the handle until there was nothing but the purest pain I'd ever experienced.

I miss you. I've taken to talking to almost complete strangers because I'm so lonely. Please come back to me.

Fuck. How was I supposed to keep this up? She was tearing me apart. All I wanted to do was text back that I wasn't that far away. That I was as lonely as she was and missed her more than I could say.

Daryl's telltale banging on my door shook me from my misery, and I trudged my aching feet and legs over to let him in, ready for him to add to my shitty moment.

"Nice to see you, Tristan. I hope you saved some of that drink for me," he announced as he brushed past me to take a seat on the old chair that filled out the living room set he'd gotten me.

"Tell me you have something, Daryl. I can't do this for much longer. Nina's texts are killing me. She's miserable, and I'm the reason she's miserable."

Grabbing my bottle of Lagavulin, he looked around for something to pour his drink into. "Get me a glass, would you? I've been working all day. I need this."

I found a glass in the kitchen cabinet and returned to hand it to him. "You're work is nothing like mine, I'm willing to bet. I ache all over."

He poured himself a healthy glass of scotch and sat back in the chair, grinning broadly. "Never did an honest day of work in your life, did you? Now you know how the other half lives."

Seated across from him, I watched him relish my physical pain and admitted he was right. I hadn't worked like this ever before in my life. "Yeah, but can we get to how we're going to get me back to my real life?"

"Right. I spent the last few days working on this Cordovex business. I still don't know what I'm looking at, but I can say without a doubt that whatever it is, it's buried under intentional layers meant to keep prying eyes out."

"Do we know yet if it has anything to do with my family or Stone Worldwide? I'm worried you're chasing shadows and wasting time when we could be much closer to finding out what Karl wants if we focused on something else."

"Like what?"

Shrugging, I silently admitted I didn't know. It just seemed too far-fetched to believe that some heart drug had anything to do with Karl or the reason why he wanted me and Nina out of the picture. "So what did you find out?"

Daryl took another swig of his drink and set the glass down on the table a little too heavily. The man was just clumsy. His lack of grace made me laugh, confusing him.

"Cordovex is a prescription heart drug, but it had a rough time of it after getting FDA approval. Seems it was killing some people. From what I can tell, it shouldn't have gotten approval, but somehow it made it through the process in record time."

"How's it doing today, four years later?"

"That's an interesting question. You know how it's doing, or at least you should know. If you've watched TV at any time in the past few months, you've seen ads for it."

"I haven't seen any commercials for anything called Cordovex."

"Yes, you have."

"No, I haven't. Stop talking in riddles, Daryl."

"All right. Well, from what I can make out, Cordovex has been resurrected as Cardiell now. Ring any bells?"

Not that I had watched much TV in the past few months, but even the little I'd seen had been peppered with advertisements for Cardiell. Smiling middle aged men and women actively pursuing life and all its wonders were the hallmark of every Cardiell ad. They were slick and looked like they'd cost a fortune to produce, easily convincing sick people desperate for help with a heart problem that the drug was the answer to all their concerns.

"Who makes Cardiell?"

"A pharmaceutical company named Rider Pharmaceutical, but there's a problem. I checked out Rider and it's a front—nobody seems to actually work for Rider. There's no physical address for the company. Some other company is the parent, but that's going to take a little more digging."

I grabbed my laptop from the end of the couch and began searching for the company's website. What came up in my search was a site as slick and well-produced as their commercials, complete with success stories and implied promises drug makers always included. At the bottom of the page, Rider Pharmaceutical was given as the maker of the drug, but it was a facade hiding the true business that produced Cardiell.

Daryl leaned over to look at the screen. "Nice site, isn't it? They spared no expense to make it look professional and welcoming, except for the fact that it's meaningless."

"How can a drug that was killing people a few years ago be back on the market with just a new name and some new fancy site?"

Daryl shook his head. "I have no idea. Makes you wonder about the drugs we all take, doesn't it? Give me a few more days and I think I can find what company is behind Cardiell. Then we'll know if it's something or not, but my guess is that we're going to find this is what Karl is worried about."

"Fine, but I can't wait much longer. Every time Nina texts me, I want to run across that field, jump the fence, and march right up to the house to find her. I don't want to do this to her anymore."

Standing from his chair, Daryl gave me his best "I'm working on it" look, but I saw in his eyes he didn't understand what Nina and I were going through. "Give me a couple days. That's all I think I'll need."

"Fine, but no matter what you find out, I'm going home after those couple days. This can't go on."

Rolling his eyes, he left mumbling under his breath about young lovers or something else he didn't understand. At least now I could tell myself there was an end to this whole thing. Whatever happened, Nina and I would be together soon. That's all that mattered.

An afternoon of pretending to have the hots for my bodyguard had left me feeling like a wrung out dishrag. While Gage seemed to be taking on the part of my boyfriend as if it were second nature, I still struggled with our fake relationship. In fact, instead of getting easier to act like he was the man I wanted, it was getting harder each time he and I had to parade in front of the press looking like two young lovebirds. Guilt did that to me.

I knew it wasn't his fault, but I took it out on him anyway. In just a short time, what had been a budding friendship between us had morphed into something full of resentment for me. Gage wasn't to blame, but it didn't matter. Every moment I spent with him in front of the world playacting was a moment I betrayed Tristan. Each loving gaze and touch of his hand on mine filled me with guilt and added to my shame over kissing him in my bedroom.

He saw it too. It was in the way I had to stop myself from glaring when we were in public or wouldn't look at him when we were alone in the car after our public displays. I nearly oozed contempt for him.

This was a great plan to Daryl, but to me it was torture. Thankfully, at least it seemed to be working.

Karl hadn't made any attempt to reach me, so perhaps it was all worth it, but every night when I laid my head on the pillow next to Tristan's, I hated myself for what the world thought. One mention of Gage and me on Page Six after our first outing called us "Cinderella and Her New Prince." The implication wasn't lost on me—I was nothing but a poor working girl before meeting Tristan and now that he was gone, I'd taken no time at all in replacing him with another man.

Nothing like being seen as a heartless, disloyal bitch by everyone who read Page Six.

Skipping dinner, I headed for my room to curl up in a ball and dream about a time, hopefully in the near future, when Tristan and I were happily married, living in this house without bodyguards, maybe even with a baby. Would that time ever come? On nights like this, as I lay alone missing him like a part of myself was absent, I doubted we'd ever truly be together again. So much had happened since the last time we were in each other's arms. Would we still be the same two people we were then?

I slid out of bed and made my way to his closet. Part of my nightly routine, I slipped one of his dress shirts from its hanger and held it to my nose. Even months after the last time it was against his skin, it smelled like him. Closing the closet doors, I completed the next part of my ritual and took a strong breath of his cologne that still sat next to his sink in the bathroom. Musky, woodsy, and slightly floral, it was all Tristan.

No one on Earth knew I did this every night. I hid each shirt until there were enough for a full wash and ran the load by myself when it was ready instead of letting Maria see my pathetic madness. It was okay. I knew it was crazy to do these things. Maybe I was going mad because I thought it was all right to sniff someone's clothes and cologne, but I'd heard that smell was one of the strongest senses when it came to memories. The vision of something might slip someone's mind, and a voice may be forgotten, but a smell associated with the past could bring it right back, closing the space of time and distance.

Climbing into bed, I leaned back against the headboard and with my phone in hand, completed my nightly ritual with a text to Tristan. *Is it night where you are? I'm in bed, even though it's barely 7. I miss you more every day. New people come into my life but still no you. I've begun learning sign language to speak to the new gardener. I'm sure you know about him from Daryl. I think he's a relative of his. They have similar beards.*

I read over my text and lightly snorted a chuckle. It sounded like a crazy person wrote it. That was okay. It wasn't like I'd get an answer anyway. The texting just made me feel like I still had Tristan's ear, except now he spoke even less than usual.

Clicking Send, I waited as I always did for a message back, but none came. It never surprised me but instead just added a tiny new layer of disappointment to everything else I'd felt for months. As I did occasionally, I added a text to Jordan in the hopes that she'd answer back. She never did anymore, but it was always worth a shot.

Hey you! I hope this finds you doing great. I'd love to hear what you're up to these days. Nina.

When no text came back after twenty minutes, I stopped staring at the phone and covered my head with the sheet, preferring to hide away and hope that tomorrow would be a better day.

Not an hour after waking up, I knew my wish for a better day had been shot to hell. I'd barely gotten out of the shower and Daryl was knocking at my bedroom door like the house was burning down. I quickly tied a towel around me and threw open the door, a combination of irritation and dread coursing through me.

"What? What do you need from me now that requires the damn banging on my door before ten o'clock in the goddamned morning?" I barked at his shocked face.

"I just wanted to remind you about the Stone Foundation groundbreaking today. As the appointed representative of the foundation, you need to be there."

I took a deep breath and adjusted the knot in my towel so I didn't give Daryl a show right there in the hallway. "It doesn't seem like poor form to you to have me attend a Stone Foundation function with Gage right at my elbow?"

I wanted to go to this groundbreaking of the newest Stone Foundation center in Poughkeepsie like I wanted someone to break off my right arm and beat me with it. Tristan's family had established a foundation to help local food banks across the country when he was a small child, and since the plane crash, he'd been the representative of the foundation. With his disappearance, somehow I'd been chosen as the one person to attend functions, even if I stuck out like a sore thumb around all those well-dressed men and women there to ironically celebrate helping starving people each of whom could probably live an entire year on one of their fur coats.

Daryl twisted his face into an expression that told me he was considering what I'd said. "Fair enough. Maybe you should do this without him as the boyfriend, but he and West will still be there as your bodyguards."

At least I didn't have to perform my rendition of the whore of Babylon again. That was something.

"Fine. What time do I have to be ready?"

"The groundbreaking is at eleven, and the luncheon is at noon."

"Do I have to attend both? I'm not really what people want at these kinds of things anyway."

Nodding, Daryl agreed with me for the second time that morning. "No. I think you can leave after the groundbreaking ceremony."

"Thanks. Do me a favor and tell everyone I'll be ready to go in a little while," I said quietly as I closed the door on Daryl and all the responsibilities of the world.

A half hour later, I'd transformed myself into the well-dressed representative of the Stone Foundation, complete with charcoal grey designer suit, black pumps, and hair up in a bun. Whenever I dressed like this, I felt like an actor in a costume. I wasn't a suit kind of woman, especially these days when I spent more time in yoga pants than in anything else. However, this was what was expected, so this was what I wore.

I saw by the looks on my bodyguards' faces that they were surprised by my look too, but unlike when Gage and I pretended to be together, I said nothing, preferring not to discuss the performance I had to give today. It seemed like I was constantly acting these days. If it wasn't trying to convince the world that I'd moved on, it was trying to make everyone around me believe that I wasn't falling apart a little more every day Tristan stayed away.

All this acting was exhausting.

Hiding behind big sunglasses, I smiled for the camera as a group of men in suits symbolically dug gold shovels into the ground for the new center, and then I quickly tried to escape the entire affair. As I stepped back into the shadows behind a tree and away from the throng of people who loved occasions like this mingling on the lawn, I ran into a woman and her son I'd noticed when I arrived. They were obviously out of place, dressed in clean but inexpensive clothes that looked nothing like what any of the other attendees wore, including myself. The mother appeared to be in her thirties, but I couldn't be sure because her face was wrinkled far more than most women's that age. Her dark blonde hair was brushed back into a barrette clipped at her nape, and she wore a navy blue pantsuit and black flats. The little boy couldn't have been more than six or seven, and he wore dress clothes, which looked completely out of place on him.

I apologized for bumping into the woman and saw the hollow look in her pale blue eyes. Instantly, I knew what she was there for. She and her son were to be the day's poster children for the success of the Stone Foundation. Cleaned up from what her life was in reality, she was there to act as much as I was.

Looking down at her son, I smiled. "What's your name, little man?"

"Michael," he said sweetly. "Michael Williams."

"It's nice to meet you, Michael. Are you having a good time?"

"Yeah. We're going to have lunch soon," he said with a grin, proudly showing off the space where his missing front tooth used to be.

I lifted my head and smiled at his mother. "Thank you for coming. The Stone Foundation appreciates it."

She smiled at me and extended her hand to shake mine. "Thank you. I'm Gloria Williams. My son and I are thankful for all the help your foundation has given us. We're getting back on our feet now, and it's the help of the people with the Stone Foundation that's made that possible."

I didn't know why, but I felt the need to tell her the truth about how much the foundation wasn't mine. "It's actually my fiancé's family's foundation. I'm sure he'd be happy to see that it was doing the work it was meant to."

"Please tell him thank you for us."

I smiled at the thought of telling Tristan anything. "I promise I will."

A hand gently touched my shoulder, and I turned to tell Gage that I was fine and didn't need to be rescued from this woman and her son. I knew he was just doing his job, but neither of these kind souls were a danger to me in any way. Ready to chase him away, I saw instead Karl Dreger standing there looking down at me, one eyebrow arched and making his expression sinister looking. His snakelike eyes peering out of his large head instantly terrified me.

"It's lovely to see you again, Nina. When do you think you'll be able to tell your fiancé about the good work the foundation is doing?"

Swallowing hard, I struggled to form any real answer to Karl's question, my mouth suddenly too dry to allow my tongue to work. Everything we'd done—all the playacting and being seen by the press that had made me feel like a traitor to the man I loved—all of it had been for nothing.

Gage swooped in to whisk me away seconds later, acting more like a lover than a bodyguard and saying something about looking forward to when we got home, but it was too late. I'd ruined everything with my stupid slip up.

By the time we reached the car, I could barely hold back the tears. Gage tried to follow me into the back seat as Jensen started the engine, but I pushed him away.

"Nina, I should be seen leaving with you so people keep believing we're together."

"No!" I cried as I tried to close the door. "It doesn't matter now. I've fucked it all up. Karl knows I'm not with you and Tristan isn't gone for good."

"It doesn't matter what he thinks. We need to keep up the act," Gage protested as I continued to tug on the car door.

"Let me go! It's over now!" I screamed, forcing him to back away enough to allow me to grab the door from him and slam it shut. Slumping back against the seat, I closed my eyes as the tears began to roll down over my cheeks and sobbed, "Jensen, please take me home. I want to go home."

As he raced over the roads of Dutchess County, I texted Tristan the bad news. *I'm sorry I messed up. I didn't mean to. Wherever you are, please know I love you and never meant to ruin everything. I'm sorry.*

For the first time in all of this, I was scared.

I expected to see Daryl waiting for me when I got back to the house, but there was no one except Ethan who stood trimming the shrubs on the side of the house near my bedroom. Even though I had no idea why, I was drawn to where he was, needing to talk to someone about all the emotions tearing through me after my encounter with Karl. I knew it was ridiculous. He couldn't even hear me, but it didn't matter. Maybe it was better he couldn't hear what I had to say.

He watched me as I walked toward where he stood, putting down his clippers when I stopped in front of him. For a moment, he looked confused, but then he just smiled and I could have sworn he reminded me of Tristan.

God, I was losing my fucking mind.

Signing, I asked, *Do you mind if I sit here with you while you work?*

He shook his head and smiled again. Very slowly, he finger spelled, *T-h-i-s i-s y-o-u-r h-o-u-s-e.*

It was. Actually, without Tristan, it felt more like my prison than my house. I still loved it for the memories we'd made here, but now it felt empty without him.

Like me.

Ethan signed *Do you want to talk?* and I shook my head. I did want to talk, but the one person I wanted to talk to was nowhere to be found.

He didn't seem to know what to do, so he just stared down at me until he signed, *How was the g-r-o-u-n-d-b-r-e-a-k-i-n-g?*

All of a sudden, the real fear that I was standing in front of someone spying for Karl exploded into my brain. That would explain how he'd known I'd be at the groundbreaking that morning. I hadn't attended any Stone Foundation functions in months. Why would he think I'd be at the one today?

"How did you know where I was?" I asked, forgetting to sign until I saw the confused look on his face. I asked him again through sign language and watched as he signed, *One of your bodyguards told me.*

There was something wrong now that I stood there with Ethan. Daryl might believe he was okay, but I didn't. Signing, I said, *Take off your glasses, please. I want to see your eyes.* I needed to see exactly who this person was who seemed to know things about me.

He seemed reluctant to do as I ordered, so I told him again what I wanted. Slowly, he slid them off his face and squinted as his eyes adjusted to the sun. I studied them for a long moment, sure I'd seen eyes like his before but unable to remember where. They were a deep blue color, but not dark like Gage's. If he didn't have such a scruffy beard, I imagined Ethan would be quite attractive, even though his hair was much longer than I liked.

That didn't mean I felt any less uncomfortable about him, though. I couldn't put my finger on it, but there was something about him now that made me question why Daryl had made such a point of my firing Chip in favor of this guy.

All sorts of terrible thoughts swirled in my mind. Was Daryl the one who'd told Karl I'd be at the groundbreaking? Had he been keeping Tristan and me apart all this time? Was Tristan even safe, wherever he was, as Daryl had continually claimed all these months?

Ethan signed something, but I couldn't understand any of what he said and left to find Daryl to get some answers. I found him waiting for me in the dining room, looking like he always did as I stormed in, ready to demand he tell me exactly what the hell was going on.

"Nina, I heard what happened. You should have let Gage come with you."

Pointing my finger at him, I barked, "You better start explaining what the fuck is up, Daryl. How would Karl know I'd be there? Something's pretty fishy about all of this. I want to know where Tristan is right now!"

"You know I can't do that, Nina. I have no idea how Karl knew, but I'd never put you or Tristan in danger."

He wasn't going to tell me anything more than that, so I left to go back to Ethan and see if he was easier to crack than his friend. I found the hedge clippers on the ground next to the shrubs, but he was gone. Looking around, I spied him walking quickly across the lawn toward the property's edge.

Where the hell was he going?

I took off after him, hampered by three inch heels and the ridiculous suit I still wore. His much longer stride made catching him impossible, but at least I was able to see him. I thanked God we hadn't seen much rain recently as my heels barely sank into the still solid ground that in late April hadn't forgotten the cold of winter quite yet.

He walked right off the property through a hole in the fence, and I followed him into a field full of much higher grass and weeds. His pace never slowed down, so by the time I found myself in Millbrook, my stockings were torn and my suit was covered in thorns and pickers.

Why he was going home in the middle of the day I had no idea, but I fully intended on finding out. I watched as he entered an old building, presumably his apartment building, breaking into a full run so I didn't lose him. Following him up the wood stairs, I saw him enter a door at the end of the hallway and stopped to catch my breath.

When I finally could breathe normally again, I brushed off my clothes and marched myself down to his apartment. I stood at his door, my hand ready to knock, when I realized he wouldn't be able to hear me. Reaching into my purse, I found one of Tristan's letters to me and tore off a piece of the envelope. But what was I supposed to write? Hi Ethan, I followed you and would really like you to open the door and I promise I'm not a crazy stalker seemed wrong.

Finally, after lurking in front of his door for almost five minutes, I wrote what I hoped wouldn't make me seem like a crazy woman. *Please open the door. It's Nina. I need to talk to you, Ethan.* Crouching down on the old wood floor in his hallway, I slid the torn piece of envelope under his door and waited, hoping he didn't call the police.

He didn't wait long to open the door, and I saw immediately that he looked nervous. Signing, I tried to assure him that I didn't want to bother him. I just wanted to talk. He let me in and quickly pushed by me to clean up the things on his coffee table and a laptop on his couch. Taking a seat on an old chair, I signed, *Please forgive me for following you to your house. I need to ask you a question.*

Nodding, he smiled, so I asked, *How did Daryl find you to be my gardener?*

Ethan finger spelled that Daryl knew he was looking for a job and thought he'd be perfect. That told me nothing, so I asked, *But how do you know him?*

He gave me a tiny smile and signed, *That's two questions.*

In a flash, the memory of when Tristan said that same thing to me that first night on our ride out to the house flooded through my mind and before I could stop myself, I was sitting there in my gardener's apartment crying like a baby. I couldn't do this anymore. Being without Tristan was breaking my heart and I was falling apart.

When I finally stopped crying, I tried to explain what the hell was wrong with me, but all I did was ramble on about missing the man I loved, not that it mattered since I was talking and didn't even bother to try to sign all the messed up shit that was coming out of my mouth.

"I'm sorry. You must think I'm crazy. I'm not. Or maybe I am. I must be since I'm sitting here in your living room bawling my eyes out over something you said that probably shouldn't mean anything to me, but it does."

I wiped the tears from my cheeks and continued to explain my bizarre behavior. "You see, my fiancé said something like you just said the first night I met him, and I miss him so much. I don't know where he is or even if he's okay. He hasn't contacted me in months, except for the other day to tell me to do something that broke my heart to do. I'd hoped he'd message me after

I did what he wanted, but there was nothing. I just don't think I can do this anymore."

The tears began flowing again, and before I knew it, I was sobbing with my head in my hands as poor Ethan stood there probably thinking he should run away or at least call the authorities to have me committed. I couldn't stop crying once I started this time, even when I thought I heard someone say my name. I was losing my mind, after all.

"Nina, honey, stop crying."

I had heard someone say my name. Dropping my hands from my face, I looked up to see my gardener standing over me speaking instead of signing. He looked like he always did wearing jeans, a long sleeve T-shirt, and work boots, but his eyes weren't the blue they'd always been. Now they were that unmistakable color of melted milk chocolate I'd only ever seen in one person.

Tristan.

Staring up at the man who stood in front of me, I sobbed, "Please tell me it's you. Tell me I'm not losing my mind. I don't think I can handle it if you're a dream or some kind of mirage."

"It's me, Nina."

I drank in the vision of the man I adored finally standing in front of me again after so long. "Oh, my God! Tristan, it's you!"

Hyperventilating, I was unable to control my emotions any longer. His voice washed over me like a refreshing rain, quenching my heart and soul so long mired in drought from his absence. He knelt down in front of me and looked up into my eyes with those beautiful brown eyes I'd missed so much, whispering, "I'm sorry, Nina. I didn't mean to hurt you."

"Oh, Tristan, I've missed you so much," I cried as I wrapped my arms around his neck and drew him to me.

"Don't cry," he whispered in my ear. "It's okay. No more being apart. I promise."

After all those months without him, just the feel of his arms around me, holding me tight, made all sadness fade away and for the first time in so long, I was happy.

ELEVEN

TRISTAN

Nina sat trembling in my arms, quietly sobbing as she clung to me. Every so often, she'd try to pull back away from me to say something, but I didn't want to let go. It had been so long since I'd held her in my arms that I was afraid if I let her go again, I might never get her back. I'd made that mistake once. I wouldn't make it again.

Quietly, she whispered against my chest, "Tristan, I came here because I blew it today. Everything we worked all this time for is ruined. I'm sorry. I didn't mean to screw up. I had no idea Karl was standing behind me at the groundbreaking. He heard me say I'd tell you something. He knows you're not gone for good."

I lifted her chin and kissed her tenderly on the lips. Pressing my forehead to hers, I tried to reassure her. "It's okay. We'll handle Karl. I'm just glad that's what you meant in your text."

She leaned back and studied me for a minute. "What did you think I meant?"

It tore me up to admit what had crossed my mind when I read her message. "I thought you meant something happened between you and Varo."

Nina hung her head for a moment, making me think my paranoid worrying about her with another man hadn't been so paranoid, after all. Lifting her head to look at me, she cupped my cheeks and smiled. "I would never do that. Not with Varo. Not with Cal. Not with anyone. You're the only man for me, even if I don't like this beard one bit."

"No love for the beard?"

"Yeah, it needs to go," she said with a chuckle. "You remind me too much of Daryl this way."

"Then it definitely needs to go."

Her smile faded, and before I could ask what was wrong, she slapped my face so hard tears came to my eyes. "That's for leaving me here all alone for months. You asked me to promise I'd never run, and then you did."

"Jesus, Nina!" After a minute, the shock wore off. "You're right," I admitted sheepishly as I rubbed the sting out of my cheek.

Nina narrowed her eyes to slits and pointed her finger at me. "You're lucky I love you, Tristan Stone. Other women would have taken all that you gave me and when you didn't come back after a few days would have jumped on the nearest good looking guy around, which incidentally is the man you and Daryl have had me pretending to play house with."

"Don't remind me. You should know I never liked the idea anyway."

"That makes two of us. I'm not sure I can forgive you for making me kiss Gage in front of all those photographers."

"Gage?" I asked, my jealousy quickly ratcheting up.

"Well, you didn't expect me to stay on a last name basis with the man I'm supposedly having great sex with and quickly falling madly in love with, did you?"

I sighed, angry with every part of the situation Daryl's grand plan had created. Not at Nina, though. I was to blame if she had any feelings for the bodyguard. That didn't make it any easier, though. "So you and Gage are close?"

"We're as close as you wanted us to be, Tristan."

"What does that mean?"

A gentle smile spread across her lips, and her eyes grew wide. "I think you're jealous, Mr. Stone."

"You're playing with me, aren't you? Fine. I have it coming. You know how I get, though. Varo will be lucky to have a job tomorrow if you keep this up."

Nina sat back in her seat. "So now you're jealous? Not when you had me kiss him so everyone in the world could see?"

"Are you done yet?" I asked, tempering my anger.

"Will you promise never to leave me again like you did?"

"Absolutely."

She leaned forward to kiss me sweetly. "Then I'm done." Nina sat silently for a long moment, staring into my eyes, before she said, "Hmmm. What do you think about me running out for some razors, shaving cream, Tony's pizza, and the flattest birch beer in the world?"

"I think this is exactly the reason I'm so madly in love with you. Call for the pizza and I'll wash off the grime from my half-day as a gardener."

I stood to head into the shower, but she pulled me back down, smiling a wicked grin. "In a minute. First, I think it's about time my soon-to-be husband gave me a proper hello after months of being away."

Leaning in, I kissed her for the first time in so long it felt like our first kiss that night after I'd taught her how to tie a Windsor knot. Every inch of my body felt alive like it hadn't in so long. I'd let myself get used to being alone and forgotten how much I truly needed Nina.

Far too soon, she pulled away and shook her head. "That beard has to go. It's picky."

"So much for our reunion," I joked. "A slap across the face and not even a decent kiss for your long lost man."

"Back to Plan A. You get in the shower, and I'll order the pizza. While I'm out, I'll get some razors and we'll get that gorgeous face of yours back to how it's supposed to look."

"Not without someone going with you, and that someone is me."

Raising her eyebrows, she gave me a look of disbelief. "Is that really necessary?"

"Karl came close enough to speak to you today, Nina. It's absolutely necessary."

"Fine. I'll tolerate the protective boyfriend thing for now."

I stood and smiled down at her. "You'll tolerate it until I become the protective husband. Are we clear?"

Grinning, she asked, "Where did the mild mannered gardener go to? I barely remember this man."

"Get used to him," I said as I walked toward the bathroom to clean up before we headed out. "He's back to claim his life and all that he's missed, and that includes you, Miss Edwards."

"Oooh, I do love it when you go all alpha on me," she said with a chuckle as I closed the door.

After an entire pizza and a two liter of birch beer that was strangely flat even though we weren't at Tony's, I sat back on the couch, more satisfied than I ever thought I could be there in my cheap apartment eating fast food. Nina leaned on me, softly humming some song, and I wished we'd never have to leave this spot that had become the most precious place on Earth since she arrived.

"What are you singing?"

Raising her head, she looked up at me. "A song my mother used to sing to me." She looked away and shook her head. "I think so, at least. Maybe it's just something I've dreamed up because I know so little about her."

The memories of the hours I'd spent in her father's storage unit surrounded by the only things left of Diana Edwards' life flooded back as I watched Nina's wistful expression. It was time I told her that I'd found some good in that ten by ten room.

Gently, I pushed her up until she sat next to me and I began. "I think I need to tell you some things.

We've spent enough time with me hiding the past from you. I don't want to do that anymore." I saw the concern in her eyes and softly touched her shoulder. "For once, it's not bad."

"Oh? Well, I'm all ears then. I just don't think I could have handled hearing you say you had a wife you hadn't told me about or something like that," she said with a forced smile.

"No, it's nothing like that." I took a deep breath and continued. "I found your father's notebook in a safe deposit box, but he has a storage unit right outside Philly that I searched. I'm sorry I didn't tell you, but I was hoping that I could find out why my father had done what he did and bury that in the past and then someday take you to see the storage unit."

"A storage facility? I know nothing about this. Did Kim know?"

"I don't know. Your father stored your mother's things there after she died and visited it the last time just before his death. I think it might be nice if you took a look at what's there."

There was pain in her eyes as she smiled at me. "I've always wished I could know my mother better. My father never really wanted to talk about her after she died. I don't blame him. Losing the one you love is like losing a part of yourself. It hurts so much that you just want to curl up into a ball and push the world away."

I heard in her words that she wasn't just talking about losing her mother or father. She was talking about losing me all those months. Pulling her toward me, I wrapped my arms around her and whispered what I'd wanted to say since the first day away from her. "I'm sorry I left. I didn't think there was any other way. I didn't mean to hurt you, Nina. I thought you'd be safer without me around."

She sniffled once and then again, signaling she was crying. "I might have been safer, but I needed you and you weren't there. Then when Jordan left, for the first time in my life, I was alone. Every night I'd scroll through my messages to you, forcing myself to believe that you got every one and wanted to respond, even though you didn't."

I tilted her head back, cradling her face in my hands. "I did get every one and every time my phone vibrated, another piece of my heart was cut out knowing that you were unhappy. I know I fucked up, but I promise if you give me the chance, I'll be the man you deserve. Maybe not right now, but I won't give up until I've become that man."

Nodding, she smiled. "Okay."

"But you need to accept that life with me is going to be hard for a while. I stayed away because I'm a target. I don't know why yet, but Karl is playing some deadly game and I'm the prize. That means you're in danger too. We may have to leave home and hide out in places that are nothing like the hotels I own until Daryl and I figure out what's going on."

"I don't care how hard life is with you. All I know is it's impossible without you. You're the one I want to spend the rest of my life with, Tristan. So what if that means we have some rough times? Every couple faces those."

"Not every couple has to deal with someone wanting to kill them, Nina. I need you to understand that things could get rough. I've made sure that if anything happens to me, you're taken care of for the rest of your life. I promise you don't have to worry about that."

A look of horror crossed her face. Jumping to her feet, she cried, "Don't say that! I just got you back. I can't think of you being gone again."

Taking her hand, I looked up into those eyes so sad and worked to fix my blunder. "Baby, I wasn't saying I was going anywhere. I never want to leave you again. It's just that I need you to know I've taken care of everything."

"Well, now I need you to take care of me. Money and everything else you have don't mean a thing to me, Tristan. All I want—all I ever wanted—was you."

I stood and took her into my arms, nuzzling her neck. "I'm all yours, princess."

Squirming out of my hold, she pointed her finger at my face. "Good. Now that we got that straightened out, that beard has got to go. It's time to bring the real Tristan Stone back and put this Daryl twin in the past.

She pointed toward the bathroom, and I nodded. "Your wish is my command."

Thanks to a pair of scissors, after nearly a half hour, I was just about back to myself. All that was needed was a good shave and the real Tristan Stone would return. Nina sat on the edge of the bathtub watching me do my best gardener act on my beard and stood when I finished lathering my face with shaving cream.

Wrapping her arms around me, she whispered, "I've always had this fantasy of shaving a man. You up for making this one come true?"

She was so sexy standing there with one eyebrow arched and a cute twinkle in her eye that I couldn't say no. I followed her arm as she pointed to the toilet and sat down on the lid. "Have you at least watched someone do this? I don't want to bleed to death here in this tiny hole-in-the-wall apartment."

Razor in hand, she smiled down at me and winked. "You're talking to a woman who's shaved three-quarters of her body for years. Have faith. You're in good hands."

If there was anyone I could trust with a razor next to my throat it was Nina, so I angled my head up toward her. "I think this could be much sexier if you were doing this in that babydoll I bought you."

She gave me a sexy grin and licked her lips. "How about bra and panties? Does that work for you, Mr. Stone?"

"Ms. Edwards, I like the way you think."

She placed the disposable razor on the sink and turned her back to me as she slid her suit jacket off, flinging it out into the living room. Turning her head to look over her shoulder, she smiled. "I think this would be better with music."

Her skirt fell to the floor and I sang my best stripper song. "Ba-da-da-da, da-da-da-da." I ducked as her clothes flew toward my head, thrilled to see her standing there in just her bra and panties. And ripped stockings.

"You planning to leave those on? I mean, they might be sexy since they look like they go with a garter belt, but now they just look like some wild chipmunks attacked you."

Nina spun around and put her hand on her hip. "Well, maybe if my gardener hadn't led me through a jungle of picker bushes, I wouldn't look like this." Shaking her head, she looked at me sweetly and asked, "Not sexy enough?"

I left my perch and took her into my arms. "Baby, you're always sexy enough."

"Yeah, yeah. Now get back on the toilet so I can finish this shaving a hot guy fantasy of mine."

Taking my seat on the lid again, I muttered, "That's some sexy talk there. And I think you've become bossy in my absence, Ms. Edwards."

Nina smiled down at me as she ran the razor up my neck in a single long stroke. "Then maybe somebody needs to show me who the real boss is, Mr. Stone."

That was exactly what I fully intended on doing just as soon as she finished cleaning off months of hair from my face. I couldn't keep my hands off her she looked so hot standing there, the same Nina as she was that first night in mismatched bra and panties.

Cupping her full ass, I struggled to control myself as she worked diligently to get rid of the rest of my beard.

"Tilt back," she ordered sweetly as she pushed my head back to shave over my Adam's Apple and under my chin. "When was the last time you shaved, Tristan? This beard is like wire."

"I had no reason to shave."

The simple truth that without her in my life I had no reason to care for myself enough to even shave stopped her hand's movement, and she gave me one of those gentle smiles that never failed to melt my heart.

"I love you, Tristan."

"Well, finish this and I'll show you how much I love you."

With a wink, she made quick work of the rest of my beard, only cutting me once or twice in her haste to get done, and in just minutes I was back to looking like myself again. I rinsed what remained of the shaving cream from my face and stared into the mirror to see the man I hadn't been since the night I left Nina.

"I missed this face," she said sweetly as she wrapped her arms around me from behind.

"This face missed you." Turning toward her, I kissed her deeply for the first time in what felt like forever. Her soft lips yielded to my eager mouth, desperate to taste her after being away for so long.

Fisting my hand in her hair, I tugged her head back, unable to wait any longer. I wanted her, right there in that tiny apartment bathroom. It wasn't lavish and it wasn't the type of reunion I'd dreamed of all those months, but it didn't matter. Nina was back in my arms.

That's all that mattered.

My hands slid over her petal soft shoulders and down her back to unclasp her bra. I threw it off to the side and lowered my head to take one deep pink nipple between my lips. Sucking it gently into my mouth, I reveled in the feel of its pebbled softness against my tongue. Nina moaned gently, and I bit down gently at the base of her nipple, remembering how excited it made her.

My gesture was rewarded with a gentle tug of my hair, and my cock throbbed at the sound of her sexy moan. Pulling away, I wrapped by arms around her hips and looked up at her to see her biting her lower lip. She was ready.

"Nina, I want you so fucking bad. Every night I was gone, I thought about this. I wanted this to be everything for us, but I don't think I can wait until we return to the house or one of the hotels."

Shaking her head, she smiled that sweet smile that never failed to do me in. "Tristan, it wouldn't matter where we were. Tiny apartment, grand hotel, our room at home—it doesn't matter as long as you're back with me."

She held out her hand, and I stood up and placed my hand in hers. "Tell me we can be what we used to be, Nina. It's the only fear I have—that I can't make up for the mistakes I made. Nothing else in this world terrifies me more than not being able to have you back. Truly back in every way."

Without a word, she walked out of the bathroom to the bedroom. When she finally turned around, I saw the answer in her eyes. She wasn't sure about us anymore.

"Tristan, I love you. I think I have since the first moment I saw you. It's just been so hard between us. And your leaving me alone for so long hurt more than you can ever understand. I want so much to trust that you won't go again. You say you want me back in your life, really back, but what does that mean?"

I pulled her close and held her to me as I opened my heart. "It means I want all of you. I want you to still walk down that aisle and be my wife. I want you by my side, no matter what. I want to be the man who makes the world a better place for you. I want to be the man who protects you." I stopped and looked deep into those blue eyes so full of uncertainty. "I want us to finally be happy in that house that meant nothing to me until the night you stepped foot in it."

"I can handle the not talking thing you do, Tristan. I get that you don't share what's inside you a lot. That's not what makes me doubt you love me. It's the hidden things, though. Not emotions or how you feel about me, but the secrets. I can't handle those."

"Nina, you know everything about me. That I don't like to talk a lot. The drugs. What my father and brother were. It's all out there—the bad and the ugly. I swear there's nothing else to know."

Frowning, she slowly shook her head. "That's not true, Tristan. There's more to you than that."

"I promise. There's nothing more, Nina."

Cupping my face, she looked up at me and shook her head again. "There's so much more to you than those things, and I'm not talking about the beautiful outside. You're good and kind, no matter what you want to think, and I love you. That's why it breaks my heart to even think of you leaving again."

I covered her hands with mine. "No more leaving. I can't promise it's always going to be perfect, but no more leaving."

None of what I said was a lie. I didn't want to leave her side ever again. Months away had made me realize I was nothing without her. I didn't want to hide anything from her anymore either. All the bad inside that had convinced me I'd never find anyone was exposed now, and she'd accepted me, even after she found out about what my family had done. Now I wanted to deserve her.

Nina pulled my face toward hers and kissed me softly. "Together, no matter what. That's all I needed to hear."

Pressing my forehead to hers, I whispered, "Together."

Her acceptance of who I was made me need her more than I'd ever believed I could need another person. Moaning her name, I lifted her onto the bed and gazed down at the perfect creature who'd agreed to be mine. Her legs opened slightly to allow me to slide her panties off her, leaving that beautiful cunt for my eyes to feast upon. I wanted to taste her, to slide my tongue over the tender skin between her legs and savor her juices as she came for me.

I nipped at her inner thigh, aching to be inside her but wanting to prolong our reunion. My cock pressed full against my belly, but now wasn't the time to plunge into her but to take my time and show her how much I adored her.

She moaned softly as with every kiss I inched closer to my goal. Her hands entwined in my hair, and she urged me to give her what she wanted. I softly placed a kiss where her leg met her body and whispered, "We have forever. No need to rush."

"But you're driving me crazy. Please don't make me wait," she begged in such a sexy voice that I nearly gave in.

I ran my tongue over the spot I'd just kissed. Looking up at her, my gaze met hers. "I never want this to end. I know it has to, so I'm going to make this last as long as possible. I want you to never forget this night."

She tilted her hips off the bed, tempting me to move faster, and I was lost. I covered her with my mouth, my tongue lapping against her clit as her hands pulled me into her. Her pussy, wet and needy, tasted so good on my tongue. Sliding one finger inside her, I reveled in how slick her cunt already was, ready and waiting for me to fill her.

Easing another finger into her, I pressed my fingertips against her tender walls, knowing the effect this caused in her. I wanted her to explode from my touch, drenching my fingers until my tongue replaced them to lick her tender folds until her body shook in ecstasy.

"Oh, God…please don't stop…" she groaned above me, her pleas making me want her even more. Her fingernails dug into my neck as her cunt tightened around my fingers, and in seconds, her release raged through her. Bucking and grinding against my mouth, she rode my tongue as if she depended on it for her very happiness.

Against her trembling pussy, I moaned, "Let yourself go, baby. Don't hold back."

She wrapped her legs around my neck, crushing my head between them until all I breathed was her. But I didn't care. If I died right there at that moment, I would have died a happy man. Her pleasure was everything.

When her body finally stopped shaking from her orgasm, I eased back onto my heels to look at her sated expression. Licking her lips, she smiled. "God, I've fantasized about that for months. I love that tongue of yours. You know that?"

I ran my finger up her moist slit to her swollen nub and grinned. "Then that must mean we're meant for each other because I love going down on you. See? A perfect match."

Crooking her finger, she said, "Come up here, and you should be naked already."

I slid up her body and kissed her hard on the mouth, my tongue snaking in and out to tease the tip of her tongue. Her fingers fumbled with my zipper, tearing at it as my cock ached to feel her touch. Finally past the last barrier between us, she tugged my pants down my thighs and wrapped her fingers around my stiff cock.

"No more waiting. I want you inside me," she whimpered as I ran the swollen head of my cock over her needy clit. "Please…Tristan, give me what I need."

Denying her was impossible, even if I wanted to, which I didn't. I wanted to devour her, to take everything she was into me so if I ever had to be without her again, I wouldn't suffer like I had for months. She silenced my demons and created new ones to take their place—new ones ten times as powerful that threatened to take me over now.

I needed her. I wanted her. I couldn't do without her.

I felt my control slipping away. With each touch of her hands on my body, she seared herself into me, stripping every defense I'd worked years to perfect from my mind until all that was left was her everywhere in my thoughts.

My mouth covered hers seeking the feel of her tongue against mine. I loved that mouth—that mouth that had questioned me so often with words that held me responsible for my actions. Those lips and tongue that brought my body pleasure greater than anything I'd ever thought possible. I wanted to possess that mouth that I'd made her kiss another man with and claim it as only for me.

Nina slid her hands over my back until they came to rest just below my hips, and she pulled me into her, tilting her hips to take all of me. I slid into her hot body so willing and eager for me and thrust hard until there was no space between us. She moaned a tiny noise as the base of my cock touched her slick pussy, her body arching to accommodate all of me.

I buried my face in softness of her neck and reared my hips back to plunge into her again. The demons she'd created spurred me on, screaming in my brain to claim her so no other man could ever see her and not know every beautiful and gentle inch of her was mine. I struggled to hold them back, but they controlled me, and I pushed into her over and over, harder and harder each time trying to force out all the pain I caused her.

My hands slid up her arms and pinning them above her head, I weaved our fingers together, needing as much to have her hold me as I wanted to hold her. Wrapping her legs around my waist, she stared up into my eyes as her body matched each plunge of my cock into her with a desire for more.

The intensity of her need surprised me, and I slowed my pace, not wanting to rush toward the moment each of us craved but to savor the journey we shared. Her heels dug into my spine and she groaned, "I don't want it slow and easy. Show me you were desperate without me like I was without you."

Her words set my mind and body on fire, and I released my hold on her to flip her over onto her stomach. Pulling her by her hips, I set her on her knees in front of me and thrust my cock into her cunt. There was no more me or her. Just us starved for one another.

Our need spurred our fucking to a place it had never been before. I slid in and out of her faster and faster, pistoning into her as she moaned into the pillow. The gentle squeezing of my cock told me she was close, but I wasn't ready to let this moment go yet. Slowing down, I eased out of her and leaned down to gently wrap my hand around her neck. In her ear, I whispered, "I want this night to last forever. I want to fuck you until you know how much I can't live without you."

In a tender voice that hit me deep inside, she said the only word that could undo me. "Yes."

No other words came between us now.

Pushing back against me, she silently begged for me to fulfill my promise. In seconds, I was balls-deep inside her again, thrusting and retreating from her cunt until neither of us could hold back anymore. She came first, her body milking my cock with its sweet tightening as her orgasm tore through her. Before she was finished, I felt my own release begin and pulled her up against me as I came inside her, the sweet sound of her cries of pleasure mingling with my panting until we collapsed onto the bed together.

When we finally were able to speak, she wiped my sweat drenched hair from my forehead and whispered against my cheek, "I missed you so much."

I pulled her close to me and held her in my arms, loving the feel of her next to me. Her body fit against mine perfectly, meant for me and me alone. She nuzzled my neck, her warm breath tickling my skin, and I spoke the words I'd held in all those months as I read her texts full of love and anger.

"Don't make me live without you. I can't do it, Nina."

She looked up at me with a gentle gaze, and I saw my life in her eyes. "I promise."

TWELVE

Nina

Opening my eyes, I squinted from the morning light and rolled over in Tristan's full size bed, crashing into him and waking him up. Looking down at me, he gave me a sleepy grin. "I forgot how sleeping with you is like bumper cars."

Propping my head up, I rolled my eyes. "Says the man who rarely spends the whole night next to me. Are you saying I move around a lot when I sleep?"

He smirked and looked left and right to prove his point. "Well, not usually this bad, but then again, we're usually in a much bigger bed."

"Yeah, yeah. Aren't you Mr. Romance this morning?"

Tristan pulled me close and nuzzled my neck. "Even with you taking up all the room and stealing the covers, I'd rather be here than anywhere else on Earth." Looking up at me, he smiled. "Better?"

I gently pressed my lips to his and whispered, "Much."

We laid there for a long time, silent except for the sound of the two of us breathing, but my mind raced with questions and confessions I knew I couldn't keep inside me for much longer. Our reunion reinforced in me how much I loved him, but this was a fresh start for us and I didn't want it based on lies or misunderstandings.

I had to know he wasn't the Tristan I'd seen that night at Top, and I had to tell him about Gage.

Tracing my fingertip over the tattoo above his heart, I cleared my throat and took a deep breath. Forcing a smile onto my lips, I sat up and began. "Tristan, I want us to be completely honest with one another. I need to know a few things and have some things to tell you. It's important to me that this time we're truthful with everything."

He knitted his brows as he always did when he was concerned and turned to face me. "Things to tell me? Like what?"

"I'd rather begin with what I need to know from you. Like, for example, I need to know that whatever was going on with you at Top that night I found you there isn't going to be a part of our life together. I can handle a lot of things, Tristan, but being in love with a cokehead isn't one of them. I need to know that isn't going to be part of us from now on."

His expression softened, but his eyes filled with pain. "I'm sorry about that, Nina. That's not who I am or want to be. Coke was a way for me to lose myself for a long time. I'm not going to lie. I got lost in that again when I was away from you, but I made a choice to not be that person."

"Okay. Now I need you to promise me you'll tell me the truth, no matter how awful it is. I know you like to handle things on your own and think you have to protect me, but we won't work if you lie to me."

Shaking his head, he grimaced. "I can't promise all of that. I love you, Nina, and to me that means I'm supposed to protect you. The world you're in now is full of people who would think nothing about hurting someone to get ahead. I'm going to shield you from that as much as I can, but if I can't, then I'll protect you from it, and that might mean not telling you everything."

His insistence on protecting me like I was some unknowing child filled me with frustration. I just didn't know if I could be that kind of girlfriend and someday, wife. Sighing, I shook my head. "Why do you think I always need protecting? I'm not a little girl, Tristan. I'm a grown woman who knows the man I love. Do you think I don't understand people at your level?"

"It's not like that and you know it. This has nothing to do with social class. It has to do with me protecting the woman I love, Nina. Why is that so bad?"

"Because it gives you carte blanche to lie to me! We just spent all those months apart and now you're telling me you can't promise you won't continue to lie. How can we be together like that?"

He sat up and leaned against the headboard, pushing the hair out of his eyes. "Nina, I can't change who I am in this. I'm not the bad guy because I won't dump all the shit in my world on you. Most women want a man to protect them."

"From bad guys and people wanting to kill them. Not from everything else. I just want you to say to me that you'll treat me like a full partner in this relationship and not some second class citizen who's forced to react when you make decisions and I have to deal with them."

"This is about me leaving you alone for months."

My mouth fell open. "Of course it's about that! You left me here, all alone, and never once answered any of my messages. All those times when I was missing you so much all I wanted to do was curl up in bed with one of your shirts, I texted you and waited for you to answer but you never did."

"I couldn't answer, Nina. I was trying to protect you."

"Again with the protecting me! Would it have been any less protection for me if I was with you, wherever you were, so you could keep me safe and not break my heart?"

I tried to stop the tears from coming, but it was no use. After the sweetness of our reunion the night before, the reality of how much he'd hurt me was right there in front of us in the harsh light of day. I couldn't go on with Tristan if our life together was going to be like this.

He took my hand and squeezed it gently. "I know I keep making these mistakes. That you've stayed with me this long still amazes me. I hate that what I do makes you sad. I just don't know any other way to be."

Wiping the tears away, I looked at him sitting there, his beautiful eyes so full of sadness. There had to be some way to make him see what I meant. "I love that you want to protect me. If there's ever a time that someone's trying to mug me or kidnap me, I want you to jump in and rescue me. But you're not keeping me safe when you leave me in the dark. I sat in that house surrounded by people and barely alive because I missed you so much. You left me and I didn't know why. Was it me? I didn't know. It doesn't matter if I have bodyguards if you're the one who keeps hurting me by breaking my heart."

"I'm sorry. I never meant to do that. I did what I thought would keep you safe, but now I see that I'm the one who was hurting you the most. I'm sorry, Nina."

He looked away, but I gently tugged his face back toward me. "I just need you to promise you'll protect me from the bad guys but still tell me about things. I want to be your wife, not some childish girl you keep around."

Closing his eyes, he said quietly, "I promise. No more keeping things from you." He opened them and stared into mine with a gaze so direct I feared what he might say next. "I lied and hid things out of fear that if you knew about them, you'd never stay with me. I just want you to know that I come with a lot of fucked up shit. I didn't know if you'd want to be my wife knowing all of it."

I cradled his face and pressed my forehead to his. "I know what you are, Tristan Stone. No matter what bad things you think you have inside you, I know the man you are is good and kind. I love you, and that means all of you. The good, the bad, and the ugly."

He nodded and for the first time in our conversation, smiled. "I love you. I always have, Nina. From that first night we drove up the Taconic, you've been the one person I knew I couldn't deal with losing."

"You're not going to lose me, Tristan. I promise."

He leaned back away from me, and I saw the icy veil he wore so often descend over his features. "So what things do you have to tell me?"

"What's that face for?" I teased, nervous about what I had to tell him.

"I'm just wondering what else you have to say."

He wasn't stupid. He knew I had something to confess in addition to everything else we'd already talked about. It was probably written all over my face. Swallowing hard, I said, "Just one more thing. About that kiss with Gage..."

"What about it?" he asked flatly, his eyes boring holes in me with their accusatory stare.

"Don't look at me like that. You're the one who made me do it."

"I really don't want to talk about that, Nina. The idea of another man kissing you isn't something I ever want to think about again."

"Fine. I can certainly understand. I don't like thinking about you kissing that cheap waitress at Top that night either."

I was messing this up big time. Instead of simply telling him I'd kissed Gage and it meant nothing, I'd ventured into the jealous waters of "you did this and I did that." Never a good place to stumble into.

Tristan simply continued to stare at me as he waited for me to continue, very wisely saying nothing about the Brandi kiss. "I just want to clear the air so we never have to talk about this again. You kissed her, which bothers me, and I kissed him, which obviously upsets you."

"Then we never have to speak of it again. It was only once, and I didn't even kiss her back. Gage was only once, and it was just acting, so that's that."

I nervously bit my bottom lip and struggled to work up the courage to tell the man I loved that I'd kissed another man and it had nothing to do with acting. "It happened another time. Neither one of us meant it. I was upset about you finally texting me back only to tell me to kiss him. It meant nothing, but I don't want this to be between us."

When all the words had finally left my mouth, I held my breath and waited for their meaning to sink in. Tristan said nothing, but stared straight ahead, his face emotionless. I knew he'd heard me, but his lack of response confused me.

Finally, after what seemed like hours of waiting for him to say anything, he turned toward me and took a deep breath. Letting it out slowly, he shook his head. "I know I put you in that position and I know I have no right to be angry, but I am. I can't stand the idea of you with him. I need to know just one thing. Did you sleep with him?"

"No. I swear, Tristan. It was one kiss. That's it."

"Then I don't want to hear about it again."

Never before in my life had any words sounded so final. His expression hardened for just a moment, as if he were working it out in his mind, and then he was back to being that same man I'd fallen in love with.

So ready to move on, I asked, "So, what should we do today?"

Tristan brought my hand up to his lips and kissed the back of it. "I think it's time for my resurrection, don't you?"

I followed him through the front door of the house, noticing he stopped for just a moment to look around the enormous entryway. Quickly, I headed to our room to change into some fresh clothes. Tristan changed into his usual suit and tie and waited for me. When I was ready, he grasped my hand, clutching it as if for support, and guided me to his office where Daryl, Jensen, West, and Varo sat waiting for us. Tristan took his place behind his desk, and I stood beside him as each of the men in front of us waited for him to begin. Pulling me close so I sat on the arm of his chair, he rested his hand across the top of my thigh. "Surprised to see me, gentlemen?"

I scanned each of their faces, and except for Daryl, all of them looked stunned to see Tristan sitting there before them. Daryl must not have let them in on the secret.

"We didn't realize you were back," Varo said quietly.

Smiling, Tristan directed his attention to the man I'd explained less than an hour earlier was the one I'd kissed. "Well, I am back, so you can go back to being merely the bodyguard. Thanks for your service, though. I'm sure Nina appreciates your diligence."

And with that, I knew Tristan wasn't quite as comfortable with my confession as I'd hoped. Varo understood his meaning instantly, if the look of shock all over his face was any indication. I felt bad about that. He'd been a good guy about everything. He hadn't even been the one who did the kissing. It had been all my fault. I gave him a weak smile, hoping it made up for Tristan's sharp words.

"And West, I'm concerned with how you guard Nina. I've told both of you I want you to stay in the background."

West looked to Varo on his left and then back at Tristan. "We always are. If she hadn't been told that we were guarding her, she still wouldn't know."

"Really? I watched you and your giant form spy on me behind trees half your size one afternoon recently. Didn't realize I was Ethan, the gardener, did you? If that's any indication of how you stay out of sight, I'm not impressed."

West grimaced as if in pain as Tristan dressed him down. I considered coming to his defense since I'd never noticed either him or Varo around me any time I went out, but the sharpness of the rebuke told me to not get involved. Tristan continued to explain how clumsy West had been one day as he'd attempted to spy on the new gardener, delineating each problem he'd seen as the bodyguard's embarrassment and anger simmered.

"From now on, gentlemen, you are to be neither seen nor heard as you guard the most important person in my world. Am I clear?"

Both Varo and West nodded their understanding of Tristan's decree and quickly rose to leave when he waved his hand to signal they were dismissed. As they reached the door, he snapped, "And make sure the hole in the fence at the back of the property is fixed. You're supposed to be our security here."

Leaning down near his ear, I whispered, "Was it necessary to be like that with them? They're supposed to want to save me, if I ever need it. I'm not sure after that little pep talk they'd want to get me drink of water if I was in the middle of the desert."

Turning his face toward me, he smiled. "Don't worry. They just hate me right now. They'll get over it."

I leaned away from him and studied this new Tristan. "Are you always like this with the people who work for you, Mr. Stone?"

Arching one dark eyebrow, he grinned. "Only with the ones who don't understand my orders and those who've kissed my fiancée without my permission, Ms. Edwards."

"Tristan..."

He angled his head toward Daryl and whispered, "Nina, we still need to talk to Daryl and Jensen."

"Then we'll discuss the whole situation with West and Varo later?"

"We can discuss my issue with West later, princess. Right now, we have two people waiting."

Usually when Tristan called me that nickname, I took it as a term of affection, but now the edge in his tone said princess was just his way of expressing his jealousy over Varo. Getting the hint, I looked over at Daryl and pasted a smile on my face.

Grinning back at me, he asked, "So how are the happy couple doing today?"

Directing his attention to the driver, Tristan softened his voice from how it had sounded with my bodyguards and smiled. "Jensen, as always, I'm nothing but pleased with your service. I want to thank you for handling your job admirably, especially with what I'm sure was a stressful drive from the groundbreaking yesterday. I'll be heading into the city soon, so I'll let you know when I'm ready."

Nodding his head, Jensen smiled meekly. "If I may say so, it's nice to have you back, Mr. Stone."

For the first time since he sat down, Tristan's smile was genuine as he listened to Jensen. "It's good to be back. Thank you."

The driver was dismissed with another thank you, and we were left alone with Daryl, who seemed to be practically bubbling over with eagerness that morning. I hoped he had some information to help us figure out what the hell was going on and how we could stop Karl.

"Let's get down to business. What have you found out about Cardiell?" Tristan asked, immediately confusing me.

"What's Cardiell?"

Tristan looked up at me and smiled another genuine smile. "I forgot you haven't been with us with all this." Turning to face Daryl, he said, "For Nina's sake, give us the Cliff Notes version of Cordovex and Cardiell."

"Got it. Cordovex was a heart drug approved by the FDA a few years ago, and it seems that it wasn't as good at keeping heart patients healthy as it was at killing them. Eventually, Cordovex was pulled from the market, but the company which produced it, Rider Pharmaceutical, still held the patent to it. Fast forward to earlier this year and now Rider has a drug named Cardiell out. The problem is they're the same drug. Chemically, they're the exact same, which means a drug which was killing people before is back on the market."

"What does this have to do with Karl and why he wants to hurt either of us?"

Daryl nodded. "Good question. Your father mentioned Cordovex in his notebook Tristan has, so I began digging and found out what I told you. We think Karl is behind the break-ins at Tristan's homes, all except here, and he's looking for that notebook. Your sister gave him copies of the notes he had on Victor and Taylor's wrongdoings, but she didn't give him anything on those notes that come after in your father's notebook."

"Why?"

Tristan squeezed me gently. "Because your father didn't make copies of those pages. Karl doesn't know that, though, or doesn't believe it, which is why I made sure Kim and her family are hidden away so he can't find them."

"Are they okay?"

Daryl chimed in. "They're fine. The girls love playing on the beach and your sister and brother-in-law are enjoying a much needed vacation. By the way, I found out that their house has been broken into in the past few months too."

Tristan started to say something, but my phone vibrated in the pocket of my yoga pants. Taking it out, I saw Jordan's name flashed across the screen. Showing it to Tristan, I whispered, "I have to take this. I hope you understand. I haven't heard from her since she left."

Smiling, he slid his arm from around me. "We'll wait for you. Tell Jordan I said hello."

I jogged out into the hallway, eager to hear Jordan's voice again. "Hello?"

"Hey you. What's up?" she said with hesitation in her voice.

"Tristan's back. We just got home."

"Oh, that's great, Nina!" The phone fell silent, and after a long pause, she said, "I'm so sorry. I don't know why I said what I said that night. I was so out of line, sweetie."

I couldn't stay angry at Jordan. I just couldn't. She was closer to me than anyone but Tristan. "It's okay. I understand."

"When I finally pulled my head out of my ass, I knew I was wrong. I just didn't know how to fix it.

We've never fought over a guy, and I had no right to accuse you of something with Varo, especially since he never even gave a damn about me."

"That's not true. In fact, I think he does like you. I have to get back into a meeting with our favorite mountain man, but what do you say to meeting me later this week? We can catch up and put all this in the past."

"I'd like that a lot. Thanks for being so cool with me since I was the world's biggest asshole to her best friend."

I chuckled at her attempt at being self-effacing. "Don't say that. Anyway, I guess we were due for a big fight. Most friends don't go years and years without one, so it was time. Let me call you later and we'll set up a time to get together."

"Okay. I love you, Nina. Life just wasn't the same without you."

"Ditto. I missed you, Jordan."

As I hung up, my heart swelled from the return of the other person so important to me. My mind raced with all the details I had to tell her, especially about Gage, who I hoped would now have the chance to ask her out. First, though, I had to be at Tristan's side as we figured out what the hell Karl was up to and how to stop him.

THIRTEEN

TRISTAN

Daryl pointed at me and shook his head. "No more beard. What a shame." His frown deepened and he continued, "You planning to keep the hair?"

"No," I said as I smoothed my hair back off my face. "There's no way I can speak to the board looking like this."

A deep laugh exploded out of his face. "No Bieber hair for you? So how's the homecoming? All better now?"

"I'll be all better when Karl is out of our lives for good. I'm hoping you have something to tell us today because I'm ready to get on with my life and that doesn't include this bullshit with him."

Nina returned to stand next to me, and I wrapped my arm around her again to pull her close. This time it wasn't to make a point like it had been earlier but because I wanted her with me in this. When she'd asked to be treated like an equal partner, I'd immediately dismissed the idea, even if I hadn't told her that. Equal partner with me meant she was going to have to deal with the vipers and sharks that made up my world. I didn't want her around them.

The problem was that she was going to be around them as long as she was by my side. The people who would see me out of power at Stone Worldwide would use anything and anyone to achieve their aims, and that included the one person who meant more to me than anyone else in the world. So if she was going to be my wife, I had to let her in and make her my equal.

Looking up at her as she sat on the arm of my office chair, I watched her sweet expression as she talked with Daryl like they were old friends. As closed off and cold as I was, she was open and kind—the type of person the bastards I dealt with every day loved to devour, using her gentle nature against her. Even the thought of that happening to her made my blood nearly boil, and I instinctively squeezed her closer to me.

She looked down at me and smiled. "I guess Tristan is ready to go, Daryl." Leaning down, she whispered, "And I think you look more like Johnny Depp than the Biebs with your hair like that."

"What?"

"You know. In that movie Chocolat. He wore his hair like yours is now."

I had no idea what she was talking about, but she looked so sweet that I didn't have the heart to tell her. "Daryl, let's get back to what you found out."

"You bet. So the two drugs are the same from the same company. Rider Pharmaceutical. The problem is that Rider is just a front. It's a company in name only. I knew there had to be a much bigger company behind it, so I set about looking for what that could be. Take a guess what the name of the company controlling Rider is."

"One of the major pharma companies?" I guessed.

Daryl shook his head. "No. Much closer to home."

"Don't tell me I own Rider Pharmaceutical."

He made a smacking noise with his lips and grinned. "Yep. I'm looking at the proud owner of Rider right now. Seems your little business was a gift to none other than Karl himself."

"Who gave him a company?" Nina asked.

I could have told her. As soon as I heard it was a gift, I knew my father had given it to Karl. Why I could only imagine. I let Daryl continue his story, though.

"Courtesy of Victor Stone, the former CEO of Stone Worldwide and the father of your intended, Nina."

"So what's the big deal? Karl runs Rider, which Tristan owns. All he has to do is fire Karl, right?"

Nina's eyes searched mine for the answer. "It's not that easy. Since legally, my father made him the director of Rider, which is what he must be if he's been given the company to run, I can't simply get rid of him. The board of directors will have to get involved."

"And Karl's likely been hard at work on them in your absence. They're unlikely to just let you make that huge change and once they get involved, Karl's going to have the upper hand, " Daryl added.

"I don't understand. Why would he have the upper hand?" she asked.

Daryl stroked his beard, pulling it to a point. "Because we have no proof that he's doing anything wrong with the company. Without that, there's no legal basis for getting rid of him."

"What I need to know is what's happening with Cardiell."

"Nothing yet. Hopefully, we can find out what's going on and stop Karl before anything bad starts again," Daryl said more seriously than I'd ever heard him before.

"I don't care what's going on. If Cardiell hurts one person and I could have stopped it, I won't be able to forgive myself."

Nina slipped her fingers through mine and squeezed my hand. "Then we just have to figure out what he's up to and stop him."

Daryl nodded his agreement. "It's my guess he's looking for that notebook because he thinks there's something in there that might cause him a problem. Now we know that's not the case, but that means that we need to find that missing sheet of paper someone tore out of your father's notebook."

That was easier said than done. If ever there was a case of trying to find a needle in a haystack, this was it. We had no idea where to even start looking. "Daryl, we need to eliminate any place we can if we ever want to find this piece of paper, assuming it even exists at all."

"I agree, so let's tick them off one by one. Your offices. Any chance it's there?"

Shaking my head, I dismissed this idea quickly. "No. The only files in my office are ones that I've been through hundreds of times before. I can promise you it's not there."

"Okay. Your penthouse. Any chance his goons have missed it there?"

"No. I had the place cleaned out before I moved in. Until I met Nina, there wasn't anything but a few suits, shirts, and ties."

Daryl took out a pencil and began crossing things off in his little notebook. "Miami and LA are out. The places are basically empty. No files there."

"What if we aren't supposed to be looking for files? What if that sheet of paper is in an envelope or something?" Nina asked.

Looking up from his notes, Daryl cocked one eyebrow. "What do you mean?"

Nina stood and walked over to the painting hanging on the far wall. Lifting it, she held it up for Daryl and me to see. "What if the paper was hidden someplace like this, like you see in mysteries? Not a file cabinet or anything like that but just someplace it could be hidden where no one could find it."

As she ran her hand across the back of the picture frame, Daryl nodded. "She might have something there. Can we still cross off the penthouse, the other houses, and your office if we think about things that way?"

I ran through each place in my mind, mentally scanning each room of each location. My office had no artwork or anything hanging on the walls. I had no diploma or commendations to replace my father's, so once I took his down, the spots they'd once covered remained bare. Only the art Nina had chosen hung in the penthouse, and there was nothing left in the other houses.

That only left this house.

"I don't think there's anything in those places, Daryl. I think if it exists, it could be here."

Nina walked back to stand next to me. Sitting on the arm of the chair again, she said, "Then we need to check every room in this house. Just that one room alone with the secret room next to it has at least half a dozen pieces that could be hiding what we're looking for. And don't forget the attic."

I shook my head. "There's nothing in the attic. Trust me. Just some old things that were my mother's."

"No, Tristan, that's not right. There are all sorts of letters and pictures up there. And that's just in one trunk. I bet there are tons of places we can look."

Nina and Daryl began to draw up a plan of attack for searching the house as I wondered why she knew so much about the attic. I hadn't been up there since I'd moved in. Rogers had been responsible for storing things, so I'd had no reason to even think about it.

"Let's head upstairs," Nina said in a chipper voice as she pulled me from my chair. "I feel like Sherlock Holmes."

"Does that make me Dr. Watson?"

Standing on her toes, she kissed me and smiled. "A very sexy Dr. Watson. Now let's go find this evidence so you can nail that bastard to the wall."

Her blue eyes were ablaze with determination. I'd missed her presence in every part of my life. Even when she tried to be tough, she was still my Nina—sweet and gentle, no matter what.

The attic was very much like every other attic in the world. Stacks of boxes, some reaching nearly to the beams that transected the ceiling, and trunks ranging in size from small to enormous lined virtually every square inch of space. A seamstress's mannequin stood silently watching guard in the corner near the south window, giving that area an eerie feeling despite the rays of light that brightened up that section of the space.

Nina lowered herself to the wood floor in front of a large trunk and looked up at me. "I think we should start here."

Looking down, I watched as she lifted the lid and began rummaging through stacks of papers and pictures. "How did you know these were here?"

A sheepish look crossed her face, and she held her hand out. "Sit with me. I want you to tell me about these pictures. I hope you're not mad at me for coming up here."

I lowered myself to the floor next to her. "When were you up here?"

She stopped looking through the trunk and sighed. "Right after I moved here last year. I swear I wasn't snooping. It was just that I was lonely out here all alone with no one but Rogers and Jensen to talk to and I went exploring."

The mention of Rogers' name made a flood of memories rush back into my brain, and I saw by the look on Nina's face that my expression had changed.

Taking her hand in mine, I brought it to my lips in a kiss. "I don't think you were snooping. It's okay."

My forced smile didn't fool her, and she took my hand to kiss it in return. "You're still hurting over him, aren't you?"

I shook my head, trying to lie. "It's okay."

She kissed the back of my hand again and gave it a gentle squeeze. "I'm looking forward to hearing about these pictures. I want to know if the stories I made up were anywhere close to the truth."

Taking the largest photo out, she held it up and looked over at me. "How old were you when this was taken?"

I studied the portrait of my parents, Taylor, and me posing when I was no older than four or five. As with every picture ever taken with the four of us, I sat in front of my mother and Taylor sat in front of my father. Dressed identically, I grinned for the camera while Taylor sat looking so serious, as he always did, and our parents' expressions told the story of their marriage. Self-satisfied and smug looking, my father's presence in the picture bordered on overwhelming, too much strength and not enough kindness. My mother's expression was the one she wore nearly every waking moment of her days. Her mouth appeared to form a smile, but on closer inspection, anyone who knew her could see the sadness in her face.

"I think we were five then," I answered, struggling to remember anything of that day.

"Your mother was beautiful. You have her eyes, but your brother doesn't."

I turned to look at Nina and chuckled at her comment. "Taylor and I were identical twins. I think if I had eyes like hers, then he did too."

She shook her head and smiled. "Nope. Look closely. See your mother's eyes? They're brown, like yours and Taylor's, but they're softer than his. Yours are like that. His eyes look a little harsher. Not yours, though."

For a long moment, I stared at that picture and finally saw what Nina had seen. So many people had always told Taylor and me that they couldn't tell us apart, but now I saw that it was a simple matter of looking into our eyes. "You're right. How did you see that?"

Nina stroked her palm over my cheek. "How could I not? It's impossible to miss. You look like your mother, at least in your eyes. The rest of your face may look much more like your father's side, but those eyes are all her."

Propping the portrait up against the back wall of the trunk, she looked for another picture while I kept my gaze on the four of us. I didn't remember the day we sat for that picture, but the fact that my father even appeared in it was noteworthy. Only formal portraits included him. Any other time a picture might be taken, he was absent, at work or on a business trip that was likely anything but.

"I have a confession to make, though. I didn't notice how much like your mother you were until now. The first time I saw this picture, I thought you looked like your father."

"I did," I admitted, knowing Nina had every right to hate that in me after what my father had done. I didn't like that truth any more than she likely did, but it was the truth. Taylor and I both looked more like Stones than my mother's family.

"It's expected that you'd look like your parents, Tristan. It's okay."

Happy to avoid the comparison between the man who had her father murdered and myself, I reached inside the trunk to lift out a stack of photographs I recognized as pictures from when I played sports as a child. Each one showed me smiling and happy, a winner every time.

"You looked so cute with all your trophies. It's hard to imagine this guy who wears a suit all the time playing anything."

"Then I'll have to take these pictures when we leave so I can remind you from time to time," I joked. "Right now, we need to look through the rest of this trunk."

Nina picked up a pile of letters wrapped in a red ribbon. Holding them up to show me, she read the name on the top envelope. "Tressa. Were these your mother's? I'm guessing from your father. At least you're like him in that."

I shook my head, unable to believe my father had ever written my mother anything. He couldn't even be bothered to call her on most days, so the thought of him writing love letters seemed unlikely. "My father wasn't the type of man to write anything down, unless it made him money."

Handing them to me, she smiled. "Well, just in case, I don't feel right looking through them. It's more appropriate you do it. But why are they here?"

"I took a lot of their things after the crash. Rogers must have brought them here." I looked down at the letters sitting in my palm and wondered if they'd been from an old boyfriend before my mother and father married. The idea of my mother happily in love with someone made me happy. All those years with my father had been so filled with misery for her. The neglect. The rumors of infidelity. The coldness he seemed to enjoy showing only her. That she might have been in love with someone who cared enough for her to write his feelings down so she could forever look back and remember their time together gave me hope that at some point she'd truly been happy.

I unwrapped the bow and slid the first envelope from the top of the pile. Turning it over, I slipped my finger under the flap and easily opened it to find a single sheet of paper inside. Unfolding it, I scanned the page and found the words of a lover. Had it been my father, after all? Maybe before they'd married he'd been the kind of man she deserved.

I hated having to leave you last night, Tressa. I know it's not forever, but it's away from you all the same. Write me and let me know when we can see each other again.

The letter was unsigned and gave no indication who the author was. Turning it over, I saw nothing on the back to solve the mystery of who had written it.

"Who's it from?" Nina asked as she leaned over to take a glance.

"I don't know. There's no signature."

"Try another one. They're probably all from the same person."

Placing the letter back in its envelope, I opened another one and read words similar to the first. Whoever the letter writer was, he'd met my mother and missed her when she was gone. I read two more letters that sounded almost identical to the first ones and wondered if any of them in this stack would be signed.

"Do they have a date on them?" Nina asked as she took the last one I'd read from my grasp.

I opened up another and searched first for a date. None was written anywhere on the paper. Shaking my head, I shrugged. "Looks like another mystery for us."

"Do you think they're from your father?"

"I have a hard time believing that, Nina. My father and mother weren't in love that I remember. He wasn't the type to love anyone."

Looking down, I read an entirely different letter that left me sure it wasn't my father who'd written any of them.

I can't stand even the thought of you with him anymore, Tressa. He isn't worthy of your love. Leave him and come away with me. I may not have his money, but I can give you what he can't or won't. I love you and don't want to live without you another day.

Nina reread the words to me and studied my face for my reaction. "Is this from your father?"

"I don't think so, but if not, my mother was having an affair."

"Maybe it was before she married your father."

Nina's attempt to help me think better of my mother was unnecessary. If she had cheated on my father, as far as I was concerned, all the better for her. At least she'd found love with someone.

"While you read the next one, I'm going to look for her letters to this mystery man. Maybe she had them hidden away too."

The next letter was another plea for her to run away with the letter writer, but it did provide me with a general time period when the letter may have been written. A mention of my brother and me meant that it was definitely an affair. Closing my eyes, I silently thanked whoever this mystery man had been for at least giving her love and the chance for happiness. But had she not taken that chance because of Taylor and me?

I became convinced the name of the man my mother had fallen in love with would forever remain a secret. That wasn't a bad thing, though. Some things should remain hidden.

The next letter's tone was distinctly different than the others. Near the bottom of the pile, it signaled a change between him and her.

I won't let you go. If all I can have is stolen moments with you, then I'll take them for now. I won't let you leave me, Tressa. We make each other happy. Just hearing you say we should end what this is nearly drove me mad last night. I won't let you do it.

I tapped Nina on the shoulder and showed her the letter. "She wanted to leave him. Any luck finding any letters from her to him?"

"Not yet. Just pictures of you all over the place. I swear your brother must have been camera shy, Tristan."

Folding the letter, I slid it into the envelope. "He wasn't much for pictures. Or sports, for that matter."

"Who took all these pictures of you and your mother? Your father?"

The memory of the one time my father attended any of my games for a mere fifteen minutes passed through my mind. "No. Rogers always took the pictures. It was him who came to see every one of my games and matches."

Nina rested her hand on my arm. "I'm sorry, honey. At least you know Rogers cared about you. I think he did."

"I thought so too."

She returned to searching for my mother's letters to her mystery lover without a word, and I focused on the next to last letter in the pile next to me. My eyes scanned the lines that told of their impending break up.

Nothing is more important than love. No matter what excuse you give, I'll give a better one to show we should be together. I won't let you go, Tressa. I can't. Why won't you give in to what you know makes you happy? Come away with me. Leave him and be mine forever.

He was losing her. I sensed it in every word. He knew it too. She probably had told him their affair had to end, and he was just holding on to what used to be.

"I think I might have found something." Nina leaned over the front of the trunk and groaned as she buried her head inside. When she straightened up, she was holding a silver tin in one hand and its lid in the other. Inside the tin were more letters but no envelopes.

She set the box between us and lifted one out for me to read. Opening it, I read one of my mother's letters to the man she loved. Her words were tender and kind, and if my father had ever seen them, he would have made her life a living hell. Suddenly the thought that he had learned of her affair occurred to me.

I sit here alone as the boys play with the nanny and wish there was a way we could all be together, but he'll never let me go with them and I can't leave without them. I'm their mother. They need me. My love for you may be what keeps me going each day, but I can't give in to that and sacrifice them.

"She stayed because of us," I said quietly as I placed the letter back in the tin.

"That's a good thing, Tristan. She loved you. You're lucky to have a mother like that."

"But she was unhappy, Nina. It's all over these letters. She was stuck in a loveless marriage. I knew that from the moment I was old enough to compare my parents with other people's. They never kissed or hugged or held hands. She could have had happiness if she ran away with this person."

"You don't know that. She was breaking it off with him. She had to have a reason, and I doubt it was you and your brother. His letters make it sound like she wanted out for another reason."

I read through more of my mother's letters, hoping to find what Nina said was in fact the truth. I hated thinking she'd given up a chance at real happiness for us. Each one read like the first, some telling him she couldn't leave because of her children and others simply declarations of love.

"Tristan, did you read this last one of his letters? He wasn't going to let her go. Do you remember her acting differently or saying anything to indicate she was frightened? He was threatening her. Listen to this."

He knows, so what's the point of hiding anymore? I know you still love me. After all these years, I know you do. It can be like it was in the beginning. The boys are older now. They don't need you like I do. I won't let you leave me. Not now—not ever.

Nina looked up from the letter. "Do you have any idea when this could have been?"

"No. I never knew about any of this."

The truth was I had never been the kind of son she deserved. I knew she was unhappy, but I never bothered to consider that something other than my father had caused that sadness in her.

"Can I read the letters in the tin to see if we can figure out what happened?"

I shook the cobwebs of memories from my head. "Sure." I didn't want to read any more of the past. The letters had only served to confirm what I'd always believed and shown me it was even worse.

Watching as Nina read letter after letter, I saw her expression change when she reached the last one. "What's wrong? Is there something in that one?"

Turning to look at me, she shook her head. "I'm not sure. Listen to this."

It's over. Take what he's given you and be thankful. He means it to be symbolic. That's why he named it Rider. He's giving you a company he doesn't care about to show you that you'll never have me. Only a company he named after me. Take it and make it yours. I can't see you again. Accept his gift and know he'll never forget this. Be careful.

"What does she mean 'that's why he named it Rider'? What does that have to do with this?"

My mother's words hung heavy in the air as I attempted to process what Nina had just read. My mother hadn't just had an affair. She'd had an affair with my father's best friend.

Karl.

Nina gently shook me by the shoulder. "Tristan, what does this mean? Who is Rider?"

"Ryder with a y. It was my mother's maiden name. Tressa Ryder. My father must have changed it to Rider Pharmaceutical when he bought the company before he found out she cheated on him. That he'd give Karl a company with the same name as my mother's is exactly what she thought. It was supposed to be symbolic. My father would do something like that.

Karl could have some company that meant nothing to him, but he couldn't have the woman that my father didn't give a damn about."

"Are you saying your mother was in love with Karl, the guy who wants you and me out of the way?"

I'd been as surprised as Nina was at first, but it all made sense. The holiday dinners when I was a child when Karl would be all smiles as he teased my mother or told her stupid jokes. How sweetly she'd always acted toward him. In my mind's eye, I could see him then, the far more charming younger man he was instead of the odious bastard he was now.

"I guess so. That's the only answer since it involved Rider Pharmaceutical."

"I don't understand. If he was so in love with your mother, why would he do this to you?"

As Nina returned to searching the trunk for what we were looking for, I tried to reconcile Karl Dreger's hatred for me with how much he'd loved my mother. It made no sense, no matter how much I wanted to pretend it did.

FOURTEEN

Nina

I rummaged through more pictures and mementos as Tristan sat silently next to me, obviously rocked by the news that the man who was busy doing everything possible to make his life a living hell was also the man his mother had loved, even to the point of endangering her own welfare. I found another portrait the family had sat for years later that showed the life Tressa Stone had accepted. In her expression was etched the sadness of a woman who'd chosen to sacrifice her own happiness. Those brown eyes so similar to Tristan's looked out blankly, even as she smiled for the camera.

Lifting the picture out of the trunk, I propped it up against the lid. "When was this taken? You look like a teenager here."

Tristan focused on the image and nodded. "I remember that day. Taylor and my father barely made it in time for the photographer to get the photo. Not that I was much better. My mother had reminded us every day for a week, but her need to have a family picture meant little to us."

"You were a teenage boy. They never care about things like that. Don't beat yourself up over it."

"Look at her, Nina. She was married to a man who didn't give a damn about her and actually gave the man she was cheating with a company, even though I don't think he gave her one present after they were married. Even if he hated Karl, he treated her worse. And my brother and I weren't much better."

"Don't do this to yourself, Tristan. You were a kid. I'm sure your mother understood that."

He faked a tiny smile and nodded. "Anything else in there?"

Pushing pictures and frames across the bottom of the trunk, I lifted my head and turned toward him. "Not that I can see. I think we should move to some of the boxes and trunks around us."

"Okay. I'll check the boxes. Take a look at that trunk near the wall."

Tristan silently moved toward the floor-to-ceiling stack of boxes nearby still wearing a frown from the news he'd read in his mother's letters. I could understand. It's as if he'd lived all his life thinking one thing, and now he had to grapple with the fact that what he'd believed wasn't true at all.

The image of Tressa Stone's sad eyes stayed in my mind as I searched through the second trunk. I admired her, even though I'd never met her. Whatever her life had been, she'd stayed for her sons, and to me, that made whatever else she did unimportant. That one son turned out to be a monster wasn't her fault. The blame for that belonged on her husband, not her. And Tristan was proof that she'd done something right. That thoughtless teenager had grown into a wonderful man. Her influence was obvious, even if he couldn't see it.

The trunk contained blankets and clothes, but as I pushed my hands through them to see if any papers were hidden there, I realized I was searching through baby things. Holding a newborn onesie up in front of me, I sat amazed at how tiny the little blue outfit was. Had Tristan worn this as a baby?

"You don't look like you're doing much searching over there," he joked from behind me.

Turning around, I displayed the onesie for him. "Was this yours? It's so cute!"

For the first time in nearly an hour, he looked happy. Reaching over, he took the clothing and held it up to examine it. "No, this must have been Taylor's. See? His name is sewn into it just under the tag."

I looked and there was the name Taylor sewn in on a tiny piece of fabric near the collar. "Is that how your mother told your clothes apart?"

Tristan chuckled. "Yeah. And it was more like that's how the nanny knew whose clothes were whose."

"A nanny, huh? I want you to know that I don't plan to have a nanny for our kids. I hope you're okay with that."

He threw the onesie back into the trunk and leaned down to place a tiny kiss on the tip of my nose. "Our kids?"

"Yeah. I thought we should have some after we get married. You know, like lots of people often do."

Twisting a strand of my hair around his finger, he leaned down and kissed me, this time on the lips.

Smiling, he said, "Kids it is, but I can't promise normal."

I looked up into his face and for a moment thought I saw a trace of fear in his eyes. "No problem. I've got perfectly normal and average covered, so our kids will be fine."

"Do you remember what I said to you that first night in the car?"

I thought back to that night for a moment. "No. What?"

He tucked my hair behind my ear and gave me that look that always made me feel like lava was pooling in my abdomen. "You said you were ordinary, and I told you you're anything but."

"Yeah, but you knew nothing about me then."

"And I still saw it in you. So forget about this average business. You're anything but, Nina Edwards."

"Well, Tristan Stone, I'll have to keep that in mind."

"Don't worry. I won't let you forget."

I loved seeing him like this. These moments when he was relaxed and playful were so infrequent, but when they happened, they made me realize all over again why I was so crazy about him.

"Did you find anything in those boxes?"

He shook his head and frowned as all the playfulness disappeared. "Not yet. We better get back to it."

Something in the way his shoulders sagged when he turned back to begin searching the boxes again showed how much this was affecting him. I wanted to take him into my arms and tell him everything was going to be okay, but until we figured out how to stop Karl, nothing was going to be okay.

Except us. We would be okay. I knew that in all my heart.

I focused on a trunk next to the one I'd just finished searching and prayed to God that we'd find something soon. Smaller than the previous two, this one contained what appeared to be old Christmas and birthday cards, some from as far back as before Tristan and his brother were born. Although I knew Tristan wouldn't mind me reading them, I felt oddly like an intruder on the private notes and cards from his family.

One handmade card of a wreath made out of silver and gold foil sat on the bottom of the trunk, reflecting the little light that reached it. Lifting it out, I ran my fingertip over the edges of the wreath, impressed with how beautiful it still was after years hidden away. The card's creator had taken care to make folds in each piece of foil to simulate movement in the wreath. Tilting the card up and down, I watched as the light from the window danced over it.

I turned it over but saw no writing or name. Carefully, I pulled the edge of the card and found it opened to reveal a barely legible handwritten Christmas greeting.

May the blessings of the season fill your days with joy.

There was an initial just below that line I couldn't make out. Smudged, it looked like a K or a D. K would make sense if it was from Karl to Tressa, but something about the card seemed distinctly unlike one a man would give to a woman. Setting it aside, I sifted through anniversary cards and birthday cards belonging to Tristan's mother. All store bought, unlike the Christmas card, they were from Victor Stone to his wife. None showed much thought on his part, and none even contained the word love. Tristan's assessment of his parents' marriage seemed to be correct.

Inside one of the cards were three small, white envelopes addressed to her in what looked like a man's handwriting. I couldn't be sure, but it didn't appear to be either Victor Stone's writing or Karl Dreger's. Had there been another affair?

I quietly slipped the letter out of the first envelope, not wanting Tristan to hear the rustle of paper. Not that I disapproved, but I wasn't sure how he'd handle finding out his mother had cheated on his father with yet another man. Some things didn't need to be known.

Looking over toward Tristan, I saw he was busy beginning his search of the next box, so I turned my back toward him and began to read Tressa's letter. I knew from the first sentence I'd been wrong. This was no love letter.

Dear Tressa,

I know it's been years since we last spoke. I've never forgotten how wonderful you were to my girls when their mother died. It's because of that kindness that I'm writing you today in the hopes that by doing so I can lessen the pain of what I must now do.

An investigation into what I thought was merely a simple case of a workplace lawsuit at Stone Worldwide has unearthed a story I have to believe you know nothing about. It's with a heavy heart that I must tell you that I cannot keep this information secret much longer. Please know that if I could spare you the pain I know this will cause you, I would.

Your husband is at the center of my investigation that shows he was responsible for a bombing at a coffee shop in Atlanta that killed innocent men, women, and children. The intended victim was the judge in a sexual harassment case against Stone Worldwide, but the story goes far deeper. The judge's daughter, a fifteen year old, had become pregnant with your son Taylor's child and when he abandoned her, she committed suicide. The judge knew what your son had done and would have made sure the case went against Stone, so your husband made sure that never happened.

Tressa, I wish there was another way to tell you this, but I didn't want to put you in harm's way. I'm sorry. Be careful and if you need to reply, do so only to the address on this letter. Your husband and the men surrounding him are dangerous.

Take care.

Joe

I sat stunned at what I'd just read, unsure of how it was possible that my father had written Tristan's mother. Thinking back to when my mother died, I couldn't remember her coming to see us. How had she known my family then?

Nothing seemed to make any sense. Had my father and Tressa Stone had an affair before my mother died? Just the thought of my father cheating seemed wrong. If not, how had they known one another?

Looking up from the letter in my hands, I saw Tristan finishing with a box and motioned for him to come over. I held the letter up and shook my head.

"What's wrong? Did you find something?" he asked, his voice full of concern.

"I don't know. I...I don't understand this letter. You read it and tell me what's going on."

My hands shook as his eyes moved across the page reading the words my father had written. When he finished, he looked up, his expression telling me he was as confused as I was.

"What does this mean? Your father knew my mother?"

"I don't know."

"Are there any other letters from him?"

I handed him the other two letters I found inside the card. "I found three letters. They're addressed to your mother at somewhere in Pennsylvania. Did she ever live there?"

Tristan nodded as he silently read the address. "My mother was from Gladwyne, right outside of Philadelphia. The address this was sent to was my grandparents' house there. It was left to her when they died."

"How would my father know to send her a letter there?"

"I don't know. Maybe we'll find something out in the other letters."

I watched as he read the next letter, silently hoping it would tell us that my father hadn't been unfaithful to my mother. Lifting his head, Tristan smiled. "I think I know what you were thinking, but it's not like that. Listen to what he wrote."

Dear Tressa,

Diana would never forgive me if I didn't tell you first, and I hope you understand what I must do. We're a long way from the nights when you and she would sneak out of your dorm at Bryn Mawr to come see me at the News Gleaner, aren't we?

You asked me if there was anything you could say or do to convince me to keep what I've found to myself. I wish I could. My investigation has uncovered many secrets around your family. I promise you that the only details that will come out will be those related to my investigation. Please know that I would never intentionally hurt you or your family. You're the reason I met Diana, and I've never forgotten that wonderful favor.

Take care to keep yourself safe. Do whatever you must to protect yourself and your family, but know that I have no choice now.

Joe

The news that my mother had been Tressa Stone's friend and had met my father because of her touched my heart. To me, my parents had always been older. To think of them younger seemed odd, but as Tristan read my father's letter, I imagined the three of them as college friends. The idea left me with more questions than answers, though. Had they remained close after college? How had Tristan's mother met my father and later introduced him to my mother? Sadly, none of them were around to answer any of my questions.

"It seems that your father knew far more than just what my father and Taylor did," Tristan said with a smile.

"They were college friends. My mother and your mother. Do you think we met as kids? My father mentioned that she was wonderful to Kim and me when my mother died. Maybe she brought you along."

"Maybe. Maybe I fell in love with you all the way back then," he said with a grin.

"Now you're just making fun of me. You're terrible! I don't care what you say. I like the idea of us meeting when we were kids and falling in love years later."

"I know what you were thinking, though. You were worried that my mother and your father had been together."

"I was. That's sort of creepy, don't you think? A little too close for comfort for me."

Tristan shrugged and shook his head. "People love who they love, Nina. If my mother was in love with your father, I don't see anything bad in it, especially if he was anything like you. She deserved someone good in her life since she sure as hell didn't have that with my father."

"Then why was she with Karl, of all people?" I asked, still puzzled at how someone so good could be with someone who wanted to kill us.

"I have no idea."

I pointed at the third envelope. "There's one more letter we need to read."

He slipped the letter out and began reading it aloud.

Dear Tressa,

I've found evidence that Stone Worldwide is the maker of the heart medicine Cordovex. The company that produces the drug, Rider Pharmaceutical, is a subsidiary company of Stone run by a man named Karl Dreger. I don't know if anyone in your family knows what Rider is guilty of, but people are dying because of it.

I can't wait with this part of the story. I'm sorry if your family is innocently tied up in this. As I've promised, only what I must reveal will come out.

Joe

"My father tried to warn her. What do you think she did with this information?"

"I don't know, but there are other sheets of paper in the envelope." He pulled the pages out and showed me the first one. On it, Karl's name was written over and over, along with references to Cordovex. "I think we found what he's been looking for."

"That's it. That's what he thinks is in my father's notebook. He had no idea he'd sent the information to your mother instead. But why would he send it to her?"

Tristan shook his head as he read the second note.

"What's that one say?" I asked as he stuffed it back inside the envelope.

"Just more about the Cordovex business. We better find Daryl."

Suddenly, Tristan seemed uneasy. I couldn't put my finger on it, but his expression had changed. Standing up, I took his hand in mine. "You okay?"

"I'm fine. Just a lot to take in."

"I don't think you should judge your mother too harshly, if that's what you're thinking. I don't think she knew about any of what your father or Taylor were doing, and I certainly can't imagine she knew what Karl was doing."

Tristan lifted my hand to his lips and kissed the back of it. "I don't blame her. Of all the people involved in this, only she and your father were innocent. I guess some people would argue that she was responsible even in some small way since she benefited from what Stone Worldwide did..."

His words trailed off, but I quickly tried to ease his mind. "That's bullshit. Your father was responsible for what happened with his company. From what you've told me, she wasn't involved at all. None of the blame is hers, Tristan."

"I know. I do. It's just hard to find out that the woman you thought you knew had all these secrets."

We walked hand-in-hand downstairs and found Daryl peeking behind pictures in the game room. He'd found nothing, but at hearing the news of what we found, his burly face twisted into a clownish grin.

"Good. At least now we know what we have. Any idea how all of that got up there?"

Tristan sat down on a barstool and pushed his hair out of his eyes. "I imagine Rogers took it up there. He was responsible for all of that."

"Well, thank you, Rogers. Now we need to decide what you should do next. You can't get the authorities involved in the whole Cordovex-Cardiell thing until Karl's out of power with Rider," Daryl said.

"Then it's time for Karl to be out of a job. Call Michelle and tell her to schedule a board meeting for three this afternoon."

"Got it."

I watched as the sadness at the mention of Rogers' name slipped from Tristan's face. Stepping close to him, I ran my hands through his hair and kissed his cheek. "Three gives you a little time. Any plans?"

Turning toward me, he winked. "A few things, but first this hair has to go. Time for the Tristan Stone Karl knows all too well to finally be back in full force."

FIFTEEN

TRISTAN

After I'd run a few errands and gotten rid of the boy band angst hair, I was finally back to being myself again, and it was time to return to the building I hadn't seen in over four months. The lobby looked the same with its white marble floors and dark wood walls, and as I passed through security I saw the guards' eyes widen just a little as they recognized me. The oldest one, a man named Bill who'd worked for the company since before I was born, gave me a tiny smile, as if to let me know that he was glad to see me back where I belonged.

Not that I necessarily believed being back at the helm of Stone Worldwide was where I belonged. As I waited for the elevator doors to open to take me to the twenty-fifth floor and my office, I looked at the reflection of myself in the metal panels. The same old Tristan Stone I'd been every day of my time in that building looked back at me wearing my usual suit and tie, but I didn't feel like that man anymore. My time in exile had given me a lot of time to think about my life, and the thought of spending the rest of my adult years in this building no longer seemed right. After the coke and the booze, I finally found out who I was in that old home my mother had loved, and it wasn't the man in front of me now.

That didn't mean I was ready to hand over the company to the likes of Karl, though.

I exited the elevator on the floor that housed my office suite and saw Michelle's face light up as she realized her prodigal boss had finally returned. I could only hope that the reception I received from the Stone Worldwide Board of Directors was half as terrific.

Michelle stood from her desk, obviously excited and with a big smile said, "Mr. Stone! Your office is just as you left it. No one has stepped foot inside, not even security or maintenance. Just as you instructed."

I stopped at her desk and responded to her welcome with a smile of my own. "Good afternoon, Michelle. Thank you for holding down the fort. I'm sure it wasn't easy."

"Mr. Dreger was an almost constant visitor, but I never let him in. He certainly was persistent, though."

"Thank you for taking such care to make sure of that." I turned to head into my office and noticed that there was something different about my assistant. My eyes traveled down her body to a slightly noticeable baby bump. Michelle was pregnant.

"I've been gone a long time, haven't I?" I asked as I pointed to her stomach. "When's the happy day?"

She rubbed her hands over her belly and smiled. "I didn't know the last time we talked. I found out in January. We're due in early August."

"Congratulations, Michelle. Does this mean I'm going to lose you?"

"For a little while, at least. I'm hoping to return after my six week leave, but we're going to have to find care for the baby. It's a big change. We need to find a new apartment first, though."

Michelle paused and a blush came over her cheeks. "I'm sorry. Here I am chattering on about me while you have a big meeting ahead of you. I did as Daryl said and notified all the members of the Stone board that you wanted a meeting at three today. The ones who are out of town will be teleconferencing, but they all said they'd be there."

Chuckling, I said, "I'd rather talk about you than the meeting with the Board, but thank you for handling it. I have a few minutes before I have to head down, so I'm going to gather my thoughts so I'm ready."

"Yes, Mr. Stone."

Michelle sat down and got back to whatever work she had after months of me being absent. Before I walked into my office, I stopped and thought about what she'd just said. Never once had she called me anything but Mr. Stone, but now, it felt wrong. Mr. Stone was my father. I was Tristan.

"Michelle, do me a favor, would you?"

She spun slowly in her chair to face me and nodded. "Of course, Mr. Stone."

"Call me Tristan. We've known each other long enough that you should call me by my first name."

A broad smile spread across her face. "Thank you, Tristan." Hesitating, she added, "That's going to take some getting used to."

"Well, let's hope you have the time to. We'll see after the meeting today," I said as I headed into my office for the first time in months.

The fact was there was a real chance the Board of Directors would inform me that I was no longer able to handle the CEO position, in their opinion. My absence might just have been too much, and if they did move to replace me, I honestly didn't know if I wanted to fight it. I should have wanted to, but as I stood there in my gorgeous corner office looking out the windows at the city below, I wasn't sure. I had enough money to take Nina anywhere her heart desired every day for the rest of our lives.

Why would I stay working in that corner office for another of those days?

Michelle's voice interrupted my thoughts to let me know the time had come. "It's nearly three, Tristan."

Without answering her, I took one last look around my office, just in case that was the last time I could call it mine. As much as I wanted to run off with Nina and never look back at this office and everything about the company, something inside me wasn't quite ready to give up yet. I'd never been meant for this, but after taking the responsibility on, it had become part of me, part of who I truly was.

Michelle was waiting for me with a supportive smile, and as I walked by, I heard her say under her breath, "Knock 'em dead." That's exactly what I intended on doing.

The conference room teemed with board members all ready to discuss the future of Stone Worldwide. The sea of faces turned toward me as I took my seat at the head of the long polished wood table. Never before had I looked at these people and seen them as strangers like I did at that moment. They looked like me in their expensive suits and silk ties, older than I but sitting there like me in comfortable leather chairs discussing topics that until today I actually tried to care about, but now I felt like we had nothing in common.

Noticeably absent was Karl, however.

Lawrence Meister, the chairman of the Stone Worldwide board, sat to my right halfway down the table and nodded silently at me to give the signal it was time to begin. "Tristan, we're happy to see you're back. We look forward to hearing what you have to say."

I took a deep breath and began. "I've never felt close to anyone on this board, unfortunately. If I had, my time away may have been different. That being what it is, I'm here today to let you know that if this board is planning on removing me from my place here, you're going to have a fight on your hands. I am Stone Worldwide. When the world thinks of this company, it thinks of me, just as it thought of my father before me. Each of you may think you can take my place and do a better job, but the fact is, you can't and you won't have the chance."

"Tristan, I'm not sure what you thought, but no one here wants that," Lawrence said as he scanned the surprised expressions on the faces of the men around him. "We're here to find out what you plan to do now that you're back."

"First, I'm curious where Karl is. He's got some supporters on this board and his actions need to be discussed."

A few of the board members whispered to one another at my mention of Karl, but no one volunteered any information to explain his absence. Lawrence's expression showed he knew nothing of what I suspected were Karl's plans to take my place at the head of the company.

"Karl contacted me when this meeting was called and informed me that he would be late. What's going on here?"

I opened the folder Daryl had given me containing all the information concerning Rider Pharmaceutical, Cordovex, and Cardiell. Taking the first packet off the top of the pile, I passed the rest to my right for each member to have for their own. As each man scanned the facts surrounding Rider and its heart drugs, their eyes grew wide in horror. Even the members I'd suspected of backing Karl looked shocked at the information Daryl had gathered.

"What you're looking at is the information the Feds will have concerning a subsidiary of Stone Worldwide. My father gave Rider Pharmaceutical to Karl Dreger to run, and for years he handled the company without a misstep. However, just after my father died, leaving his position to me, Rider found itself in trouble with Cordovex. As you can see on page two, the drug was deadly. The FDA knew, and Rider pulled it voluntarily, but it still held the patent."

James Sheridan, one of the members I'd believed supported Karl in his takeover plans cleared his throat and asked in a shaky voice, "Is this company responsible for Rider's actions?"

I knew what he was afraid of. As a Stone Worldwide stockholder, Sheridan worried more about his portfolio than helping Karl climb over me on his way up the corporate ladder. Nodding, I spoke the truth that no one in that room wanted to hear. "Of course. This board will have to answer for its actions in this matter also, especially considering how accommodating you've been to Karl Dreger's ambitions over the years."

Whatever support he'd had evaporated as they read page after page of his malfeasance as the head of Rider. While the members of the board began to mutter their disbelief, Karl himself came through the conference room doors full of confidence and oblivious to the shitstorm he'd just stumbled into.

He stopped next to my chair and looked down at me, his beady eyes telegraphing his smugness. "Nice to see you again, Tristan. A few days more and you may not have had that seat."

Leaning back, I stared up at him and smiled. "We were just talking about you, Karl. Sit down. I think you'll be very interested in this. Perhaps you'd like to give us a rundown of how Rider Pharmaceutical is doing."

He pulled up a chair and sat down as I slid one last copy of Daryl's report toward him. He hadn't read more than a few words before his hands began shaking.

"Rider? I think you'll find it's doing just fine," he sputtered out. Looking up from the stack of papers with enough proof to cost him everything he'd earned, Karl scowled. "What the hell is this? You all aren't believing this, are you?"

"Yes, they are, Karl, and so are the Feds. Killing people is not only bad business. It's wrong. When it comes out that you knew what Cordovex did and still brought it back as Cardiell, you're going to be the one to pay."

His eyes darted around the room, searching for an ally that no longer existed. Looking like a trapped animal, he swallowed hard. Sweat beaded on his brow, even as the fight inside him struggled to overcome his fear. Thrusting his chair away from the table, he stood upright and shook his head violently.

"This is fucking bullshit! I'm not going to stand here and take this. That company was nothing when I took over. It was nothing!"

Lawrence shot me a glance and calmly spoke up. "Karl, I think it would be better if you got your things in order and spoke to counsel. What we're seeing in this report means you'll have to go."

As if the chairman's words set something off inside him, Karl turned toward me and spat out, "You don't know who you're fucking with, son. You're not going to take me down. No fucking way."

"Time's up, Karl. And don't call me son. I'm Tristan Stone, son of Victor and Tressa Stone."

I watched as the mention of my mother's name made his eyes flash with rage, and he stormed out of the room, slamming the doors behind him. While the members of the board sat in stunned silence at what they'd seen, I stood and leaned down to place my hands on the table. "Gentlemen, if you'll excuse me, I have a mess to clean up."

"Before you go, can you tell us if anyone died this time? There were no details in the report about Cardiell," James Sheridan asked, obviously concerned.

Shaking my head, I said, "Not that we know of. Hopefully, we've caught this early enough."

Sheridan slumped back in his seat, his expression one of disbelief. "My mother takes Cardiell. To think that bastard knew what it could do and still let it be sold to people."

"If you'll excuse me gentlemen." Even though I understood his horror, I had to deal with Karl and the repercussions that would inevitably fall in my lap. Returning to my office, I asked Michelle as I passed her desk, "Can you get Harvey on the phone? Tell him I'm going to need him on this Rider thing."

Dialing the phone, she said, "Daryl had me call him earlier. He made sure to send what he'd found over to his office so he'd be ready when you called."

"Good. Let me know when you get him."

I opened the door to my office and heard her say behind me, "Is everything going to be okay, Tristan? They're not going to blame you for this, are they?"

With a shrug, I tried to downplay how concerned I truly was. "What's that saying—the buck stops here? As CEO, I needed to know what Karl was up to. I didn't. I don't know what they'll do."

The truth was I really didn't know what they'd do, but whatever happened, at least Cardiell would be off the market and Karl wouldn't be hurting anyone anymore.

"I have Harvey on the line," she yelled in as I sat down at my desk.

Raising the receiver to my ear, I pressed the blinking button on the phone. "Harvey, you got the information Daryl sent over?"

"I did. This firm will take care of it. Don't worry."

"I'm not. You never let me down before, Harvey. I know things are going to get ugly before this is over, but I'm prepared for whatever happens. I have something else I need you to take care of too."

"What's that?"

"I want to sell my share in a business I'm part owner of. This isn't part of Stone Worldwide, though. This is a private business arrangement. Can you handle it?"

"Sure. We can talk after our meeting with the Feds."

"Sounds good. I'll see you in a little while."

I hung up the phone and sat back in my chair to look around my office, noticing the bare white walls that surrounded me. After all of this business with Rider was over and Nina and I were back from our honeymoon, I wanted to have her pick out some artwork for this office. It was about time I made this place my own.

SIXTEEN

TRISTAN

Hours later, I arrived home to find Nina pacing the floor in our bedroom. I hadn't made it two feet into the room before she was peppering me with questions about what happened. I'd hoped Daryl wouldn't tell her about the possibility that I'd be held responsible along with Karl for the Rider mess, but I wasn't that lucky. Leave it to that hairy son of a bitch to pick that day for true confessions.

"I've been a nervous wreck for hours. You weren't answering your phone, and Daryl was no help at all. What happened? Can your lawyers get you out of this?"

Loosening my tie, I slipped it from under my collar and threw it on the bed. "One question at a time. It's been a long afternoon."

Nina slid my jacket off, draping it across the desk chair. "I'm sorry. I'm just a mess from worrying. Why didn't you tell me about this?"

I smiled and began unbuttoning my shirt. "Because I knew you'd be like this."

She let out a heavy sigh and sat down on the bed near me. Tugging on my shirttails, she twisted her face into a fake scowl. "What happened to me being an equal and you not keeping secrets from me anymore?"

Lying hadn't been what I'd intended, but she was right. Looking down at her, I hoped if I flashed a smile I could lessen her justifiable anger. "I figured one last time I could spare you. I didn't realize Daryl would suddenly need to bare his soul."

"Don't think you're going to get out of this with that famous Tristan grin. I'm angry at you, Mr. Stone."

I shrugged off my shirt and flashed her another smile. "Then I'm going to have to figure out a way to make sure you're happy again, Ms. Edwards. Give me ten minutes and I'll tell you everything. Then I'll see what I can do to bring back that beautiful smile I love so much."

Nina ran her finger along the top of my pants, her nail grazing the skin beneath my boxers. "Ten minutes. That's it. I'll be waiting."

"You could join me."

Chuckling, she pressed her palm to the front of my pants. "That would only make you think I forgive you already. You're going to have to do a little more than that to make up for this."

Her touch thrilled me, making my cock spring to life. Wanting her more than a shower, I pushed my hips forward, causing her hand to slide down the length of me. "Forget the shower. I've got a better idea."

She pushed me away and shook her head. "No way. Now get in there and wash the day off you. I'll be back in ten minutes so you can tell me everything about what happened."

"I like my idea better."

Standing, she kissed me softly and smiled. "Don't try to charm me. I won't let you this time."

"Can't blame a guy for trying. Get ready for a great night. We're celebrating being back in our own bed and together."

"It's a deal. See you in ten."

After a quick shower, I dressed in pajama pants and prepared to tell Nina everything as quickly as possible so we could get to celebrating. I had a surprise for her I knew she'd love, but she was nowhere to be found by the time I got out to the bedroom. Thinking she may have gone to the kitchen for a snack, I made my way there only to hear her talking to someone in the entryway. When I turned the corner, I saw her standing with Varo, and suddenly all that jealousy I thought I'd conquered rushed back, filling me with rage.

What the fuck was he doing in my house?

Struggling to get a handle on my emotions, I crossed my arms and leaned against the wall to wait for one of them to realize they were being watched. Nina was talking about something concerning her garden, but it didn't matter. Varo worked for me guarding Nina. He had no business standing there talking to her about anything.

He saw me first and instantly his body language became defensive. Crossing his arms, he took a step back away from her. "Mr. Stone, we were just talking about the gardener Nina's looking for."

Nina turned around and quickly the smile she wore faded. "Hey, that was less than ten minutes."

"Be in my office at nine sharp, Varo. Good night."

With a quick nod, he got out of there before I had to say another word, leaving Nina standing in the middle of the room staring daggers at me. "What was that about?"

"What was he doing here?"

Knitting her brows, she frowned and shook her head. "Exactly what he said. I'm hiring a new gardener."

"Then I'll take care of it."

Her disgust came out in a huff, and she stormed past me down the hall. I followed her, knowing what was coming next and wanting it far too much. I found her in our bedroom pacing the floor just as I'd found her a short time earlier. Folding my arms again, I leaned against the doorframe and waited. It didn't take long.

She spun around and pointed her finger at me. "You aren't seriously going to be jealous after making me kiss him, are you? I mean, you wanted me to do that and now I have to deal with this nonsense?"

"Nonsense?"

"That's exactly what it is. You're jealous and it's nonsense. Or maybe you'd rather me call it bullshit. Whatever we call it, I can't believe you're acting like this."

"Like a man who doesn't want his soon-to-be wife hanging out with other men?"

"You're acting ridiculous, Tristan. So now there's a problem with me talking to one of my bodyguards?"

"Maybe you wouldn't mind if I had a conversation with Brandi?"

Her pacing stopped dead, and in her face I saw what I felt. Rage. Jealousy.

"What the fuck are you doing? I did nothing wrong out there and now you're acting like a jackass. A jealous jackass!"

I knew she was right, but it was like I was standing outside my body and couldn't stop the words from coming out of my mouth. My heart told me I had nothing to worry about with her and Varo, but my brain so filled with those old demons egged me on. "I'm not in the mood to discuss this, Nina. I'm replacing Varo tomorrow."

Her mouth dropped open. "What are you doing? Why? He did nothing wrong. If anyone should be fired, it's West. Varo's been nothing but an obedient employee, even when you made him pretend to be my boyfriend," she screamed. "Don't do this."

"I didn't realize you cared so much about what happened to him."

She came at me like she wanted to hit me but stopped short just inches away to stare up into my eyes, as if the answer to my madness could be found in them. Taking my hands in hers, she pleaded, "Tristan, what is going on? Stop acting like this and tell me what's wrong. Whatever it is, we can handle it. Just tell me."

Lowering my head, I shook it, unable to explain why I was acting so stupid. "I don't know. It was just something exploded inside me when I saw you together."

She caressed my cheek with her hand and said quietly, "Baby, I don't know how to convince you that you're the only man I want. I can tell you a million times, but you don't seem to believe me."

I caught her hand and lowered it between us. Looking down at it, I said, "You're not wearing your engagement ring. Why? Have you changed your mind?"

"Is that what this is about? Look at me and tell me. Is that it?"

I let my gaze travel up to hers and shook my head. "No. I'm fucked up. That's it. I don't know why."

"Well, fucked up or not, you have nothing to worry about. Remember you left me for months? I don't want anyone else, so let poor Varo have his job and stop thinking I want anyone else on Earth because I don't."

"I have a surprise for you."

Sighing, she asked, "A good one?"

"A good one. Sit down and close your eyes." She did as I said and I grabbed the box I'd picked up earlier that day. Kneeling on one knee, I opened it and held it in my palm. "Okay. Open them."

I saw in her eyes the surprise I'd hoped for. In my palm sat a robin's egg blue Tiffany's box with a new ring. It was meant as a new start, even though I'd nearly fucked it up with my jealousy just minutes earlier.

"Another ring? Why? I loved the first one," she said as she lifted the box up to examine it. "It's beautiful, Tristan. But why?"

"Maybe we had bad luck the last time. And the time before that. I want this time to go right, so I bought this ring hoping that maybe this can change our luck. Marry me."

"Of course I'll marry you. You didn't have to buy me another ring, though. I'd marry you even without one." Leaning down, she kissed me sweetly on the lips and whispered, "You do this proposal thing pretty well, Mr. Stone."

I pressed my forehead to hers as a sense of relief flooded over me. "Third time's a charm. Isn't that what they say? Put it on."

Holding her hand up, she wiggled her fingers to show me how perfect it looked on her and grinned broadly. "Is it me?"

"It's all you."

"What are we going to do with the other ring?"

"I don't know. Donate it to a charity. Get it reset in a necklace. Save it for our kids."

Nina stroked her fingertips over my shoulder and down my arm. "I like this proposal best. You're already half naked and on your knees."

"Mmm….is that a proposition from you?" I teased as my hands slowly made their way over her thighs. Making quick work of the button at the top of her jeans, I tugged them and her panties off her body in one pull, leaving her wide open for what I planned to do.

"I like the way you think," she said with a moan as I slid my finger through the folds of her wet and ready pussy.

"Lean back," I ordered. She whimpered a tiny noise at the first touch of my tongue to her clit. Sucking it gently, I eased my middle finger inside her tight cunt. Her body clung to me as I slowly added a second finger.

I stared up into her face and watched a look of pleasure settle into her features as I finger fucked her, loving the moans that flooded my ears as I inched her toward release. I wanted to make her forget my stupid mistake from before so all tonight would be in her mind was the night I showed her how much I wanted to spend the rest of my life with her.

"God, Tristan…don't stop. That feels incredible. God, don't stop!"

Arching her back, she angled her pussy toward my mouth and I obliged, running my tongue up to her swollen clit. She moaned my name, and I thrust my fingers into her hard as I flicked my tongue over her tender skin, wanting her to come apart under my mouth. Her cunt tightened around my fingers, and I quickly pulled out, replacing them with my tongue thrusting inside her.

"Yes…yes! Oh, God…yes!" she cried, pulling on the back of my head to hold me as she rode the tremors of her orgasm.

When she finally finished, her thighs quivered uncontrollably against my jaw. Turning my head, I placed a light kiss on her left leg, loving the feel of her soft skin against my lips and the knowledge that I'd made her tremble.

She lay there, eyes closed and biting her lip as she waited for me to get rid of my pants and rejoin her on the bed. I hovered over her and rolled my hips forward to slide the full length of my cock through her drenched pussy, loving how her eyes rolled back in her head when it skimmed her clit.

"Mmmm…you just love to tease me, don't you?" she said with a sexy grin.

"I love watching you come. You are so fucking sexy when I'm between your legs lapping your pussy."

Nina giggled, and a blush covered her cheeks. "Mr. Stone, you have a dirty mouth!"

I placed a light kiss just below her ear and slowly pushed my hips forward again. "You love it."

Nodding, she said whimpered. "I do."

"Good. Now be a good girl and open those legs for me. I'm not anywhere close to done with you."

"Are you going down on me again?" she asked with an innocence that made my cock stiffen to rock solid.

Sitting up next to her on the bed, I dragged my finger slowly down her swollen slit. She bit her lower lip again and moaned as I lingered there watching her. "I might. Then again, I might pin you to the bed and fuck you long and hard, or maybe slow and easy. I don't know."

She opened her legs wider, but I lifted my hand away, receiving one of her all-too-sexy pouts in return. "You are so mean. You make me wait for hours and then you tease me like this. Downright cruel is what you are."

I bent my head down and captured a nipple in my mouth, flicking my tongue over the pebbled flesh. Nina's fingers pressed into the back of my head, urging me on, but I pulled away and sat up.

"What's that wicked grin for?" she said with an edge to her voice that told me my teasing was working.

"I was just thinking about how much I want to bury my cock in your wet cunt and fuck you until you can't walk."

Stretching her arm to touch my thigh, she stroked my cock from the base and smacked her lips. "Put up or shut up, Mr. Stone. The time for teasing is over."

"Ms. Edwards, I'll take that challenge. Get up here on my lap."

Nina stood and straddled my hips, and I positioned her perfectly so all I had to do was lift my hips from the bed and ease into her. She didn't give me the chance, though, and slid down my cock until I was fully seated inside her. Tracing her tongue around the shell of my ear, she whispered, "I didn't want to wait anymore."

"Always so impatient."

I pushed hard into her and stopped, holding her hips tightly in my hands. She cried out, her fingernails digging into my shoulders, her voice filled with aching need. "Don't stop. Please don't stop. I'll beg if that's what you want. Just don't stop."

"You want me to fuck you? To slide in and out of your tight cunt filling you until you can barely breathe? To empty my cock inside you until there's nothing left of me?"

She stared down at me and knitted her eyebrows like she was in pain. "Yes. Tristan, yes."

I wanted her as much as she wanted me, and as she buried her face in my neck, I pumped into her. She met my thrusts with her own, riding me with abandon until the two of us were close to coming apart. Pulling her head down, I kissed her long and hard, wanting to eliminate any trace of every other man her lips had touched. The thought of Varo's mouth on hers tormented me, even as I tried to push it from my thoughts, and as if she read my mind, Nina broke off the kiss and said quietly as her body closed in around mine, "There's no other man I want. Only you. All I want is you."

Wrapping my arms around her, I held her tight as her release and mine exhausted us both. She was so small in my hold, a precious soul I needed to take better care of now that I was back. I couldn't let my jealousy ruin her love.

I lay there with Nina in my arms and silently thanked God for everything I'd been blessed with. I'd avoided jail time from the debacle with Rider, and as the new director of the company I'd have a chance to make sure nothing like that ever happened again under my watch. Maybe we'd even be able to truly create a drug to help heart disease patients. My business life was going to be rocky for the foreseeable future with Federal investigators combing through every last inch of Rider Pharmaceutical's actions since Karl's takeover of it more than a decade ago, but that was the price I had to pay for turning a blind eye to even the smallest part of the Stone Worldwide empire. From now on, I'd have to accept the fact that being the CEO meant I couldn't do it halfway anymore. I just hoped Nina would understand.

Our lives would have to change. For the first time in my life, I had to devote myself to the business of making money. It wouldn't be enough to playact the role of CEO of Stone Worldwide as I had for the last five years. Now, I'd actually have to be that man.

Nina's finger traced a line across my stomach, telling me she had something on her mind. It was one of the cute things she did when she wanted to talk about something but didn't know how to bring it up.

"Tristan, we need to discuss what we want to do about the wedding."

Lifting her head to face me, she looked at me intently and I knew she'd already thought about it. I pushed a stray strand of hair out of her eyes and smiled up at her. "We'll do whatever you want."

She sat up and grinned mischievously. "Whatever I want? Like if I want us to take our vows at the top of the Empire State Building you'd be okay with that?"

I knew she was teasing me, but I really hoped her plans didn't involve anything in the city. Something small at one of my hotels, maybe in Italy or Greece, was more along the lines of what I had in mind. "Whatever you want. Your wish is my command."

Her smile changed to that special kind she gave me when she was genuinely happy. "I think something small right here at the house would be great. Just a few close friends and us. We could do it sooner that way."

I thought about her idea for a moment. "How does a honeymoon in Europe sound then?"

Nina nodded her head. "I was thinking we could go back to Venice. I'd love it if we could get that same room we had last time. Do you think we can?"

I couldn't help but chuckle. "I know the owner, so I think so."

She rolled her eyes and jabbed me sharply in the side. "I'll never get used to that. Maybe it only seems normal if you're born into it."

Pulling her down on top of me, I kissed her full on the mouth. "Then that's something I need to work on. Once you're Mrs. Tristan Stone, you'll officially have everything I have."

"I still don't think I'll get used to having whatever I want, whenever I want."

"You'd be surprised how easy it is to get used to it."

"Do you have any idea about who you want to invite? I thought maybe just a few close friends."

I thought about who I'd invite and realized there wasn't a soul I'd remained close to after the plane crash. Everyone I'd surrounded myself with before had been people who wouldn't fit into the life I'd created with Nina. Maybe Michelle and her husband. "I don't know."

"Well, I'm thinking Jordan and Varo, at least. Maybe he can be your best man?"

"Maybe I'll let him keep his job and we'll leave it at that, Nina."

She rolled off me and sat up. "Then who will be your best man?"

As much as I didn't want to admit it, there was only one person who I even considered a friend. "Daryl."

Laughter exploded from her, and she covered her face as she continued to giggle. "Oh, Jordan's going to love that. I think I'll make her walk down the aisle with mountain man."

"She likes Varo. Set her up with him. He can be her date for the wedding. That should make up for having to hang out with Daryl for a few minutes."

"Then it's set. Jordan will be my maid of honor, and Daryl will be your best man. When should we do it?"

"We both have birthdays coming up. Which one works better, yours or mine?"

Nina sat silently, and I realized she didn't know when my birthday was. To be honest, I only knew her birthday because I'd had her checked out even before meeting her.

"Well, mine's on a Thursday this year, so that wouldn't work. I think we should get married on a weekend. Your birthday is on the weekend, isn't it?"

"You tell me," I said with a smile.

Tilting her head, she arched one eyebrow. "You think I don't know when your birthday is, don't you?"

"When is it?"

"Well, I'm going to guess May or early June since I met you last May after Memorial Day and starting living with you in mid-June and we've never celebrated it. I don't really know when it is, though. Does that make me a bad girlfriend?"

"No. You're still a great fiancée. It's June 2. And since yours is May 15, we're not able to do it on either day if you want to keep it on a weekend."

Nina twisted her face into a scowl and bit her lower lip. "Then what about next weekend. We're not planning to do anything big, so as long as everyone we want can be here, we're good."

Lifting her left hand to my lips, I kissed her engagement ring. "Next weekend it is. You ready to be Mrs. Stone, Ms. Edwards?"

"I am. And are you ready to tell me everything that happened with Karl today?"

"I guess I'm not going to escape explaining that to you, so yes, I'll tell you everything."

Nina crossed her legs and settled in next to me. "Good. See how nice it feels to not keep secrets?"

"We'll see how you feel after you hear everything. Things are going to change for me at work."

"I'm all ears, Tristan, and don't worry. As long as you don't change what's inside you, we'll be A-OK."

SEVENTEEN

Nina

I listened as Tristan explained how he would have to devote more time to Stone Worldwide business from now on, knowing that he feared I wouldn't want to be with a man like that. He was wrong, though. It didn't matter if he was a CEO or a doorman. All that mattered to me was that he was the Tristan I loved.

By the time he was finished, he looked like a weight had been lifted from him. Even though he'd decided to be more hands on with the company, the fact that he could shape Stone Worldwide into a business he could be proud of was important.

"So it looks like I'm going to become what I never thought I'd want to be—a real CEO. How do you feel about that? This wasn't who I was when you said yes to marrying me."

Lifting his chin with my fingertip, I looked him straight in the eyes. "Tristan, you have to do what's right for you. If that means taking on more responsibility, how could I have a problem with that? You're still the same man I fell in love with. It's not like you've decided to give up everything you've ever been and live in the wilderness without running water. That I'd have a problem with."

He kissed my hand and smiled. "I'm not much of a wilderness type of guy. I couldn't even handle the beard and long hair, and I'm pretty attached to running water myself. I just don't want you to think that I'm turning into my father. I promise I'm not."

Who Victor Stone had been was basically a mystery to me, except for what my father had believed about him. I knew nothing about him other than that he was the man I blamed for taking my only parent from me. But never once had I feared Tristan would turn into that man. I saw in the slight frown he wore as he spoke about becoming like his father that he did fear that, though.

"Tristan, you're not your father. I don't worry about you turning into him."

"I swear I never will. I won't let that happen to me or to us."

"Speaking of us, I've got a million and one things to do before next weekend. One week isn't a lot of time to plan a wedding."

"That's the good part about being the groom. All we have to do is put on the tux and be there on time."

"I thought the good part was getting married to the woman you love."

"Well, yeah, of course," he said with a chuckle. "But not having to do all that wedding stuff is pretty good too."

I jabbed him in the side. "For that comment, I hope I take up all the bed tonight and leave you with just a sliver of mattress."

Pulling me close to him, he gave me one of those truly rare Tristan smiles that told me he was truly happy. "As long as you're next to me, I don't care how much I have. All that matters is I have you."

I hit the last step to Jordan's building and struggled to catch my breath as the door flew open. Jordan stood there grinning from ear to ear, arms wide open to envelope me with a hug. "I am so ready to check out some wedding dresses. We can have lunch, gossip about all the things we need to catch up on, and, of course, find you the perfect gown to marry that man of yours in."

"Let me catch my breath! I think you might be more excited than I am about this shopping trip."

Grabbing me, she hugged me close and then held me at arm's length to take a look at me. "This is going to happen this time. I swear to God, if I have to chain you and Tristan down, it's happening."

"I promise no more false starts. This time we're doing this. You ready to go?"

Jordan looked past me at Jensen and the car waiting for us. "I've missed that old guy." Looking around left and then right, she giggled. "And where would your bodyguards be today?"

"They're somewhere. Tristan told them to make themselves scarce, so we may not see them. Don't worry, though. You'll see Gage at the wedding."

We nearly bounced down the stairs to the car, and Jordan turned toward me, her expression suddenly serious. "By the way, what other females will be there?

I need to know who my competition is for the bouquet."

I opened the car door and held it for her. "It's going to be a small affair. I promise to make sure you catch the bouquet."

"Make it look good, though. We don't want people thinking the fix was in," she joked as she climbed into the back seat.

I sat down next to her and tapped on the back of the driver's seat. "We're ready, Jensen."

"Yes, miss. We should be there shortly."

Jordan turned toward me. "So tell me what's going on with that ring. If my eyes don't deceive me, that's not the diamond he gave you when he first proposed."

I couldn't help but grin. "It is a new one. He had it for me when he asked me again last night. I didn't ask for it or anything. I was perfectly happy with the first one."

Taking my hand in hers, she studied my ring like a jeweler. "This ring looks even bigger. What is this, like almost two carets? I'm surprised you're not dragging your knuckles on the ground when you walk."

I pulled my hand away and shook my head. "Don't tease. It's not that big, and I like it. Tristan's got good taste. He knows what I like."

"Yes, he does. Simple round cut but stunning. So what are the plans? You mentioned on the phone it was going to be intimate, so I'm not going to have to mess up other women there if they hit on Gage?"

Laughing, I said, "It will be intimate. Just a few of us. You'll have all the chances you want to get to know him. I tried to get Tristan to have him as the best man, but he wasn't going for it. I'm planning to make sure there's a chance for just the four of us to spend a little time together too."

"Okay. As long as we have a plan. As for today, we're getting your gown and mine. I'm trusting that you won't put me in one of those awful bridesmaid's gowns, right? No horrible pastels like mint green or peach. That would just be cruel, sweetie."

I grabbed her hand and threaded my fingers through hers. "I wouldn't do that to you. You're my best friend in the world, so no mint or any other horrible color dress. I was thinking a nice black gown would look incredible on you with your blonde hair and green eyes."

"Perfect! I knew you wouldn't dress me in something awful. But what about Kim? What is she wearing?"

"I don't know. I didn't ask her to be a bridesmaid. I haven't even told her we're getting married."

Jordan made a clucking sound with her tongue. "I don't blame you. That girl is a drag. Do you plan to let her know?"

Sighing, I shrugged. "I don't know. Kim is never supportive of anything with me, and I don't want her to ruin this. Then I think that my father would never forgive me if he knew I didn't invite her to my wedding. I don't know what to do."

The car rolled to a stop in front of a Brooklyn boutique where I knew I could find a dress on such short notice. As Jensen got out, Jordan gave me a sympathetic smile. "Well, we don't have to think about her today. We just have to find you the world's most incredible wedding gown and me the hottest bridesmaid's gown so Gage sees that I clean up nice and sweeps me off my feet."

"I see you've thought about this a bit," I joked as my car door opened.

"Just a little. Now let's get in there and find that dress!"

My dress wasn't hard to find. I knew exactly what I wanted when I walked into the store, so it was just a matter of finding a dress that didn't look like I was stepping out of a Disney princess parade. Thankfully, I only had to try on three before I found my perfect dress. A white satin gown with a beautiful draped neckline and cut-out back, it hung like it was made just for me. I knew as soon as I looked in the dressing room mirror that it was the dress I'd marry Tristan in.

Jordan's squeals of delight when I walked out to model it for her told me I'd been right. Stepping up onto the carpeted dais, I twirled around in front of the tri-fold mirror. The coolness of the silk against my legs felt luxurious, and the back had just enough sexiness for my style.

"I love it! Is that the one you're going to get?" Jordan asked as she fluttered around behind me checking out the dress from every angle.

Stopping, I smoothed the fabric over my thighs and nodded. "I think so. It's not incredibly fancy, but it's me. I love the way it hangs on me and makes me look taller. Not poofy or prom-like. Now for the veil. What do you think would work?"

"Elbow length would be perfect," Jordan suggested as she skipped over to the rack of veils on the far wall. She choose one and held it out to me. Iridescent and lined with beads, it fit perfectly with the dress.

I placed it on my head and held my hands out as if to model the finished product. "Ta-da!"

In the mirror, I saw Jordan tear up behind me. Covering her mouth, she whispered, "Oh, honey. You're gorgeous."

I looked at the woman I was standing there in that bridal boutique, and for one of the few times in my life I thought I looked beautiful. That awkward art geek who never seemed to get the quarterback or dream boyfriend in high school was nowhere to be found, replaced by the most glamorous version of me there'd ever been.

Jordan sniffled behind me, making the moment so serious I almost cried, so I quickly turned around and changed the subject. Stepping down off the dais, I said, "Now we have to find you a dress. It's your turn now."

"I found a couple while you were in the dressing room. I don't think the saleswoman thinks much of your idea of having me in black, though. She kept trying to foist pink gowns on me, and the last one she showed me was aquamarine. Can you believe it? Aquamarine! I had to stop myself from asking how her trip back to 1987 was."

As I headed into the dressing room again, I carefully slid the dress from my shoulders. "Pink might work, if you want, but aquamarine is definitely out of the question. You sure you want black?"

I closed the door behind me just as the saleswoman came into the room with her arms full of pink, fluffy bridesmaids dresses—exactly the kind I'd promised Jordan she wouldn't get stuck wearing. From inside the dressing room, I heard her announce to the woman, "There's no way I'm going to be caught dead in those prom dresses."

I hurried out of the dress and veil before she offended the woman and got out to her just in time to stop her from explaining just how dreadful the color aquamarine was. As the saleswoman turned on her heels and left, Jordan and I burst into laughter and it was like old times again.

Thankfully, the woman wasn't too offended to bring back four black bridesmaids dresses, and after trying on each one, we couldn't decide. They were all stunning on her. Not willing to take no for an answer, the saleswoman returned with one last dress in a soft peacock blue and before we knew it, we had to admit she had something there.

Jordan hurried into the dressing room and emerged in less than a minute in the dress that made me forget the idea of black in a heartbeat. Next to her long blond hair, the blue satin was stunning. Strapless, with a cuff neckline, it showed off her toned shoulders, and in the back it laced up like a corset, a very sexy touch. Standing on the dais, she turned around to face me and shook her head. "I have to admit. That lady knows her business. She's delusional about the aquamarine, but this dress is fantastic. Are you okay with it instead of a black one?"

"As long as you're happy, I'm happy. And by the way, I think any man would bow at your feet in that dress."

"Oh, I'm happy then. Bring on the bodyguard. He doesn't know what he's up against with me in this dress," she said flashing a gorgeous smile.

"Good. Let's go grab a bite to eat. I'm starving after all this dress stuff. Hurry and get that dress off and we'll hit that little restaurant near your place."

While Jordan changed back into her clothes, I made nice with the saleswoman and paid for the dresses. I also saw Varo and West outside, and channeling my inner Cupid, approached them as they stood near the front door to the boutique. West looked surprised, so I used what I was sure was his concern about Tristan being unhappy once again with their lack of invisibility to my advantage.

"Gentlemen, we're going to head to a restaurant near Jordan's apartment. I'd like you to join us."

Varo looked at me and raised his eyebrows. I had a feeling the expression wasn't one of surprise but amusement. "I'm not sure Mr. Stone would be pleased with that. I distinctly remember him saying he wanted us out of sight."

"Well, that went by the wayside already, so let's move on to lunch and everyone can be happy."

West grimaced and turned to face Varo, who simply smiled and shrugged. "Looks like we're eating lunch today, buddy."

Jordan joined us, and as she explained that the dresses would be delivered to the house by the middle of next week, I saw Varo sneak a look at her. My inner matchmaker had hope!

Brickfire was quaint and relatively quiet, considering it was in the middle of one of the busiest parts of the neighborhood. Long and narrow, the restaurant's central feature was a deep red brick fireplace that in the winter made the place one of the coziest in Brooklyn. Since it was springtime, it was merely the restaurant's inspiration but it was no matter since the food was supposed to be some of the best in the city.

The hostess sat the four of us at a table in the back, and even though the photographers seemed to have far less interest in me now that Tristan had returned, I was thankful for the little privacy the location afforded us. Unfortunately, it took me only a few minutes to see that West intended on making our lunch like some awkward double date he'd been forced into. It was like the man knew nothing of how two people got together. Every time I attempted to introduce a topic of conversation I knew would help Jordan and Varo really get to know one another, West insisted on inserting some comment about what they were supposed to be doing instead of enjoying a nice meal with us.

The server took our order, and I tried for the third time to talk about something that could help my two intended lovebirds get acquainted. "Gage was in the Navy before he began working as a bodyguard, Jordan. Remember when we went to Fleet Week?"

Her green eyes grew as wide as saucers with surprise, and for a moment I thought she might be angry with me for bringing up the topic, but before she could say anything, West angrily excused himself from the table and stomped away.

As I watched him leave the restaurant, I wondered aloud, "What's up with him?"

Rolling her eyes, Jordan joked, "Maybe he's an Army guy."

Out of the corner of my eye, I saw Varo smile and knew instantly it was one unlike any he'd ever given me. It went all the way up to his eyes. He really did like her. Thrilled my plan was unfolding exactly as I'd hoped, I sat back and let things happen.

Just as I'd believed, he was charmed by Jordan's humor and occasional snarkiness, and if she liked him before, the mention of him in the Navy made her practically crazy about him. I saw it in her eyes. Only a few times before had I seen them sparkle like they did as the two of them sat there getting to know one another in the back of Brickfire. By the time West returned, I was convinced my matchmaking work had succeeded beyond my wildest dreams.

As we climbed into the back of the car to head to her place, I couldn't help but smile from ear to ear. Jordan was less expressive, but I knew inside she was bouncing off the walls. "Don't tell me you didn't have a great time. I know you did."

"Sure. The food was great. I really liked that fireplace. I bet in the winter it's great to have dinner there."

I smacked her arm hard. "Don't tell me you didn't love getting to know him. I know you did."

She giggled like a schoolgirl and blushed bright red. "I did. He's even better than I thought. I'm trying not to get too excited by things just in case it ends up being nothing."

"Nothing? When he sees you in that peacock blue dress, he's going to want to sweep you off your feet right there in my garden."

Jordan's expression turned serious, and she squeezed my hand tightly. "I just don't want to be let down, Nina. He's gorgeous and hot and everything any girl would want. I don't want to get my hopes up just yet."

I understood her cautiousness. Letting someone into your heart was risky business, and as we both knew from experience, it rarely worked out. I still believed she could be happy like I was, so wary or not, I had hope for her and Gage.

Jensen stopped the car in front of her apartment and with a heavy heart I had to accept my time with her was over too soon. She saw my sadness and hugged me tightly to her. "Just a couple more days and we'll be standing there in our awesome dresses and you'll be marrying the man of your dreams. No sad faces, okay?"

"Okay. See you in a few days. The wedding is set for six next Saturday, so I'll have Jensen come for you around two."

"Two it is. I love you, Nina. Thanks for being such a great friend."

I watched as she climbed the stairs to her place, already missing her. I wasn't sad so much as understanding for the first time that everything was going to change. Living with someone was one thing, but becoming a wife meant something far more serious. I knew I'd see her whenever we wanted, but my life was about to change.

By the time we arrived back at the house, Varo and the still miserable West were there waiting for us, and as I got out of the car I saw Tristan pull Varo aside near the garage to speak to him. Both wore very serious expressions, but I didn't get the sense he was reprimanding my bodyguard. After a minute or so, Varo left and I approached Tristan, happy to see him but curious about what the conversation had been about.

"Hey you! I found a wedding gown and Jordan found her bridesmaid gown, so we're all set on the dresses."

He took my hand in his and smiled. "Good. I can't wait to see it."

Looking up into his eyes, I tried to discern the meaning of his chat with Varo. "Everything okay? I saw you pull Varo aside as I drove up."

"Everything's fine. I have to head into the city, but I'll be back in a few hours. I'd love it if you'd be waiting for me," he said with a wink.

"You know I will be," I said as I stood on my toes to kiss him, missing the feel of his lips on mine after hours away. "Maybe I'll have a surprise for you."

"I like that. You're making it hard to leave, though."

"Good, but I know you have things to do, so just remember I'll be waiting when you get back."

Whispering "I love you," he kissed me again and turned toward the garage. As I watched him walk away, I thought about how I might surprise him. Maybe a nice dinner? Or me in sexy lingerie? Or a nice bubble bath for two?

I'd think of something good.

EIGHTEEN

Nina

A few minutes after Tristan left, my phone rang. Thinking it was him calling me to say he loved me, I didn't pay attention to the number that flashed across the screen and simply answered the call.

"Hello," I said in a happy, singsong voice.

"Nina? It's Kim."

Just hearing my sister's name made my mood change from blissfully happy to completely miserable. She must have had some kind of happiness radar that beeped as soon as I began to feel good in life, but this time, I wasn't going to let her ruin my great day.

"What do you want, Kim? I'm a little busy."

The phone was silent for a long moment, and then when she spoke again, her voice sounded different, almost contrite, for the first time ever. "I thought maybe we could meet."

"I've got a lot to do this week. I'm getting married, so it's not really a good time. Maybe after I get back."

I knew I was being a bitch, but after years of her being just that, I figured she had it coming. No matter how sorry she felt for our relationship, or lack of, I didn't want to hear it.

"Baby, you're getting married? I thought you and Tristan already had the wedding. You weren't going to tell me, were you?"

Just the word baby made guilt rush over me. My father would be heartbroken to know on the biggest day of my life that Kim wouldn't be there to share it with me. I heard his words echo in my mind at that moment.

"No matter what else you two are, Nina, you're family. Always remember that, baby."

"Kim, what do you want to meet about? I'm not interested in hearing you tell me I'm making a mistake. Considering the man I'm about to marry saved you and your family from being killed, I'd think all you'd have to say to me would be glowing praise for Tristan."

"Please, can we meet? I'm in Manhattan for the night."

Every fiber of my being told me not to go to her, except for that tiny part of my brain whispering that no matter what else Kim was, she'd always be my sister and I owed it to my father to give her another chance. We didn't have to be the best of friends, but I'd always wanted us to be closer. Maybe now we could be.

"Okay. Meet me at a restaurant called Malone's. I can be there in an hour."

As I gave her the address, a sense of satisfaction came over me. Perhaps this was finally the time we could be the kind of sisters I'd always wanted us to be. I felt strong enough to handle her now.

I tracked down Jensen near the carriage house to let him know we'd be hitting the road again, and as I made my way back to the house, I saw Varo. I didn't need a bodyguard to meet my sister, but if I tried to leave without letting him and West know, the hassle wouldn't be worth it.

"Since you're only seeing your sister and Karl's been taken care of, I can probably handle this without West. He seems to be feeling under the weather anyway. He's been scarce since we returned from our little lunch get-together."

I couldn't help but smile. No matter how snide he sounded, I knew he had a good time. "Yeah, don't act like you didn't enjoy it."

He smiled and I saw a sparkle in his dark blue eyes. "Always the matchmaker, Nina. I hope Jordan and I don't disappoint you. We're mere humans, after all."

"All I want is you and her to be as happy as Tristan and I am. That's all."

He chuckled at my statement, and as he walked away toward the car he and West used, he turned around. "I don't know about that, but maybe Jordan's right about that good things happening to good people thing. I guess we'll have to see."

"Just give it a chance," I yelled as I walked back to the house.

The hostess led me to where Kim sat, and I saw that her time in the islands had been good to her. Tanner than she'd been since she was a teenager, she practically glowed. I sat down and was greeted with a smile that looked so different on her. Optimism surged in me, and I was ready to begin what I hoped would be a new future with my only sister.

"Nina! You look wonderful."

"You too. You wear the tropics well."

"You should see the girls. They'd never seen so much sand. It's going to be hard for them to get used to Pennsylvania weather again," she said with a smile.

"I'm glad you enjoyed the resort Tristan arranged for you."

A sharpness crept into my voice that I hadn't intended, but I couldn't deny what lived in my heart. I wanted to repair my relationship with Kim, but that wasn't going to happen with just one dinner and it wasn't going to happen with me forgetting everything she'd done.

The mention of Tristan's name elicited a forced smile from her, and I instantly knew she was still struggling like I was. Maybe that wasn't such a bad thing. Whatever we were going to end up being to one another, I wanted it based on truth.

"It was very nice. I just wish there hadn't been a reason for us being there in the first place."

I knew what she was saying—that Tristan was to blame for a fucking madman being in our lives. Instinctively, I defended the man I loved. "Karl wasn't interested in you because of Tristan, Kim. He thought you had something he wanted because of Daddy. It had nothing to do with Tristan, in fact, so I don't appreciate your insinuation that he was to blame for any of this."

A waiter interrupted our conversation, and I quietly ordered the first dish I saw on the menu, not even sure I was in the mood for a roasted vegetable panini. Not that it mattered. I had a feeling I wasn't going to have much of an appetite tonight.

When we were alone again, a heavy silence settled in between us. I had to admit once again that she hadn't contacted me because she wanted to wish me well or to see if I was happy. As always, Kim had sought me out to be a damper on my life. I felt sad that once again our relationship wasn't going to change.

Unlike every other time I'd accepted that reality, this time I wanted to know why. Why was my happiness a thing she always had to crush?

"Nina, when Daddy died, I promised myself that I'd watch out for you. I know I haven't done a wonderful job, but I tried."

Kim sat there across the table from me wearing some kind of martyr expression, as if she'd struggled so long with me only to be disappointed in the results of her efforts. I wanted to smack that look off her face. How dare she! I'd never been the one who sabotaged her happiness. Never once had I been a hassle asking her for money or to bail me out of trouble. I'd lived my life my way and respected her for living hers the way she wanted to. Why was she acting like I'd been some kind of cross for her to bear?

"What are you talking about, Kim? I didn't need anyone to watch out for me. Why do you make it sound like I've been one problem after another for you?" I asked, feeling the defensiveness rising inside me.

She took a sip of her water and swallowed hard. "Daddy always spoiled you. I told him not to, that it was going to make things harder for you when you became an adult, but he never listened. I think he felt guilty about not finding another woman to help as you were growing up, so he gave you whatever you wanted. It would have been better if he had remarried."

"What the hell does that mean? I had nothing to do with him not marrying again. And Daddy didn't spoil me, unless you call making sure we had a warm place to live and I had clothes on my back spoiling someone."

"That's not the type of spoiling I mean. What I'm talking about is the way he took care of everything for you. You think that's the way it's supposed to be because that's the way you always had it with him."

I wasn't sure where Kim was going with all this, but I wasn't liking any of it. And I wasn't liking the way she was dancing around her true intentions. "Just say what you want to say, Kim. Don't blame Daddy if you're jealous of whatever the hell you're jealous of."

Gritting her teeth, she said, "This isn't about me being jealous, Nina. It's about our father not preparing you for the world and allowing you to be naïve for too long."

That was it. I was done. Leaning across the table, I pointed my finger at her face. "I'm not going to take this anymore from you. You're jealous because I'm not a miserable bitch full of mistrust. I'm sorry you're like that, Kim. I really am. But I didn't make you that way and nothing I do can change who you are. That's on you. I simply won't be the person you dump all your shit on anymore. Don't bother calling me again. I met you tonight because I knew it was what Daddy would want. To be honest, I hoped that we could finally change the vicious cycle our relationship has always been in, but it's obvious that's not going to happen, so don't contact me again."

As I stood to leave, she grabbed my arm to hold me back. "Don't leave. I need to tell you something. Whatever happens after that, at least I can know that I tried and didn't let Daddy down."

I glared down at her, not believing a word coming from her spiteful mouth. "Whatever you need to say, don't bother. I don't want to hear about it."

Reaching into her purse, she pulled out a sheet of paper with tattered edges that looked like someone had ripped it from a notebook. It was folded in half, and she placed in on the bread plate in front of her and looked up at me. "Just hear me out."

As if everything was happening in slow motion, I sat down again and stared at the piece of paper. It looked just like the kind of paper in my father's notebook. "What's this about?"

"Do you remember when you first told me about Tristan? I told you I'd heard horrible things about him—that he'd been responsible for someone's death?"

I raised my eyes from the sheet of paper to look at her. "Yes, and I remember telling you I thought you were crazy. I still do. Tristan couldn't kill anyone. You don't know him."

"No, I don't. I'm afraid you don't either."

Shaking my head, I took a deep breath. "You're wrong. Whatever you think that says, you're wrong. It was Tristan's brother who was responsible for that girl's death. Taylor did that, not Tristan."

She opened the folded sheet of paper and scanned what was written there. "This says Tristan. There's no mention of his brother being implicated in that girl's death. Daddy found all this out when he was investigating Stone Worldwide."

"You're mistaken. I've seen Daddy's notebook, and he knew it was Taylor who got that girl pregnant. He wrote it down himself. I can't believe you'd accuse the man I love of being a murderer again. What is wrong with you, Kim? What did I ever do to you to make you do this to me?"

"I've seen that notebook too, but before Daddy died. He ripped this page out because it wasn't part of his investigation of Tristan's father's company and filed it away. I found it when I cleaned out his house after the funeral. You know, when you were busy spending hour after hour in bed while I had to deal with everything that comes when your father dies and no one else is there to help you."

Her attack stung, and I sat there speechless as my mind attempted to process through the hurt and anger to the meaning of what she'd said. "I'm sorry I wasn't there when you needed me, Kim. I can't help how I reacted to when he died. Daddy and I were very close. His death devastated me."

"I was heartbroken too, Nina. That didn't mean I got to stay in bed, though. I had to be responsible for taking care of all the business that comes with death."

My chest tightened as I watched her expression harden. She couldn't forgive me for not being there because I was falling apart. How could we ever hope to have any kind of healthy relationship while she still harbored these feelings? "Kim, why are you telling me all of this? What does this have to do with why you wanted to see me?"

"When Daddy died, I had to go through every inch of that house, reliving all the memories of Mommy's death. I wanted to break down too, but every day I had to return to those rooms so full of the past. I had to sift through every piece of paper he kept. Do you remember how he'd always write on scraps of envelopes and cocktail napkins when he had an idea or found some fact he needed to remember? That house of his was full of them. Some I threw away, but most I kept, mainly because I couldn't let go and those were all I had left of him. So I stuck the ones I saved in a box, even though I wasn't sure what I'd ever do with them. Copies of that notebook of his you've seen were some of what was in that box, along with this sheet of paper."

"I'm so sorry, Kim. I'm sorry I wasn't there and didn't realize what you had to go through," I said quietly, hoping to at least show her we didn't have to continue like we'd been.

Her hand shook as she lifted the paper in front of me. "When you told me about Tristan, I knew something about him sounded familiar. I couldn't place it at first, but then it all came back to me. I'd seen his name on one of Daddy's scraps of paper. When I searched through that box, I found everything Daddy had discovered about Tristan and his family. How they'd done horrible things and never gotten caught or been punished, and now one of them had tricked the only family I had left into falling in love with him."

Reaching out, I stilled her trembling hand. "Kim, I know all about what Victor and Taylor Stone did. I know they weren't good people, but Tristan isn't like them. He's like his mother. Did you know Daddy and Mommy knew Tressa Stone? She and Mommy were friends in college. It was Tressa Stone who introduced Mommy to Daddy."

My sister stared at me with a look of coldness I'd never seen before in her eyes. "He's not good, Nina. He's a Stone just like his father and brother. His father had Daddy killed and he found you to make himself feel better."

I shook my head violently. "No, that's not true, Kim. I know he felt bad at first and that's why he came to find me, but then we fell in love. He's a good man. I know he is."

Without breaking her icy stare, she slid the paper across the table to me and pulled her hand back. "Then how do you explain your good man doing that?"

My heart pounded so hard that my chest began to ache. I didn't want to look down at what was written on that sheet of paper. I believed deep in my soul that Tristan was a good man and loved me as much as I loved him, and I didn't want to know that I could be wrong. I didn't want to see an indictment of who he was written in my own father's handwriting.

Holding back the tears that threatened to pour down my cheeks, I shook my head. "I won't do this with you. Whatever you think you know, you're wrong. Tristan is the man I love, and I'm going to marry him. I won't let you ruin this for me."

"Look at the paper, Nina. Look at what Daddy found out about your fiancé."

My heart ached at the thought of what I'd find, but I couldn't stop myself. I had to read it, if only to prove that Kim had it all wrong. I unfolded the sheet and there at the top of the page was his name.

Tristan Stone—August 2006—Hoboken

My eyes slowly scanned the next line, but I didn't understand my father's notes. All it seemed to be was an address with a bunch of numbers after it.

99 Garden Street NJ #0002675-2006

I looked up at Kim, confused as to what I was supposed to know from these notes. "What is this? I don't understand."

"Daddy's notes are at the top. He found out about a girl's death in 2006—a girl's death your future husband was responsible for. The notes below are Jeff's. I had him check into this when I realized who Tristan really was."

I read my father's notes about Tristan again, still not understanding them, and then moved on to Jeff's. As my eyes slid over each word, the horrifying truth became clear.

Arrest record #0002675-2006 Tristan Stone arrested for the murder of Melissa Raynard on August 13, 2006. Case dismissed after death ruled an accident.

As I stared at the words swimming before me over the lined notebook paper, I heard Kim speak. "He killed a girl, Nina. He gave her the drugs. She was only twenty-one years old and he killed her. Oh, his father's money kept him out of jail and from what Jeff says the coroner said the death looked like an accident, but if he didn't kill her, he sure as hell was responsible for her death. He was a coke addict and that girl paid the price for knowing him. I couldn't let you go on thinking he was the person he claims he is. He's bad, Nina, and you're going to get hurt or worse if you stay with him."

Opening my hands, I let the paper drop to the table and shook my head in disbelief. "No, this can't be. He wouldn't do that."

"Did you know he used cocaine back then? Did he tell you that?"

I wanted to scream, to run away from every word she uttered. Instead, I continued to shake my head, not wanting to believe Tristan could hurt anyone like that. I couldn't think of him like that person described in my father's notes.

But I couldn't help it. Maybe if I hadn't seen him sitting in front of the coke with my own eyes that night at Top, I could believe it was all a mistake or some awful, cruel ploy of Kim's to hurt me, but I had and now those notes of my father's and Jeff's seemed entirely possible.

"Nina, you've seen him do coke, haven't you? I can tell by the look on your face that you know what Daddy and Jeff found out is the truth."

My head pounded and it felt like someone was strangling the air out of me. I stood up, still shaking my head, and croaked out, "I can't do this. I can't stay here."

I ran out of Malone's into the street desperate to find Jensen. Frantically, I searched up and down the sidewalk for him, but he was nowhere to be found. Where was Varo? Why wasn't Jensen nearby like he always was? God, I just wanted to see a familiar face, someone to get me out of there and take me home.

Home where I lived with Tristan.

My feet were moving, but I didn't know where I was going. My mind spun like a top, making me dizzy and lightheaded. Nausea choked me, making me want to throw up, and I reached out to steady myself on a pole. I couldn't breathe. All I could think of were those words on that paper describing a man I thought I knew. Did I even know him at all if he could keep this from me, even after promising to tell me the truth?

"Miss, are you okay?"

I turned to see Jensen standing next to me. "I'm fine. I need to go home, though. Please take me home."

"Of course, miss. The car is just over here."

He helped me to the car, and as we drove away toward the house, I asked, "Where was Varo? He's supposed to be nearby at all times."

"He's stuck in traffic, miss. I'm sure he'll be home right after we arrive. I'll let him know we're on our way now."

"No, that's okay, Jensen. He has enough to deal with right now. Just get me home as fast as possible."

As Jensen did his best to conquer the very beginning of rush hour traffic, I called Tristan. I had no idea what I'd say, but I needed to speak to him. I needed to hear his side of the story. I tried three times, but his phone went to voicemail every time and I never left a message. There was too much to say.

By the time we reached the house, I'd made up my mind. Of all the secrets surrounding Tristan and the rest of the Stone family, this was the one I couldn't live with.

NINETEEN

TRISTAN

Hours of questions by Federal investigators had left me exhausted, but just the thought of Nina waiting for me with a surprise was enough to make me top a hundred miles an hour as I drove up the Taconic. Tapping my phone's screen, I saw she'd called three times but left no voicemail. That was nothing new. She never liked leaving voicemails.

Now that Karl was out of the picture, there was no reason to worry. Varo and West made sure she was safe, so she'd probably called just to tell me she loved me. I loved those calls and hated that I missed them, but stopping the Feds to answer a phone call wasn't an option.

Fifteen minutes away from the house, I called her to let her know I was almost home. Two rings and then to voicemail. That was odd. Maybe she was in the shower. A sense of anxiousness settled into my mind, but I quickly dismissed it. The investigators had assured me that Karl would be in custody within the hour, so there was no reason to be uneasy.

I turned onto the driveway and punched in the security code on the keypad. The gates opened, and I raced up to the house, dying to see the woman I loved. The garage door was up, but I could park the Jag later.

I didn't want to waste another minute on anything but Nina.

The sun was just setting as I walked to the front door, wondering what my surprise would be. A nice dinner and the rest of the night in bed together would have been good enough for me, but if she preferred something a little wilder, I was up for that too. After all those months without her next to me, I didn't care if we simply laid in each other's arms and watched movies all night, stuffing our faces with Jiffy Pop.

As long as she was by my side, everything was better.

I threw my keys on the table in the center of the entryway and listened for any sign of what she'd planned. The house seemed strangely quiet. As I walked down the hallway to our bedroom, I peeked into the kitchen and sitting room, but both were empty. Convinced she was waiting for me in the bedroom, I prepared myself to act surprised when I opened the door and saw her lying there in her sexy lingerie, or even better, naked and ready for me.

But she wasn't there.

Taking out my phone, I typed out a text telling her I was home and pressed Send. I slid my tie from around my neck and unbuttoned my shirt, relaxing for the first time since leaving the house. My phone remained silent, so I checked it for Nina's text back to me, but there was nothing.

Fifteen minutes went by without any message from her. Had she gone out? If she did, I knew Jensen could tell me. I made my way to his part of the house, but he was nowhere to be found. Where the hell was everyone?

"Mr. Stone? Can I help you?"

I turned to see Jensen standing behind me with a look of concern on his face. I rarely intruded on his personal life or space, so his expression didn't alarm me. The poor guy probably thought I was there to ream him out about something small.

"I was looking for you to find out if Nina went out."

"She did, but we returned over an hour ago."

I clapped him on the shoulder to let him know we were good. "Okay. Thanks, Jensen."

After a look around the entire house, I headed to the carriage house to see if Varo and West had any idea where she could be. The place was dark, and jiggling the handle, I found the front door locked. As I turned to walk back to the house, the car they used when they guarded Nina drove up with only Varo inside.

Opening the door, he looked calm. "You looking for me?"

"I came back to look for you and West, but the house is dark and the door is locked. Where's West?"

Varo shook his head. "I don't know. He said he wasn't feeling well, so I went alone when Ms. Edwards went out."

"Why are you just getting back now if Jensen and Nina returned more than an hour ago?"

"Traffic. Is there something wrong?"

I shook my head and tried to piece together what was going on. "I can't find Nina. Jensen said he brought her back an hour ago, but she's nowhere to be found."

"Did you check the entire house?"

"Yes, and now West is nowhere to be found too?"

"I'll check the grounds. See if you can find anything inside to give us a clue where she could be," Varo said as he took off into the darkness.

I hurried back into the house and went straight to our bedroom. All her clothes still hung in the closets, and there didn't seem to be anything missing in the drawers. Even her toothbrush still stood in the holder on the back of the vanity. As I checked each room again, I saw nothing in the house to indicate she'd been taken against her will either.

But something was very wrong.

Calling Jordan, I prayed Nina just decided to meet her in the city and this all was a misunderstanding. When she answered, I knew just by the tone of her voice Nina wasn't with her.

"Jordan, this is Tristan. Is Nina there with you?"

"No. She and I went dress shopping earlier today, and she dropped me off after we had lunch. Is something wrong?"

"I'm sure there's nothing wrong. I just came home expecting her here and she's not."

"Did you try her cell?" Jordan asked, trying to hide the worry in her voice.

"Yeah. She didn't answer. I sent her a text too, but nothing."

"Let me try. I'll call you right back, okay?"

I pressed End and began pacing across the width of the entryway, suddenly worried I'd let my guard down too soon and Karl had finally found a way to get to Nina. After what felt like hours, Jordan called back and I instantly knew something was wrong.

"Tristan, she answered, but I couldn't figure out what she was talking about. Her phone kept going in and out, but she said something about Kim and some girl. I couldn't make out the name, but it sounded like Alyssa or Marissa. I don't know anyone with those names. She was sobbing. Something happened. I know it. Kim did something, Tristan. I don't know where Nina is, but wherever it is, she's falling apart. You have to find her."

My stomach sank as I listened to Jordan tell me what I'd feared ever since reading Joseph Edwards' note to my mother explaining what he'd uncovered about me. Kim had finally found out about Melissa and told Nina, no doubt to hurt her intentionally. That fucking bitch!

"I'll find her, Jordan. First, I have to find her sister to figure out what damage she's done this time."

"I don't know what this is about, Tristan, but Kim is no good. Whatever she did, I'd bet a hundred bucks she did it on purpose."

"Did she tell you where she was or say anything else?"

"No. I heard something in the background that sounded like a loudspeaker, though. Her phone went out and I couldn't get her again."

"Okay. Thanks, Jordan."

"Whatever happened, you need to bring her home, Tristan."

"I will. I promise."

I stuffed my phone in my inside pocket, my hands shaking from the rage coursing through my body. If I didn't get myself under control before I saw Nina's sister, I might do just what she thought I was guilty of.

Varo knocked on the front door and walked in to explain he hadn't found any evidence of anything wrong but he hadn't found Nina either. "You won't," I said as I grabbed my keys. "She's not here."

"Are you going to get her now?" he asked, confused by my angry tone.

"I don't know where she is. All I know is that her goddamned sister had something to do with this. I'm going to see her to find out if she knows where Nina went. Call Daryl and tell him I want you two to search everywhere, including the penthouse, her old job at the gallery, and anywhere else you two can think of. I want her found before Karl or his people find her. Do you understand me?"

Varo nodded, obviously shaken by the anger I no longer even tried to hide. As I pushed past him, I added, "And find out where the fuck West is!"

I stood on Kim's front porch after making the three hour trip in less than two hours, my hatred for Kim fueling my driving with each mile. Not that it was entirely her fault. I knew that. I knew that I should have told Nina about Melissa, especially after I promised her I wouldn't keep anything from her anymore, but how the fuck do you tell the woman you love about the woman who died as a result of your actions? I never found the right moment to explain that I'd been arrested and charged with the murder of Melissa, even though I'd been innocent.

Banging on the front door, I didn't know what I planned to say. At every turn, Kim had fought me about Nina, but I'd thought that when I'd done everything I could to keep her and her family safe from Karl that she'd finally seen I wasn't a bad guy. Obviously, she'd been saving the information about Melissa for when it would do the most damage.

Kim opened the door and immediately tried to slam it shut, but she was no match for me in my mood. I threw it open and brushed past her with little effort, intent on finding out how much damage she'd done. "Don't bother trying to make me leave. I'm not going anywhere until you tell me what you did to make Nina run away."

Closing the door, she scowled at me. "You can't change things with your money this time. The truth can't be stifled by any amount."

"You just couldn't leave well enough alone, could you?"

"And let my sister marry a murderer? No way. People like you get away with things every day. I hear my husband talk about getting people off all the time, and with your money, your father no doubt had to just flash a few big bills in front of some underpaid D.A. and that was it. No more problems for his baby boy."

I shook my head at how in the dark she was. "You have no idea what you're talking about. I didn't kill Melissa. She overdosed."

"I'm sure. How much does it cost to get a coroner to say that?" she spit out at me.

"I swear to God if Nina is hurt because of you, I'll make your life a living fucking hell. You think I can buy whatever I want with my money? If one gentle hair on Nina's head suffers because of what you've done, I'll devote every last cent of what I have to making you pay. You have no idea what you might have done this time."

Kim shrugged and shot me a sneer. "I told her the truth about you. If that causes you a problem, so be it."

Balling my fists in rage, I tried to keep myself from hitting a woman for the first time in my life. "That man I made sure you and your family were safe from might have her right now. I don't know where she is, and I can only hope that the Feds have him in custody or he hasn't made bail, because if he has, he's going straight for her. All of this because you couldn't let her be happy."

"I was just doing what I promised my father I'd always do for Nina—watching out for her. Your father made sure I had to do that."

Suddenly, everything I'd been holding in exploded from me. "I'm not my fucking father or brother! I've done everything in my power to show you I'm not like my family. If I hadn't made sure you were safe all that time, Karl would have killed you and your family. I'm not a murderer. All you had to do is have your husband do a little searching and you'd know that. Melissa overdosed. I'm not saying I wasn't there or don't still feel responsible in some way still to this day, but I didn't kill her."

Kim's stood there in her living room shifting her weight from foot to foot just like Nina did when she was uncomfortable. She knew I hadn't killed anyone and still she'd told Nina about Melissa. Slowly, she moved toward the table behind the sofa and pulled a sheet of paper out of her purse.

"My father believed you were a murderer. Just because Jeff found out otherwise doesn't mean I have to believe him instead. All that lawyer talk just meant that they didn't have enough evidence to overcome your family's money."

I took the paper from her hand and recognized it as the same kind as in her father's notebook. He'd told my mother the truth. He hadn't revealed everything he'd found about our family, just as he'd promised her. He'd intended on it never seeing the light of day. That's why he'd sent her the information with that last letter he'd written.

Looking down at the sheet of paper in my hand, I read what Nina had learned about me. "Your father had decided not to disclose this information. Why did you think you had to do that now?"

"My father was a sentimental man who didn't always think clearly. He was likely impressed with your mother, probably because of her money, and didn't realize that the person he was friends with wasn't that girl he knew in college but just the matriarch of a family of murderers."

Never before in my life had I wanted to hurt someone like I wanted to hurt Kim at that moment. How anyone so petty and nasty could be related to Nina and her father baffled me, but I didn't have time to ponder what had happened to make her so vicious and jealous. I stuffed Joseph Edwards' notes into my pocket and left Kim to her misery, unsure of where I'd find Nina but sure that I wasn't going to get any help there. I just had to hope I found her before Karl did.

On the way to my car, I felt my phone vibrate and quickly yanked it from my coat, hoping to see Nina's name. It was only Daryl, though. Sliding my finger across the screen, I answered it and prayed he had some good news. "Tell me you found something," I said as I opened the driver's side door.

"Nothing yet," Daryl said in a somber voice. "Do you have any idea why she left? Varo said you went to see her sister."

I started the car and breathed a sigh of disgust, not only at Kim but at myself too. "Yeah. She found out about Melissa. Kim told her."

Daryl said nothing for a long time, and then in his indomitable way, summarized my current problem succinctly. "Well, that was pretty stupid of you not to tell her, especially since you did nothing wrong."

"Thanks. Just what I need. I know it was stupid, Daryl, but since I still think I was to blame, I just never found a way to tell her."

"Water under the bridge now. We need to find your lady ASAP. So where would she go?"

Places raced through my mind, but none stuck out as the place I thought she'd go when she was upset. "I have no idea."

Daryl made that clucking noise with his tongue he made when he was thinking and then said, "I'd suggest getting the word out to your hotels. She might go to one of them. I already checked the penthouse and no one has seen her there tonight."

I headed out of Kim's development toward home, wondering how much time I had. "What do we know about Karl?"

"What do you mean? I thought the Washington guys had him."

"I have no idea if he'll be held. If he's not, how do I know he won't find Nina before we do? And do you have any idea where the hell West is? Varo didn't know where he was, and I'm worried he has something to do with Nina's disappearance."

"Whoa! I don't think she's disappeared, and what the fuck would West have to do with that?"

Putting my foot to the floor, I gassed it and began weaving through traffic. "I have no idea, Daryl. It just seems suspicious that Nina's gone and West is nowhere to be found. I don't care where he is if he isn't with Nina, but if he is, he better fucking hope I don't find him when I finally get to her, or I'm going to fucking kill him."

"Alright, alright. Let's not get crazy here. I'm heading out to the house now. Maybe Varo found something there or Jensen remembered something about the ride home that can help us. I'll see you there in a little while, right?"

"Yeah. If you find out anything before I get there, call me. Do you understand?"

"I get it. Don't worry. We'll find her safe and sound."

TWENTY

TRISTAN

I drove like a demon over the roads and highways that led to the house I shared with Nina, my mind drifting back to the events that now made her run from me. Even though they'd occurred seven years before, the memory of them still ached like a fresh wound.

A haze of smoke hung heavy over the spacious room, a telltale sign of how long we'd been ignoring the outside world. Melissa giggled as she lay sprawled out across the bed while Sam smacked her on the bare ass. I guessed I should have been jealous since I was sleeping with her, but it wasn't anything exclusive between us and I didn't care if she liked to fuck him too.

Sex wasn't what kept us together. Coke was.

Well, coke was what kept me there. Melissa didn't like what coke did to her, preferring the more mellow high of pot or pills. But she was always good for what I wanted, knowing I liked it and eager to please me, no matter the cost.

I had no idea what the fuck Sam saw in any of this. True, he liked to smoke every so often, but nothing like how often Melissa did. I wasn't even sure I'd ever seen her straight. Not that I cared.

"Tristan, come over here. I'm all alone and Sam won't talk to me," she whined in a voice that I found cute at times other than this. She knew it and used it anytime she wanted something from me.

Sam stood from the bed and pushed her away. "I won't talk to her because she doesn't make any fucking sense. Maybe if you'd get your head out of the clouds one in a while, Lissa, I'd be able to understand what the fuck you're talking about."

This was their usual routine when Sam felt like a third wheel. To everyone but Melissa, it was obvious he was in love with her. I had a feeling he hated me and wished I'd just disappear so he could walk off into the sunset with her, happy and high as a fucking kite. I would have been okay with that, as long as it didn't interfere with what she and I had.

What that was exactly was hard to say, however.

I liked her well enough. I liked her even better when she spread lines out in front of me in an effort to make me happy. I didn't love her, though, and she knew it.

That fact never stopped her from wishing it wasn't true.

"Melissa, I don't feel like talking. I leave that up to Sam," I said with my usual curtness.

Lying there naked, she looked up at me with a stare that was supposed to make me want to fuck her. "Tristan, why are you so mean?" she cooed. "You're always so mean to me."

"You don't want to see mean," I said, hoping to put an end to her attempts to seduce me. Turning to look at Sam, I nodded my head toward her. "Talk to her. That's all she wants."

"I don't want your fucking scraps, Stone," Sam snapped before storming out to Melissa's living room to sulk as he always did.

I let my gaze travel to the bed where Melissa lay pouting. I understood why Sam would want her. Perfect body, at least as perfect as money and a plastic surgeon could buy, lots of laughs, and not a lot of frustration. For many, she'd be the perfect girlfriend.

"Tristan, he's gone. You don't have to sit over there all by yourself anymore. Come over here on the bed with me."

Leaning forward, I snorted the last line on the tray and shook my head trying to handle the sensation of the coke teasing the inside of my nose. "You should be nicer to Sam, Melissa. When I go, he'll still be here."

"Don't say that! You're not going anywhere," she cried as she rolled off the bed onto her feet to come toward me. "I won't let you."

She knelt between my legs and gazed up at me with bloodshot blue eyes. I knew what she wanted, and if I hadn't been so fucked up, I might have wanted it too. "Get up off your knees," I ordered only to have her respond by shaking her head.

"Tell me what you want and I'll give it to you. Whatever you want, Tristan. Tell me." As she spoke, her hands slid up my thighs to the crease of my legs. "I could make you happy if you'd let me."

I pushed her hands away, and she careened back into the table. "I have everything I need to make me happy."

She looked up at me and frowned. "Then why aren't you happy, baby?"

Reaching toward her, I smoothed her platinum blond hair from her eyes. "Don't try to use what you learned in Psych class last semester on me, Melissa. It's not going to work."

"When I become a psychologist, you'll see. I can be your therapist and solve all your problems."

"That'll be the day you're a therapist," I said casually without care for her feelings.

Her face fell as her eyes filled with tears. Why I was such an asshole to her I didn't know. Even if I believed what I said, I didn't have to say it. She'd never been anything other than completely devoted to me and I couldn't even muster up enough feelings to be kind to her.

Closing my eyes, I tried to shut out the truth of how much a fuck I really was.

"This isn't happy, Tristan," she whispered as she lay her head against my knee. "This isn't happy."

"Well, it's all we have. If you want happy, I'm not the person to be with. Stick with Sam."

"Someday, Sam and I will be together. I know it. He'll be in love with me still and I won't be in love with you anymore, so we'll finally be together. But then you'll be all alone, my Tristan without a soul in this world."

"Jesus, Melissa. Stop being so fucking maudlin. I have women all the time. I'm not alone."

Standing, she sat on my lap and straddled me. She cradled my face in her hands and shook her head. "You're more alone than anyone I've ever met, baby. I could change that. I want to change that for you."

My hands slid over her perfect ass and pulled her into me. "I like the way we are. You like the way we are, don't you?"

She didn't dare say she didn't and risk my rejection, and I took advantage of that fear. I saw it in her eyes, though. She loved me, or felt what she thought was love. Fuck, I didn't know what she felt at that moment.

Her hand pressed against my heart, a gentle touch that should have meant something to me. "Your heart is beating so fast."

"That's because I don't spend my time smoking that shit. You wouldn't be such a downer if you gave up the smoke and tried coke."

My vision blurred as that moment of my past came crashing full on into my present. Over and over, I had to tell myself I wasn't the murderer Kim thought I was. If only I could convince myself.

"I'd do that if I thought it would make you happy," she whispered next to the corner of my mouth. "Would it make you happy?"

I turned my head away from her. "You're too fixated on happiness, Melissa."

"Would it make sex better?" she asked before snaking her tongue over the shell of my ear.

"Yeah, maybe," I answered without any thought as to whether my answer was true and not caring.

"Then maybe I should do it," she said with a smile as she scooted up my lap, exciting me.

I stilled her movement before she got me too hot. "Then you're going to have to get more. I finished all of it."

Melissa leapt off my lap and skipped over to the nightstand next to her bed. Pulling out a vial, she showed it off and threw it to me. "You underestimate me, Tristan."

She dropped down next to the table in front of me and spread four lines out. Before I could even have one, she'd snorted two and was moving for a third. I pulled her back by the hair and pushed her hard onto the floor. "Don't be so greedy."

I saw in her eyes as they filled with tears that her feelings were hurt. She'd done exactly what she believed would make me happy and still I didn't come across with anything but nastiness. As she began to cry, something inside me softened toward her, and I pulled her up onto my lap, still unsure I wanted anything physical from her that night but hoping I could stop her tears.

Covering my mouth with hers, she teased the inside with her tongue, exciting me. Pressed against me, she moved her hips back and forth, giving me a preview of what she wanted. Her wet pussy slid over the front of my jeans, drenching them, and for a moment, I wanted her.

But she came with far too much baggage for me at that moment, and Sam was bound to return at any time. The scene he'd create alone was enough to make my cock go soft. I pushed her away and shook my head. "Maybe later, Melissa."

Stung by my rejection, she slid off me, smacking me across the face as she left. "Fuck you, Tristan!"

She kicked the tray of coke as she stormed out, sending the powder into a white cloud that slowly fell in puffs to the floor. I watched in disgust as the rest of my night was ruined in mere seconds, content to ignore both Melissa and Sam in favor of sitting alone until I figured out where I'd be able to find more coke and hopefully salvage the night.

I had no idea how long I'd sat there consumed by my own thoughts when I heard the first siren. It seemed to come out of nowhere and suddenly be so loud it drowned out everything in my head. Another and then another followed, and my instincts kicked in. Quickly, I dialed Rogers to get me the hell out of there. I didn't need another arrest for possession.

I'd barely gotten to my feet when the cops stormed through the door. There was no escaping. My guilt was obvious by the coke all around me. Pushing my hands through my hair, I tried to make myself look less fucked up, but it was no use. What was the term—caught red-handed? That was me. Again.

As they led me out, I saw the paramedics working on Melissa as she lay motionless on the floor next to the living room sofa. Sam paced back and forth, wringing his hands and praying aloud for her to be okay while a cop tried to get him to answer his questions about what she'd taken and when. For a moment, his answers, no matter how disjointed they were, scared the hell out of me, but I'd get out of it. Melissa would be okay too, assuming they pumped her stomach to get rid of any pills she'd taken.

Everything would be okay. My father's money would see to that.

I pulled off the side of the road and leaned back to close my eyes as the memory of what happened next flooded into my brain. Melissa never made it out of that apartment that night. The mixture of prescription drugs and cocaine sent her into cardiac arrest, and she died there on that floor surrounded by strangers as they took Sam and me away.

Arrested and charged with murder for giving her the drugs, I spent the night in jail before my father's attorney got me released. I didn't find out she'd died until two days after she was gone when I was finally home safe and sound in my parents' house.

I sat silently listening to my father explain in detail what would happen to me as he paced from one side of the room to the other, stopping only to glare at me and shake his head.

"What is wrong with you? You've had everything a boy could want. A good education. The best of tutors. Yet still you act like some street kid who doesn't know better. That girl died. Did you know that? You're charged with her murder."

The news of Melissa's death hit me like a brick to the face. Whatever he expected me to say, I couldn't speak. It was like all the air had been sucked out of my lungs.

"Did you hear me?" he bellowed, leaning his face down in front of mine, so close I saw the gold flecks in his brown eyes as they flashed his anger at me.

"Victor, don't do this to him. His friend is dead. He needs time to mourn her. You can talk about the rest of it later."

I looked at my mother as she spoke to defend me, knowing I didn't deserve her kindness. My father stormed out, leaving her alone with me. I didn't deserve that either.

Cradling my face in her hands, she smiled that gentle smile she always gave when she thought I needed saving. "Tristan, I don't know how to reach you. What is it that makes you like this?"

What she meant by 'like this' was a mystery to me. Like what? Any normal American twenty-two year old male? Every other person my age I knew? But I understood my role in this drama and acted accordingly. "I don't know."

"Honey, if you have a problem, we can get you help. There are places where you can get help."

I couldn't give her the answer I knew she needed to hear. She needed me to say I'd accept her help and stop living my life. I couldn't tell her that, so I just nodded, letting her think she'd saved me, at least for now. My father was right, but I didn't care. Someday, my mother would realize that too.

I shook my head to push away the memory of that Tristan. That me had been selfish and careless, thinking I was the only one whose wants and needs mattered. God, I couldn't help but cringe at who I'd been all those years ago.

Now all those terrible acts had finally caught up with me, as I always knew they would. The problem was that now when the most important part of my life was torn from me because of what I did, all I could do was hope that when I caught up with Nina that she'd see that Tristan didn't exist anymore.

I checked my phone for any message or text from Nina. Nothing. Where was she? Was she alone? Images of West or worse, Karl, holding her marched through my mind. No! I couldn't believe that. She was safe. She had to be.

My fingers tapped out a message I prayed to God she saw. *I know what Kim told you, but I swear she's wrong. Tell me where you are and I'll come to you. Don't do this. Don't let everything we have mean nothing.*

After ten minutes, I knew she wouldn't be answering my text. I didn't expect a few words to fix everything. The damage my past had inflicted on us would require far more than that. I didn't expect anything, in fact. Nina had accepted all my demons, even if she'd done so unknowingly at times, but I'd made the biggest mistake of my life by not coming clean just days before as she and I lay in bed that morning for the first time in months. She'd practically begged me to tell her everything, and I hadn't. I didn't know why. Maybe I'd hoped I wouldn't have to tell the woman I loved that I was a thoughtless, callous dick to someone who only wanted love from me, and my carelessness with her had led to her death.

Before I put the car in gear, I tried one more time, hoping at the very least she was receiving my messages and at best she was reading them. *I know I promised to tell you everything, but sometimes a man wants to have the woman he loves see him as more than he actually is. I wasn't trying to hide what happened then. Please believe me.*

I got no response.

Daryl and Varo were waiting for me outside the house when I pulled up, their faces telling the story I didn't want to know. Stepping out of the car, I asked, "Nothing? You've got no clue where she is?"

"Nothing yet," Daryl said nonchalantly as he tugged on his beard, betraying how worried he really was. "What took you so long? I figured you'd be driving at the speed of light."

Varo said nothing, but I could tell he had something on his mind. "You seem to want to say something. Speak up," I ordered.

"I think you might have been right about West. I've been thinking about how he acted today at lunch. He was angry about having lunch with Nina and Jordan. She was playing matchmaker, so I figured he was annoyed about that, but now that he's vanished, maybe it was more."

Daryl spoke up before I could. "What do you mean more? Did he have something against Nina?"

Shaking his head, Varo frowned. "Not so much something against her but something's been bothering him for weeks. I can't put my finger on it, but something's different."

"Something's bothering him? Something's different? What the fuck does that mean? Are you saying he wants to hurt Nina?" I bellowed as fear tore through my body. West may have been the older of the two bodyguards, but she was no match against him. He could subdue her in seconds and she'd be gone.

"No, no. I just mean he seemed more resentful of things once I moved into the house. Even though it was only for a short time, I think he had a problem with that. I just can't imagine he'd hurt her, though. If anything, I got the feeling his problem was with you, Mr. Stone."

"Have you tried calling her?" Daryl asked, easing the tension around us only slightly.

"No," I answered, shaking my head. "Only texts."

"What the fuck is with your generation? A phone is for talking. You know, with your voice? You think she wants to hear from you through misspelled words? She wants to hear you, man. Call her."

Maybe he was right. I took my phone out and pressed 1. Her phone rang, which was a good sign. At least I could still believe it was turned on and still with her. By the fourth ring, I'd all but given up on her answering, but then I heard her voice so full of sadness say my name.

"Tristan."

I turned away from Daryl and Varo and walked behind the car. "Nina, I'm sorry. Please tell me where you are so I can come to you."

"No, not this time, Tristan. I needed you to tell me the truth and you broke your promise. I can't do this anymore."

Her voice was barely more than a whisper. I pressed the phone hard to my ear to hear her, even as I dreaded her next words. "I know I messed up. I know. But you don't know the truth. I need you to know that."

With tears in her words, she spoke the worst thing I'd ever heard. "You've made sure I can live a comfortable life. Not happy, but secure. I just can't do this with you anymore. Maybe if I'd been brought up in your world, but I wasn't. I'm still that middle class girl, no matter how much the clothes I wear or the house I live in costs."

"Nina, don't hang up! Tell me where you are. Let me explain. Don't let everything we've been through mean nothing," I pleaded, knowing I had only the slightest chance of changing her mind.

"I can't. I love you, but we're just no good together. Goodbye, Tristan."

"Nina! Nina!" I screamed into the phone, but it was no use. She was gone.

Hanging my head, I struggled to know what to do next. I had no idea where she was, and she didn't want to see me anymore. To her, we were over.

"Tristan, what did she say?" Daryl asked behind me, but I couldn't tell him. I couldn't admit I'd finally lost her. "Tristan, did she tell you where she was?"

I shook my head and turned to face him and Varo. "No."

"Then we can use the GPS tracking software to find out."

"What? I don't have that on our phones."

Daryl smiled and for the first time since I returned, stopped pulling on his damn beard. "I'd hoped she would willingly tell you where she was, but when love doesn't do the job, technology can. I had it installed on her phone right after you left. I figured that way if she was ever in trouble, we could find her."

I couldn't stop myself from smiling. "You're not kidding? Then show me how the hell I find out."

Slipping his phone out of his pocket, Daryl tapped his finger on the screen a dozen times and turned the screen to face me. "Time for a little trip. Better get that plane of yours revved up."

I leaned forward to read the words in front of me.

Venice, Italy.

Daryl grinned like a Cheshire cat. "Don't you love technology?"

"Damnit, Daryl. I should have you put that on my phone."

TWENTY-ONE

TRISTAN

I left Varo at the hotel and set out to find Nina, unable to track her down to any specific place in Venice after she turned off her phone. Unsure of where to begin, I let my feet take me back to the one place in the city other than our hotel room that meant anything to me.

The Piazza San Marco.

It was midday by the time I reached the square. Tourists milled about snapping pictures from every vantage point possible as artisans and vendors hawked their wares to eager buyers. I paced every inch of the piazza, my eyes scanning every arch and hidden corner, but I saw no sight of her.

This place was haunted with memories of a time when Nina and I were happy. I wanted to believe we were happy then. Maybe we'd never truly been happy because I'd never been completely honest with her. If so, I was to blame for any sadness she'd felt because she'd been with me.

I could change that, though. I had to believe that or my being there in that place where I'd finally realized I could tell her how much I loved her was all for nothing.

Hours passed as I sat watching families move through the square, parents chasing after young children who hopped and skipped on their way over the stone pavers oblivious to the flocks of birds they disturbed as they played. The sun traveled in its natural path across the sky until I'd sat there long enough to see the last rays of its light as it began to set behind the Museo Civico Correr. Nina had told me about the museum's paintings, in particular one that even though it had been painted centuries ago showed the city as nearly the same as it stood today.

As I replayed her sweet attempt to educate me on Venice's art treasures, I caught a glimpse of her through an archway walking down the arcade. She wore her hair pinned up in a bun, but I'd know the shape of her beautiful face anywhere. I bolted from my seat and ran toward her, losing her when a crowd of school children paraded hand-in-hand in front of me. By the time I'd navigated around them, she was gone.

Frustrated, I scanned the area for any sight of her, finally accepting I might not see her that day. I could wait, but if Karl knew she was alone in Venice, every second she wasn't with me meant she was in danger. I needed to find her.

The final minutes of daylight highlighted the colorful mosaics on the Basilica di San Marco, and I stared in newfound awe at them, seeing for the first time what Nina had explained about them. The arches and columns of the basilica stood as they had for centuries, tributes to the Gothic style of the Middle Ages. I'd known none of this until Nina.

The crowds began to thin as people left the square for dinner and other parts of the city. I hadn't given up hope, though. If I had to search every square inch of Venice all night, then I would.

"You can't do this, Tristan."

I turned to see her standing behind me, looking more beautiful than I'd ever seen her, even in jeans and a T-shirt with her hair pulled up. "I can't do anything else. If you won't come with me because you love me, then come with me so I can keep you safe."

Sadly, she shook her head. "I have to learn to live on my own, Tristan. I can't do that if I go with you."

"I don't know if Karl knows you're here. West is missing, so I don't know if he's a danger to you."

"It doesn't matter. I have to go."

She turned to walk away, but I grabbed her forearm to stop her. "Don't do this. Let me explain, at least. Give me the chance to show you how much I love you."

Tears filled her eyes, and she looked away. "I know you love me, Tristan. I've never doubted that, strangely enough. I just can't be with someone who won't be truthful with me, no matter how difficult it is for him."

"Look at me, Nina." She shook her head, but I gently pulled her by the chin so she was forced to face me. "Look at me. I know I was wrong, but I never meant to deceive you about Melissa's death. I know that doesn't make what I did right. I know."

"Do you ever wonder why we can't just seem to be happy? Why there always seems to be something that ruins what we have?"

Quietly, I admitted the truth. "No. I know why. It's me. I'm fucked up. That doesn't mean I don't love you more than even you believe, though."

Cradling my face in her hands, she looked up at me with love in her eyes. "What am I supposed to do? We keep messing this up. Maybe we're just not meant to be, no matter how much both of us want to be together."

"I can't believe that. I've never loved anyone before I met you. I can't believe you'd be sent to me just to show me I don't deserve to be loved. I won't believe that."

Her hands slid from my cheeks as she hung her head. "Sometimes it's just not meant to be, Tristan. It's not that I don't love you. I'll always love you. We just can't seem to get it right."

I clutched her wrists gently, afraid if I didn't keep hold of some part of her she'd run away and I'd lose her forever. "I know, but give me another chance. Let me show you I can be the man you deserve." Nina tried to back away from me, shaking her head, but I saw something in her eyes that told me there was a chance. I couldn't let that chance slip away. "Hear me out. Listen to what I have to say and then listen to your heart."

Nina stood silently staring at me and finally gave me a tiny nod. "Okay. I want to know everything."

"Everything. I promise. Just as soon as we return to the hotel, I'll tell you all of it."

Nina slipped her hands from my hold and shook her head. "No. Right here. I believe you bared your soul to me the last time we were here. I want you to do that now. Tell me everything about the worst I believe about you here near that very spot you told me you loved me and couldn't live without me."

"Fine. I'll tell you everything."

We found a bench and I took a deep breath. "Her name was Melissa and she died because I didn't take care of her. But Kim was wrong. I'm not a murderer. Melissa died from an overdose of prescription drugs and cocaine. That's why the charges were dropped and I never went to trial."

Nina grimaced like she was in pain. "Did you love her?"

I thought about her question and hesitated. I wasn't in love with Melissa that night or any other night, but did that mean I didn't have a responsibility to her? I had to tell Nina the truth, no matter how it made me look.

"I don't think I was capable of love when I knew Melissa. That man thought only of his wants and desires without any care for what others needed. I wasn't even a man then. I looked like one, but I didn't act like one. A man would have taken more care with her."

"Were you with her?" Nina asked sharply, her voice full of condemnation.

"Yeah," I said, nodding.

"But you didn't care for her?"

"I cared for her enough to sleep with her and use the drugs she got me, but no, I didn't care for her like I care for you. I was a selfish boy who took what he wanted and didn't give a damn about what she wanted."

Nina's eyes searched mine. "What did she want, Tristan? Did she want you?"

"She wanted me to love her like she loved me."

There in that one statement was the indictment I deserved. A confused girl who only wanted me to love her got nothing but my callousness in return for all she gave me. And now I risked losing the woman I loved because of how I acted then.

"I think I know what she felt. You don't understand what you do, Tristan. You say so little that someone who loves you has to fill in the blanks, so of course, we fill them in with what we hope you feel. Only she was wrong. She hoped you'd love her, but you didn't. I want to believe you love me, but how do I know? You kept secrets from me. You left me alone for months and never answered my messages. You don't know how painful that was."

I took her hand in mine and brought it to my lips in a kiss. "I know. I'm sorry. I thought that was the only way to keep you safe. I never meant to hurt you. The man I am now is sickened by how I treated Melissa. But I can't change that. All I can tell you is that I wasn't guilty of murdering her. If I was guilty of anything, it was carelessness with her. That's all."

"You say that like it's some small thing. Like being careless with someone's heart is a minor offense. That girl loved you, Tristan, and what did she get in return? Nothing. No, well, she got to spend time with you. That's something, I guess."

Nina's eyes flashed her anger at me as her words cut me down to size. If she wanted me humbled, she was doing a damn good job at it. "I can't change that, Nina. All I can promise is that I'm not that person anymore. I love you—completely and more than even I thought I could."

"You know what? I'm tired of hearing that you can't change that. Someone loved you and she died because you didn't care. That's the truth of it. You didn't care enough for her and she died. Maybe it wasn't your fault, but the way you treated her was. I'm just not sure I want to risk my heart on you anymore."

Angrier than I'd ever seen her, she stood to leave—leave me, leave us. I couldn't let her. I had to make her see what we had was worth fighting for. Forcing her back down onto the bench, I dropped to my knees in front of her, knowing this was my last chance to convince her to listen to her heart.

"You promised me you'd never leave. You promised you were mine forever. Stay with me. Don't be like the person I was. Do what your heart tells you instead of what your head says. I love you. I always have. I can't do this without you."

"I'm sorry. I am. I just don't know."

Her words were like knives to my heart, each one plunging in and carving me up. "No! I can't believe that. I won't believe that. You love me like I love you. You take up every inch of brain, pushing out everything else. I can't live without you. I know I should have said these things every day, but I'm saying them now. I love you so much it hurts sometimes. The months away nearly killed me. We promised each other no more leaving. Stay. Let me show you the kind of man I am because of you."

Her hand slowly caressed my cheek as a tear rolled down hers. "How can I know you won't hurt me like you did her?"

I leaned into her palm and looked up into that beautiful, sad face. "I love you. If I ever do hurt you, it won't be because I don't care. Don't let everything we've gone through be for nothing. I swear to cherish you like you deserve, and someday I promise you'll see I'll be the kind of man who deserves you."

Nina closed her eyes for a moment and when she opened them, I saw my last chance had passed. As I waited to hear her answer, I held my breath, my heartbeat pounding in my ears. When she shook her head, I thought all was lost, but then she spoke and I heard the sweetest words in the English language.

"For a guy who doesn't say a lot, you sure do know how to say exactly what a girl needs to hear. I love you. I don't want to imagine my world without you, Tristan. I thought I could live without you, but I don't want to."

Rising to my feet, I took the woman I loved in my arms and kissed her in front of the whole world to show everyone she was mine and I was hers. As I held her in my arms, I whispered, "No more secrets, no more time apart. From this point on, I'm making it my job to make sure you're the happiest woman in the world."

Nina smiled up at me and held my chin between her thumb and forefinger. "You better."

Taking her left hand in mine, I turned it over and saw the engagement ring I'd given her. "I see you didn't take the ring off."

She let out a deep sigh and shrugged. "I guess I just wasn't ready to really be done with you, after all."

I'd made sure when I checked into the hotel that I'd gotten the same room Nina and I had the last time we traveled to Venice. She needed to know that time had meant everything to me. I might not be able to say the right words, but maybe I could show her I truly couldn't live without her.

Candles flickered in glass containers placed around the room, giving the suite a magical feeling. Nina looked around the rooms like she had the first time, her eyes full of wonder as she admired what I owned. "It's just as beautiful now as it was the last time we were here, Tristan."

Sliding my hands over her shoulders, I whispered, "All for you. Everything I own is yours."

She turned in my hold and shook her head. "I don't want things, Tristan. What I need you can't put a price on or buy. As long as I have the truth from you, I'll be happy. Just the truth."

"I can't live without you, Nina. If truth is what it takes to make you happy, then it's yours. I just hope the real me is what you want."

She wrapped her arms around my neck and stood on her toes to kiss me softly on the lips. "I'm madly in love with the real you, Tristan Stone. I know you're not perfect. I just need you to promise no more secrets. I can't live like that."

I cupped her nape and looked into those gentle blue eyes. "No more secrets. But right now, I don't want to talk about secrets or anything else. I don't want to think about anything but you and me and reliving our last time here."

Her body melted into mine as my lips covered hers in a kiss full of need. She was perfect in my arms, right where she was meant to be. I slid her shirt over her head and her jeans from her legs to reveal mismatched bra and panties. I couldn't help but smile. All the money in the world, and she still was that wonderfully unspoiled Nina who stole my heart all those months ago.

"You're laughing at me, aren't you?" she said with a sexy smile.

I slowly lowered myself to my knees and looked up at her. "No. Not laughing. Charmed."

A delightful blush colored her cheeks. Biting her lip, she rolled her eyes. "Charmed, huh?"

Hooking my thumbs under her panties, I gave them a slight tug as she wiggled her ass to help me remove them. They easily slid down her gorgeous legs, and stepping one foot out of them, she kicked them away, leaving her standing there open to me.

I licked my lips in anticipation of tasting her sweetness on my tongue, dying to feel her slick pussy grind against my face as I slowly and methodically inched her toward release. She looked down at me, so sexy yet innocent, and I couldn't wait anymore. With my hands on her ass, I pulled her to me and slid my tongue the full length of her wet slit. Her body trembled when I touched her swollen clit, and I flicked the tip of my tongue once more as she whimpered my name.

Her hands skimmed over my scalp, gently pulling me closer to give her what she desperately wanted. My mouth devoured her, loving every moment of pleasure her pussy gave me. I wanted to give her that pleasure back. I wanted to be the only man who made her body sing.

"Tristan, my legs can't hold me up when you do that," she whined sweetly above me as I sucked her clit between my lips. "I'm going to fall…"

Lifting my head, I smiled and licked my lips to taste her. "I won't let you fall. Just hold on to my shoulders. This was all I could think of the whole flight here."

I wasn't lying. To ward off the anxiety that always came with flying, I'd spent the entire time fantasizing about making love to her. It had been the best flight I'd ever had.

"You were pretty confident I'd take you back, weren't you?"

I slid my middle finger through her wet folds and sucked the taste from the tip into my mouth. "I had to hope."

Her expression softened as one finger slid slowly inside her. "I do love a confident…ohhhh...man."

Another finger made her eyes roll back. "And a man who knows how to…oh God…work with his hands."

"Hang on." While my fingers fucked her, my mouth fastened on her clit and I sucked softly, bringing her to the edge before easing back. I wanted this to last.

Nina's fingers pressed hard into my shoulders just as she was about to come, but by the fourth time, I was ready to give her what she wanted. One last thrust into her made her cunt contract, and her legs buckled. I held her there as waves of pleasure rolled through her, my fingers and mouth unrelenting as she begged me to never stop.

Finally, when her legs stopped trembling and I knew she could stand on her own, I sat back on my heels and smiled up at her. "Welcome home, Ms. Edwards."

She dropped to her knees and kissed me full on the mouth. "That's one hell of a welcome. If I didn't hate being away from you so much, I'd leave more often."

I fisted my hands in her hair, pulling it loose from the bun. "No more leaving."

TWENTY-TWO

Nina

The room was the same as last time we'd been in Venice, but we were different. The Tristan and Nina who'd found each other then hadn't been the real us. They'd been pretending. I'd thought I'd known him, but I'd only scratched the surface. Now I knew the man I loved more than anyone in the world was so much more than a gorgeous billionaire crazy about me. When all the money and possessions were pushed aside and it was just him and me, I saw how deep his emotions ran. The rest of the world could go on believing they knew him, but I knew the truth.

I knew the real Tristan Stone was the man who sat in front of me now. Imperfect, troubled, and bound to fuck up again, he'd bared his soul to show me the man he'd been and now had changed to be. That honesty was worth more than any amount of money.

And who was I on this second visit to Venice? I'd been pretending too—pretending that the fantasies of a teenage girl were reality. When I met Tristan, he appeared to be everything any woman could want. Gorgeous, wealthy, and confident, he was perfect. I'd never allowed the idea that he could be human with flaws like any regular man to get in the way of my fantasy of who I believed he was. Then, when I found out he wasn't perfect, I'd run.

Months without him had shown me I didn't want to run anymore, or so I'd thought. Then Kim's poisonous words flooded my ears and I lazily slid back into my teenage fantasies, condemning him for a past I'd never even given him a chance to explain.

Now it was time for me to grow up, to accept the fact of who Tristan truly was. The man who would fly around the world to impress me and protect me, even though flying terrified him. The man who agreed to bare his soul in the Piazza San Marco not once but twice. The man who'd promised to give me whatever my heart desired, and never once failed.

The man who even with his flaws had proven himself time and again. Now it was time for me to prove myself.

Tristan stared down into my eyes with a look that told me he had other ideas than a discussion of how I'd been a goddamned fool. As he tenderly stroked my jaw line, a look of need sparked in his eyes. "Come with me, Nina. I want to show you something."

His hand grasped mine, but I pulled him back. "Not yet. I want to say something first."

Those beautiful chocolate brown eyes filled with worry, and I watched as he knitted his eyebrows. "Okay. Say whatever you need to. We're all about truth."

I reached up and cradled his face in my hands. "It's nothing bad. I just need to tell you that I've been a childish fool. I expected you to be some perfect specimen of men, but that's not fair. I gave you a hard time when you returned to me last week, but it's been me who's run away all the time. And every time I ran, you followed me. You followed me, and I believe you'd follow me if I left again."

Smiling, he turned his head to kiss my right palm. "A good man knows when to drop the Alpha shit and chase after the woman he loves."

"I acted like an ass, and I'm sorry. I preach about telling the truth and then I don't give you chance to do just that."

"Thankfully, I have a plane that allows me to fly wherever I want to find you," he joked.

"I'm serious, Tristan. What kind of fiancée am I? I know you hate flying and I run away to a place where you have to fly to get to me. I've been such a terrible person. I'm so sorry."

"I told you. I fantasized about making love to you the whole time, so not another word about it. No more apologies. From now on, we follow the truth policy. Right now, to be honest, I'm more interested in less talking and more doing. Come with me."

He took my hand and I followed him to the first bedroom. On the nightstand sat a bottle of champagne in a silver ice bucket and two glasses. A tray of fruit sat next to them filled with every fruit I'd ever heard of, except strawberries.

"Are we eating first or drinking?"

Tristan pointed toward the bed and smiled. "Sit. I'm overdressed for what I have in mind."

As I laid back on the bed, he shrugged out of his shirt. Still leaner than before he left for all those months, his body was tight and sinewy. My gaze slid over his abs, as defined as they'd always been, and I rolled off the bed wanting more than just to watch him undress.

"Let me help," I said as I pushed his hands away from his pants.

He lifted them, as if in surrender, and looked down as I knelt in front of him. "Help is good. This is even better."

I lowered his zipper and reached my hand in to palm his stiff cock. "There's one thing I want the same as last time. Remember?"

A sexy smile spread across his lips and he nodded. I eased his pants and boxer briefs down over his hips until his cock sprang free. Positioned perfectly, I merely had to open my mouth and take him into me. Gripping it near the base, I slipped the swollen head between my lips, playfully flicking my tongue over the silky soft skin.

"Toying with me may be a dangerous choice right now, Nina," he whispered hoarsely as I eased only the head in and out of my mouth.

Staring up into his eyes full of desire, I slid my tongue up the length of him. "Turnabout is fair play."

He ran his hands through my hair and pulled me down onto his cock. "Then let's play."

I moved up and down his shaft, teasing the spot just under the head where he was most sensitive with my tongue and fingertip. Taking the full length of him into my mouth, I crushed my nose against the hardness of his muscles just below his navel and inhaled his fragrance, a combination of a musky sex smell and soap, as I swirled my tongue around the base of his cock.

"God, Nina, you're killing me, baby."

There was nothing better than hearing him groan raggedly while I sucked his cock, totally in control of his pleasure. In those moments, his walls came down and he showed me a side of him so intimate and personal the world never saw in the man so restrained all the time. Tonight, though, I could tell as his hands guided my head up and down that he wanted to control our lovemaking.

He pumped into my mouth, his long, thick cock stretching my lips to take all of him. I followed his pace, loving the sound of his moaning and panting as I brought him closer to the final edge. His hands fisted in my hair, gently at first but then sending tendrils of pain across my scalp as his body began to surrender to my mouth.

In a voice hoarse with desire, he groaned, "Oh, fuck…right there, baby."

I closed my eyes and felt the first spurt of cum hit the back of my tongue. My left hand clawed at his abs as my right hand milked the base of his cock and gently squeezed his balls. I wanted to taste every drop of him. He filled my mouth, and I swallowed as I opened my eyes to watch him staring down at me, those gorgeous brown eyes watching me give him pleasure.

When he was done, I sat back on my heels and smiled up at him. He stepped out of his clothes and led me to the bed. Easing me onto my back, Tristan slid up over my body until our faces met. His dark eyes stared into mine, holding me with his gaze. "I want you, Nina. When I thought I might never get you back, something changed inside me. You make me want to be the man I see in your eyes. You do that to me."

He pressed my legs apart with his hand and slid the length of his cock over my clit, nearly driving me out of my mind. His hand slid over my breast, cupping it as his thumb and forefinger squeezed my nipple to a sharp peak. Arching my back, I urged him to ease my need, but he was in control, not me.

"Don't tease, Tristan," I moaned as he hovered over me, grinning and licking his lips.

Leaning down to flick the tip of his tongue over my nipple, he looked up at me and whispered, "No teasing. Just pleasure." His lips closed around the needy peak, and he sucked it sharply into his mouth, sending ribbons of desire through my body.

Expert at building my need, he bit down gently, making my pussy run wet. Much more and I'd come without even having his cock inside me. I dragged my nails down his back, urging him to give me what I want.

He lifted his head, a look of pleasure on his face. "Tell me what you want." His voice was ragged, signaling any control he possessed was slipping away.

"I want you inside me. Don't make me wait."

Slowly, he plunged into my body, filling me so completely that he nearly took my breath away and ridding me of all the emptiness inside. My fingers dug into his biceps as he thrust in and out of me, his body moving over mine as he made my body his once again. I adored him. Needed him. Wanted him.

When he finally let me come, my body ached from need, able to cling to him but little else. For hours we lost ourselves in one another, him giving me delicious orgasm after orgasm and filling me as often as I came for him. We'd worshipped each other as we should have, making up for lost time.

Taking me in his arms, he held me and tenderly stroked my skin as he whispered how much he loved me. I believed him. As scary as it was to take that chance, it was even scarier to think of my life without him.

After a long while, he gently rolled me onto my back and placed a kiss on the tip of my nose. "Are you hungry?"

"I could eat. Are you?"

Smiling, he said, "I can eat. Making love for hours should always be followed by a meal in bed."

Tristan poured us champagne and lifted his glass to make a toast. I couldn't help but smile. There I was in Venice, in a gorgeous hotel suite my fiancé owned, drinking champagne in bed. Was this really my life?

"What's the smile for?"

"I just can't believe this is my life. I mean, look at us. In bed drinking champagne. Do people really do this?"

He kissed me tenderly on the lips. "They do, and from now on, we do."

When he said that, it seemed so natural. What was a girl to do with a man like this? "Then let's toast to our life of champagne in bed."

"I have a better toast. Here's to us finally accepting the happiness we've been running away from for so long."

Raising my glass, I met his with a clank. "And more time in bed."

Tristan dangled a bunch of grapes just above my mouth. I craned my neck to grab one with my teeth but only ended up biting the air. Taking one grape off the vine, he held it between his teeth and smiled. "Do you remember that first night I fed you?"

Nodding, I said, "Yes. It was the most erotic thing I'd ever experienced." Plucking the grape from his mouth, I popped it into my own. "I think it's time I fed you."

He swallowed the last of his champagne and leaned back against the headboard. "Mmmm, I like that."

Climbing on top of him, I took the glass and grapes out of his hands. "Then this is perfect. I'll be the last woman to do that for you."

He gave me a devilish grin and looked up at me as I straddled his hips. "I really like that."

I grabbed a chunk of pineapple and placed it on his tongue. "Here's to us being the first and last of many things for each other."

His face grew serious, and he stroked his thumb over my cheek. "I love you, Nina. Don't ever doubt that, no matter how I screw things up. I love you."

Leaning down, I kissed him lightly on the lips and slipped another grape into his mouth. "No more talk about messing up. We're in Venice, in love, and in bed eating fruit and champagne. And when we get up tomorrow morning, I'm holding you to a promise you made the last time we were here. That means museums, Mr. Stone. It's time you see Venice for what it really is."

He smiled and I knew he remembered his promise. "It's isn't the Louvre, but it's a deal. First, though, I have all night with you before we head out to the museums. I plan to make the most of it."

Some problem at the hotel forced the concierge to interrupt us just as we planned to leave for our museum tour, and I was forced to wait in the suite for hours while Tristan cleared up the mess. Just when I believed we'd miss the chance yet again for me to show him the art wonders of Venice, he returned, ready to learn all about what he'd been missing in the art world.

As we walked hand-in-hand to the Piazza San Marco, I explained my plans for the rest of the day. "I first want to take you to Ca' Rezzonico. There's an entire floor dedicated to paintings that show what the city was like in the eighteenth century. Then we can visit the museum you found me at yesterday, Museo Civico Correr."

"We can go wherever you want. I told you it's about time I get some culture."

Climbing the massive marble staircase to the first floor of Ca' Rezzonico, I asked, "Did you know this was a palace before it became a museum?"

He shook his head and smiled. "No, I didn't."

"It was. In 1936 they opened it as a museum, but it was first built in the mid-1600s. Wait until you see the way they arranged it. The entire place looks like it would if it was still a palace. It's really quite beautiful. Oh, and the Triumph of Zephyr and Flora..."

My words trailed off as I watched a man hurry away from the top of the stairs and through the first floor. I hadn't assumed we were alone, but something about him seemed odd, as if he hadn't wanted us to see him.

We reached the first floor and I couldn't see him anywhere. Tristan squeezed my hand, and I turned to face him. "Nina, what's wrong? You look like you've seen a ghost."

I forced a smile, not wanting to ruin our museum tour. "It's nothing. I thought I saw someone."

"The man in front of us a second ago?" he asked as he looked left and right for the man.

"It's nothing. It's just that last time I was here—remember you were supposed to come with me and I had to go with that giant bodyguard instead? Well, I met a man here who said he knew my father. That man we just saw looked like him."

Tristan took me by the shoulders and stared down into my eyes with an intense look that frightened me.

"Nina, I need you to think about this. What did that man say to you?"

I hesitated for a moment and he repeated his question. I didn't want to say what that man had told me and bring up all the terrible things from the past, but finally, I said, "He told me he thought it was a shame the people responsible for my father's death were never charged."

"And you think that man was the same person as the one who just nearly ran away when he saw us?"

I didn't know. It could have been him. He did look similar to him, especially his tanned skin. I wasn't sure, though. "You're scaring me, Tristan. I don't know if it's the same man. It could be. I just don't know."

"I'm not trying to scare you, but I think we need to get out of here. Something's wrong. I feel it."

We hurried back down the stairs and out the museum doors. Tristan didn't say anything, but I knew he was far more worried than he wanted me to believe. We walked along the Grand Canal for as long as we could with him looking behind us every few feet. Finally, I realized that we weren't going back to the hotel.

"Where are we going? The hotel is back there."

"Just keep walking," Tristan said, his tone serious.

"What's going on?"

He pulled me into a dark corner and shook his head. "I thought they had him. I thought we'd be safe. Nina, no matter what happens, I won't let anything hurt you. Trust me."

His words were meant to calm me, but I saw fear in his eyes. "You're scaring me. What's going on?"

The sound of footsteps on the stone walkway told me someone was coming. Tristan's hand tensed on my arm as they came closer, and he pushed me behind him. A large man came around the corner and for a moment I held my breath until I heard a familiar voice.

I peeked around Tristan and saw Varo standing there. "I've been looking for you. You lost me at the museum. We need to get you out of here. The plane's ready to go."

Tristan held my hand tightly. "What's happened?"

"Daryl called me. He's worried about Karl. He's been released."

"Released?" I asked as I moved to Tristan's side. "Is he here?"

Varo looked around and shook his head. "I don't know. We need to leave here."

Tristan didn't question my bodyguard's order, which told me he believed we were in danger. If I had any doubt, the gun in Varo's hand put any uncertainty to rest. As Tristan asked him if he remembered something or another, I began to get scared.

TWENTY-THREE

TRISTAN

Varo followed us as I led Nina and him along the streets of the city looking for a water taxi to take us to Marco Polo. As long as we got to the airport, we'd be safe, at least until we got back to the States. There I knew I could protect Nina much better than in Venice.

As we walked quickly back toward the Grand Canal, we ran into crowds of people flocking out into the night, making it harder to look out for Karl and whoever he had with him. I hadn't seen his face yet, but I knew he was there. I'd taken everything that mattered to him, and now he planned to do the same to me.

My heart raced as we weaved through tourists and Venetians, all out to enjoy a beautiful night. They had no idea that among them was a man who wouldn't think twice about killing two people just like them.

Nina held my hand like she was afraid I would let go, squeezing it harder when she heard a loud noise or when someone pushed against her as they passed by. My eyes scanned the crowds as we wound through them, every person appearing guilty as the minutes ticked by.

"We should try to find a water taxi," Varo said behind us. "The sooner we get to the plane, the better."

I saw a taxi coming in our direction, but it was on the other side of the canal. To catch it, we'd have to cross one of the bridges. Pointing toward the nearest one, I tried to make Nina believe everything was going to be okay. "What's the name of this bridge? You know all about Venice."

Her eyes grew wide, and I knew she wasn't buying my act. "It's the Accademia Bridge, not that it matters. Why are you acting like everything's okay?"

"Because it's going to be. Now tell me all about this bridge so we can at least pretend our tour of Venice was successful."

As Nina gave me chapter and verse about the history of the Accademia Bridge, we began crossing over to the other side of the canal and I saw my first glimpse of Karl. We were too late.

Before she could realize what was happening, I stopped and turned toward Varo, who had seen him too. "I need you to do what you said you would."

Varo simply nodded, and I turned to face Nina. "I need you to go with Varo now. He'll get you to the plane and keep you safe. I'll be there in a little while."

Her eyes flashed panic, and she looked around to see what was making me send her away. When she settled back on me, I saw tears in her eyes. "No, don't do this! Don't send me away. You promised no more running. Don't do this, Tristan!"

I cradled her face in my hands as the tears rolled down onto my skin. "Baby, I won't let them hurt you because of me. Go with Varo so at least I can know you're safe."

"No! He's going to hurt you or worse, and then I'll never see you again. Please don't send me away."

I leaned in and kissed her as Varo moved around me to take hold of her arm. "I'll see you soon. Don't worry."

She fought him off, but it was no use. He knew what he had to do. I'd made him promise that if she was ever in danger and I couldn't protect her that he would. I needed to believe he'd live up to that pledge now.

Nina's eyes pled with me not to send her away, nearly breaking my heart, but I had no choice. For one of the first times in my life, I was doing the right thing, no matter how much it was killing me to watch her as Varo took her away.

Karl stood on the other side waiting for me. Dozens of people separated us, each in danger if I didn't find some way to get off that bridge. I took off in the direction Varo and Nina had gone, hoping to at least reach the walkway, but one of Karl's henchmen was waiting. Terrified they'd already gotten Nina, I frantically searched for any sight of her, finally seeing Varo leading her into a building and hopefully to safety.

From behind me, I heard a familiar voice. "Son, I told you not to fuck with me. Like father, like son." I turned and saw Karl's face twisted into an angry smug expression as a man grabbed me from behind to hold me. "Take him to the room."

"Planning to kill me in one of these hotels? Is that supposed to be ironic, Karl?" I asked, hoping to gain some time for Varo to get Nina out of Venice.

"I'm going to do even better, Tristan. I'm going to kill you in one of your hotels. Or maybe I could do it on your plane. I like the symbolism of that too."

"Way to keep it classy, Karl. You always were new money. Never did understand your level, did you?" His answer to my question was a hard right to my face. After a few moments, I could see straight again, if not a little blurry. I knew I had to keep him there as long as possible. A couple more insults might give Varo the time he needed to get Nina to the plane. "No wonder my father only gave you a nothing company. He knew your true worth, didn't he?"

But Karl didn't take the bait. "Always the clever one, Tristan. Take him to the room, and West, find your buddy and that girl now!"

I turned to see West standing behind me. How long had he been working for Karl and living just yards away from Nina? I watched him take off to hunt down Varo and Nina and prayed to God I'd given them enough time to find their way out of the city. I heard two men start to say where to search for them and then all I felt was pain in the back of my head before everything went black.

"Wakey, wakey. Time to rise and shine."

I opened my eyes and saw the familiar gold and burgundy décor of a Richmont Venice room. Karl sat in front of me with a cigar between his teeth, like some kind of evil villain character from an old cartoon. My hands were tied behind me, so I had to blink the sleep from my eyes. "Tie any women to train tracks recently?"

"Still clever, even just minutes before I finally get rid of you once and for all. I have to say, Tristan, you are one tough foe to eliminate."

Shaking my head, I wasn't sure I wanted to have this be my last conversation of my life, but he left me with little choice. The guy was a homicidal madman but even more, a colossal asshole. "It didn't have to be like this, Karl. You were my father's friend."

He blew cigar smoke in my direction and let out a deep laugh. "Friend? You don't know much at all, son. I would have figured that by now you would have found out I was never your father's friend."

"Then you were my mother's lover. One would think that would count for something. I can't imagine she'd want her son killed by the man she loved."

The smug expression slid from his face, replaced by a hint of sadness for only a moment. But then the nasty fuck was back again. "Oh, so you know about that?"

"I know she loved you and you seemed to love her."

"I adored her. I may not have had the money your father had, but I could have made her happy."

"It would have been nice if someone did," I said quietly, unsure how I felt about agreeing with the man about to kill me.

"But she left me. For him! I couldn't have that. I couldn't," he said with venom in his voice.

"She had no choice. Once Taylor and I came along, she had to stay. She's been dead for five years. Maybe it's time to forgive."

Karl stood from his seat and walked over to the bar to pour himself a drink. When he turned around with the glass in his hand, I was struck at how much he reminded me of my father. The few times I'd watched Victor Stone conduct business, he'd had a glass of scotch in his hand each time. That's what this was to Karl now. Business. But it had a lot of the personal involved too.

He walked back and took a seat in front of me again, the ice cubes in the amber liquid clanking against the side of the glass. "Sometimes there can be no forgiveness, son. Sometimes all you're left with is hatred as pure as the blood that courses through your veins."

"So you won't forgive my father or mother and decided to kill me instead? Seems pretty fucked up. You have nothing left, Karl. Can you possibly hate me so much that you have to kill me? Does the fact that you loved my mother mean nothing now?"

He drank a gulp of scotch and took a deep breath before he exhaled slowly, as if some weight had been removed from him. "If only she'd met me first. You know, I used to wish that you and your brother were my sons. Twins ran in her family, so maybe we could have had twins. I never liked your brother, Tristan. Presumptuous fuck that he was, he thought he was too important to deal with the likes of me, even as a teenager. You were different, though. More like me. He was all books and studying, but not you. I could have liked you. I did like you. You're a lot like her. I see her in your eyes, even now."

"You mean the one that's nearly swollen shut or the other one your men haven't started on yet?"

"Your one flaw—do you know what that is?"

He took another drink of scotch while I shook my head, not interested in helping him in whatever the fuck this was. "Boyish charm?"

"Smart ass. Your one flaw is that you get attached to things, people. The drugs when you were younger. This girl now. She's the reason I have to do all this."

I chafed at his mention of Nina, tugging at the ropes that held my wrists behind me. "Don't blame Nina for your being crazy, Karl. At least be truthful with yourself. You're killing me because I found out about Cordovex and how Rider's drugs were killing people. Nina had nothing to do with that."

"But that's not true, Tristan. If only you'd left things well enough alone. You couldn't, though. That's your mother in you. You found out about Joseph Edwards and then you saw his daughter. That getting attached thing, remember? Your weakness. All you had to do was throw some money at her. It wouldn't have taken much. A middle class girl probably would have been happy if you paid off her fucking student loans. But no, you had to ride in on the white horse and save her. You did this."

"My father had Joseph Edwards killed. Once I was CEO of Stone Worldwide, it was the least I could do to try to make up for that." Why I felt the need to explain my actions to this psychotic madman was beyond me, but I did.

A laugh exploded from Karl's face, startling me. "Your father never had a damn soul killed. He couldn't be bothered. You think he was some kind of shark, but the truth was he was just a workaholic. Nothing more. Well, work and those goddamned secretaries he liked to sleep with. It was the work he loved more than the people around him, though. Hell, he loved work more than he loved Tressa. He made it easy for me to get to her."

"The least you can do now is tell the truth, Karl. I know my father ordered Nina's father to be killed. He'd gotten too close to exposing the story of Judge Cashen and his daughter's deaths and Taylor's part in that. I know all about the sexual harassment case and the Judge's part in that."

Slowly, Karl shook his head. "Right puzzle, wrong pieces, son. It's true that Taylor got that girl pregnant. That smarmy fuck thought he could do a teenage girl, but he wasn't smart enough to wear a fucking condom. That he didn't want her was no surprise. She was a fucking child. A throwaway lay. But your father had nothing to do with her father's death. That was me. I ordered his death and Edwards'."

The realization that my family hadn't directly ruined Nina's family stunned me for a moment. All this time the guilt I'd shouldered had been wrong. My father hadn't been a saint, but at least he hadn't killed Nina's father. "Why? Was it because Edwards was getting to close to the dirty laundry my father wanted hidden? Did he tell you to get rid of Cashen and Nina's father?"

Chuckling, Karl lifted his glass and swallowed the last gulp of alcohol. "You have a misguided view of who Victor Stone was. A semi-talented businessman, his real skill was as a worker. He knew more about business than most men because he spent hours learning about it, but he would never have a threat eliminated. He preferred to fight it out. The competition is what he liked."

As he stood to refill his glass, I asked, "Then why were they killed if my father wasn't worried about losing the case or what Nina's father had?"

With his back to me, he answered. "Rider Pharmaceutical."

"What?"

He turned around and smiled, repeating his answer. "Rider Pharmaceutical. The success of Cordovex wasn't going to be ruined by some nosy journalist or your father's inability to keep his dick in his pants. So they had to go.

"All of this over Rider and Cordovex?"

"That competitive streak in your father extended to your mother too. When he found out, he gave me that tiny, pissant company named for her maiden name. I knew what that meant. That was his way of saying I couldn't have the woman I loved but I could have some useless company to remind me every day that he'd won. Over the years, I'd been able to make it into something and then Cordovex came. We got it through the FDA with an acceptable level of problems, but no amount of hope changed the fact that it wasn't what we wished it would be. Your father found out and fired me. He was nice enough to give me some time to come up with a way to save face when I left Stone. That's where his mistake was."

I wracked my brain to remember any evidence of Karl ever being fired, but if there had been any proof, I'd never seen or heard about it. Whatever he was going on about was fiction to feed his demented ego. "My father never fired you. This is all just to make you feel like you weren't some low level operative in a company run by a bigger man."

"So I found a way to make sure I didn't have to leave. I couldn't be forced out if the man doing it wasn't around anymore."

Karl's words slowly sunk into my brain and I suddenly realized I wasn't breathing. It couldn't be true. He must have been lying.

"I see by the look on your face you don't believe what I said. Believe it. I needed to find a way to get rid of your father and Taylor, since he'd take over the minute your father was gone. That your mother would have to suffer for staying with him was poetic justice, but I knew I'd have to find some way to get rid of you too. I figured I could deal with that later. Tressa had secretly told me that Victor planned to fire me over the Cordovex thing your girlfriend's father had found out about and thought convincing him to take a few days off would give me the chance to leave the company quietly. She told me you didn't want to go. Something about some party you didn't want to miss."

As he spoke, I remembered that time like it was yesterday. I'd told my mother I had no interest in going away with them but at the last minute, I'd given in to her constant asking me to change my mind, thinking a few days in the islands would at least offer a chance to party there with much better drugs. My mother had been so happy when I finally relented.

Rage coursed through my veins as the truth became clear. Karl had killed my family over his petty ambitions and now planned to kill me and Nina because he was a megalomaniacal fuck. "You bastard! You killed them over a fucking job?"

"I deserved that job! I made Rider Pharmaceutical a company worthy of respect and he wanted to shut me out of everything! I deserved everything he was taking away."

"You killed my entire family over some bullshit company the Feds would have ruined anyway. Cordovex would have been the end of Rider," I said quietly, still unable to process the actions of the monster in front of me.

"Not true. Rider only had to pull the drug voluntarily. The FDA is nice like that. Then it was just a matter of playing the waiting game for a few years and reintroducing it onto the market. I just had to make sure that reporter was handled. But then you didn't die in the crash."

A look of disappointment crossed his face and he shrugged nonchalantly. My living through the plane crash had put a damper on his big plans. At least I could know that even though I didn't know about it at the time, I'd been a thorn in this fucker's side.

"But then you disappeared a few months ago and all my plans could be set in motion once again. It was like God was smiling down on me from Heaven. So Cardiell was born, and I had it all, but once again, one of you fucking Stones ruined it."

Karl's face turned bright red, and he jumped up from his chair to begin pacing as he rambled on about how he'd been treated unfairly, first by my father and then by me. With every word, he sounded more and more like a madman out of his mind.

It didn't matter, though. None of his men had returned to report their success in finding Nina and Varo, which meant they'd found a way to escape. As long as she was safe, I could handle anything Karl did.

As long as I believed I'd protected her, I could die with some sense of peace.

TWENTY-FOUR
Nina

No matter how hard I tugged my arm, I couldn't break Varo's hold on me. I had no idea where he was taking me, and with each step away from Tristan, I feared I'd never see the man I loved again. I tried once more unsuccessfully to yank my arm free from his hand around my wrist, but he pulled me harder down walkway, hurrying me to some unknown place.

"Varo, you're hurting me! Let me go! We need to go back to help Tristan."

"We're going to the plane. He'll meet us there," he said coldly.

I stopped walking, forcing him to drag me. "No! I won't go without Tristan."

For the first time since we left Accademia Bridge, Varo stopped walking and turned to face me. "Nina, I gave him my word that I'd keep you safe. That's what I'm doing."

"I don't care what he made you sign when he hired you. That means nothing to me. We need to go back to help him."

"I can't let you do that. This has nothing to do with anything I signed for a job. He asked me before you left to come here to promise that I'd protect you if he couldn't. I made that promise, Nina. You just have to trust that he'll be okay."

I hung my head in frustration. "He's not going to be okay. Karl's going to kill him. Why don't you see that?"

"I can't help that. I have a job to do, so let's go."

There had to be a way to get through to him. I knew he wasn't the heartless bastard he seemed to be at that moment. That sweet guy who'd helped me when I didn't think I could pretend to move on had to be in there somewhere.

"Gage, I know this is more than a job to you. You're a good guy. I believe that in my heart. Please help me save Tristan. He needs us."

"Nina, I can't. Tristan needed to be sure you'd be safe. Just trust that he'll be okay."

I couldn't fight him like this. "Do you understand what it's like to be so in love with someone that you don't feel like you can go on without them?"

He looked away and said in a low voice, "Don't."

"It's like if they're not in the world anymore, you don't want to be either. Like if you lose that part of you, you'll never be whole again."

I saw by the look in those dark blue eyes that I was getting to him. He knew what it felt like to lose someone from when he lost Angela. It was a shitty thing to do, but I needed to manipulate that soft spot in his heart if I ever expected to get him to help me.

"Tell me you wouldn't have given anything to save Angela if someone was trying to kill her. I know you would."

"Nina, it's not the same thing."

"Yes, it is! You loved her, and if she was ever in danger, you would have given your life to save hers. How is that different from this? I'm not asking you to sacrifice yourself, but don't tell me it's wrong for me to do. I love Tristan more than I ever thought I could love anyone. Just help me find him. Please."

He let out a heavy sigh and shook his head. "I can't let you get hurt, and I have no idea how we can help him. I don't even know where they took him."

The thought of Tristan already dead and floating face down in a side canal somewhere made my chest hurt. He might be dead already, but I had to try to find him. I had to save him, if I could. "There has to be a way for us to find him, Gage. He needs us. Please. There's got to be a way."

Gage was silent for a long time before he shook his head once again. "I can't think of anything, Nina. They could be anywhere in Venice."

His grip loosened, and I tore my arm from his hold. "I can't give up on him. He needs me now, and I won't just leave him. Don't worry. Your conscience is clear. You did what you could, but I won't go with you."

Turning, I set off running toward the bridge, unsure of where to find Tristan but sure I'd never give up until I did. I heard Gage yell my name and then I felt his hand on my arm again. "No! Let me go!"

"I remembered something, Nina. There might be a way to find out where he is. Just stop so we can check."

He held me tightly, giving me little chance to run, so I stopped trying to escape. "Tell me what it is and how we do it."

Gage reached into his pocket and in seconds he was on the phone. "Daryl, they got him. We need to know where he is."

Daryl said something that sounded like it was about me and Gage nodded. "Yeah. I know. Can you find out?"

As he waited for Daryl to answer his question, I looked around, worried we might be caught before we ever found out where Tristan was. "Gage, we don't have time for this. We have to go."

He nodded again and smiled. "Thanks, Daryl. You might be right about technology. I'll tell Tristan you said hi." Gage stuck his phone back into his pocket and pointed down the sidewalk toward The Richmont Venice. "They have him at the hotel."

"How do you know?"

"I don't, but if his phone is still on him, that's where he is. Did he have it when he left the hotel earlier?"

I nodded, unsure of how Gage knew Tristan's phone was there but thrilled at the hope that he could still be alive. "Yes, he had it. He showed me a picture on it as we walked toward the museum."

Taking my hand in his, Gage smiled. "Then let's hope it's still on him. Now we just have to figure out where in the hotel he is and how we get in without Karl's thugs grabbing us."

A tour group of what looked to be at least thirty people milled about the Richmont Venice lobby waiting to check in, so we attempted to blend in with them as we figured out where Karl could be holding Tristan. Unsure if the hotel staff were helping Karl and his men, I pulled Gage behind a marble pillar farthest away from the concierge desk to plan what to do next.

"There are any number of places he could be," I whispered into his ear as I peered over his shoulder to make sure nobody had spotted us.

"The suite you two are in is on the fifth floor. There's only one other suite on that floor, so I think we should start there and eliminate that possibility. The problem is how are we going to get up there without being seen? The main staircase is in the center of the building, and there's no way we can get upstairs and not be noticed, even with all these tourists."

My mind flashed back to something Tristan had told me the first time we visited the hotel. I closed my eyes and replayed the conversation that night after we'd made love and spent hours in each other's arms. Suddenly, I remembered. "There's a back staircase that's only used by staff. It used to be a secret staircase back when this was a palace."

Two women I recognized from the concierge staff walked past us trying to herd all the tourists toward the check-in desk, but one seemed too interested in Gage and me as we stood huddled behind the column. Her stare lingered just a second too long on us, making me worry. Did she recognize me from when Tristan and I returned to the hotel?

I turned my back to the crowd and whispered, "Gage, we need to get to that back staircase, but I don't know where it is. All I know is that Tristan told me it existed."

Gage moved to shield me and nodded his head toward a hallway that transected the lobby. "If this is the front stairway, then maybe the back one is down that hallway."

"I think that could be right. We just need to get past the concierge, who I think might have recognized me from last night."

An elderly female tourist backed into a large ornamental vase and knocked it from one of the lobby's tables with her oversized purse at that very moment, and with its crash to the floor, we had a perfect diversion. She screamed in surprise, and the crowd formed in around her to see the results of her clumsiness, including the two hotel employees. Quickly, I yanked on Gage's arm to lead him away from the scene. "Let's go!"

We raced down the hallway until we reached a door that looked like a closet. Opening it, he found our back staircase. "Come on. We've got four flights of stairs to climb."

Compared to the front staircase with its gorgeous caramel colored marble walls, ornate cut outs, and candle sconces lighting the way, this staircase was sorely in need of repair. Old plaster peeled from the walls and except for a few small windows, the staircase was dark.

Perfect for someone trying to sneak around Tristan's hotel.

We reached the top floor and quietly entered the hallway connecting the two suites. Listening near the door to the one Tristan and I shared, we heard no noises. I pointed to the room and shook my head to let Gage know I didn't think that's where they were holding him.

He whispered, "Did you see the people who were staying in the other suite?"

I shook my head again. "No. How are we going to find out who's in there?"

Gage pointed to an alcove behind two columns on the left side of the hallway. I followed him there and watched as he moved toward the suite's door. "What are you doing?"

He raised his hand to knock on the door. "Ding dong ditch."

I hid behind the column and peeked my head around just enough to see him knock on the door and run behind the column across from me. After a few moments, a young blonde wearing very little opened the door and looked around to see who'd knocked. From inside the suite, I heard a man with a voice that sounded much older than she looked ask who it was.

"Nobody. I guess they were looking for the suite down the hall, honey," she answered in squeaky voice and closed the door, leaving us standing there at least knowing Tristan wasn't being held on that floor.

"I guess we can rule that out," Gage said with a smile.

"Onto the fourth floor," I said as we hurriedly crossed the hall and entered the back staircase again.

The floor below wasn't going to be as easy to search. Unlike the top floor, this one had twenty rooms instead of two suites. Thankfully, it had alcoves too where we could hide as we searched, but ding dong ditching twenty rooms seemed like a poor way to find out what we needed.

Gage held the door as we exited the staircase in the middle of the floor and hurried to the nearest alcove. Five middle aged hotel patrons stood outside a room at the end of the hall as one man fumbled with the room key. They left immediately, so at least we could guess that room wasn't where Tristan was.

"How are we going to find out if he's in one of these rooms? This is going to take forever, and we don't have that kind of time," I said in frustration as we watched them walk by us.

Before Gage could answer, I saw his eyes grow wide as saucers and followed his gaze to someone getting off the elevator. I recognized him immediately. West. He walked quickly to a room at the opposite end of the hallway and knocked.

I leaned in close to Gage and whispered, "He's in there! We need to get in there!"

Nodding, he held up his hand to calm me. "Give me a second to figure this out."

The door closed and tears began to well in my eyes. Hanging my head, I leaned against the pillar, devastated. "We missed our chance, Gage."

"You didn't think we'd just barge in there, did you?" He put his hand on my shoulder to comfort me and quietly said, "Don't worry. I'll think of something."

"No need, buddy. I'll get you in there right now."

Terror raced through me, and I looked up to see West standing there with a gun to the back of Gage's head. We were lost. Tristan would be killed and then they'd do the same to us. I'd blown it.

West led us down the hall into the room, and my first sight of Tristan nearly took my breath away. His left eye was black and blue and practically swollen shut from a beating. Blood trickled down his chin from a deep cut in his bottom lip. Even with all that, he was immediately worried about me.

"Nina, why are you here? Why didn't you just leave with Gage?" he asked as he groaned in pain.

The man I recognized as the one from the museum grabbed my arms tightly, and when I moved to help Tristan, he roughly pulled me back, hurting me. I opened my mouth to answer, but Karl spoke up before I could say a word. "She didn't leave because she loves you, Tristan. Now she'll pay for that love with her life."

"Why are you doing this?" I cried, finally needing to know what the hell I'd ever done to make this person hate me so much.

Karl turned to face me, his snake-like eyes scanning me from head to toe. "Why am I doing this? Because you're the reason why everything fell apart. Just like your father and his fucking investigation.

Because all Tristan had to do was throw some money at you to ease his guilt over your father and you would never have ended up here. He'd still have to die, but you wouldn't be here. You'd be back in your little life serving the art world in your inconsequential way. But he didn't do that. He fell in love with you and now we're here at the end of the road."

Tristan hung his head and said quietly, "I'm sorry, Nina. I'm sorry I ever waited for you that night in the alley behind the Anderson Gallery. If I hadn't…"

His voice trailed off and he closed his eyes. I couldn't let him think that I regretted one moment of our time together. He deserved better than that. "If you hadn't, I wouldn't have met you and fallen in love with the most incredible man in the world."

"How touching. Now if we're done with the staging of Romeo and Juliet, it's time for this to end. You'll be dead, and in a few years, I'll be the head of Stone Worldwide. In the meantime, one of my friends on the board will make sure my company thrives in my absence."

A large, bald man who looked nearly the size of Gage stood behind Tristan and violently yanked his head up, and Karl aimed his gun directly at him. I scrambled for anything to delay—to give Gage time to stop him—and blurted out, "Wait! Tell us how you got Rogers to turn on Tristan. He loved him like a son. He wouldn't hurt him unless you did something horrible to him."

Karl smiled, his gun still aimed at Tristan. "Ah, Rogers. I have to tell you, son, you certainly do have some very loyal people around you. Your girlfriend's right. Rogers didn't come easily. You were his world. He loved you more than your father did. It took me forever to figure out the angle to take with him. Nothing worked. Money didn't matter. Threats didn't work. But you know what did? When you fell in love with her, Rogers couldn't take it. He was jealous. Go figure. Out of all the emotions to manipulate, I only had to wait for jealousy to rear its ugly head. Once it was obvious that you were going to marry her and wouldn't need him anymore, he was putty in my hands."

Tristan's frown deepened as Karl detailed why the one person he'd always trusted betrayed him. It tore my heart apart to know I'd been the reason he'd lost Rogers.

"And then you killed him. Why, if he was helping you?" I asked.

"It seems those paternal feelings he'd always had never left after all. He was weak, and when you told him to get out of your life, I knew I couldn't trust him to handle things anymore."

I watched as Tristan hung his head and said sadly, barely above a whisper, "You made sure you took everyone from me."

Karl smirked. "Not yet, son. Not yet."

Just when I was sure he'd given up, Tristan looked over at West and said, "Obviously not everyone around me is loyal."

Karl turned to look at West and smiled. "Oh, West? He was easy. Right, West? Not everyone thinks a man your age should have everything his heart desires."

West mumbled something about Tristan being a spoiled rich boy, and then out of the corner of my eye, I saw Gage's arm move. In a flash, I heard a gun go off and the man behind me released my arms. I dropped to the floor and covered my head as two more shots rang out. It all happened so fast. Somebody yelled "Get him!" and I heard the most terrifying sound I'd ever heard in my life. A body fell to the floor and a man's voice moaned until another shot exploded and everything fell silent.

I opened my eyes and saw Karl and West on the floor in front of me and blood everywhere. Gage stood over another man in the corner of the room who looked like he'd only been grazed by a bullet. Frantically, I searched the room for Tristan and saw him slumped over in the chair he'd been tied up in. Blood covered the side of his face, and he looked unconscious.

Running over, I knelt in front of him and looked up to see a bullet had hit his right shoulder and his left eye was bleeding. "Gage! Tristan's been shot! He needs help!"

Behind me, Gage called for help while I gently lifted Tristan's head. He didn't respond to my touch, and the real fear that I'd lost him settled into my brain. Shaking my head, I let the tears roll down my cheeks as I pleaded for him to stay with me. "Tristan, don't leave me. I can't do this without you. Don't leave me here all alone. Please, Tristan! Open your eyes. Open your eyes and let me know you're going to be okay."

His eyes remained closed as I sat there praying he'd survive. I heard the ambulance in the distance as it raced up the canal toward us, piercing the night with its shrill emergency cry. "The paramedics are coming. Just hang on for me, Tristan. Don't leave me. Don't leave me, baby."

Gage pulled me away as the paramedics entered the room, and I watched as they took him away, barking out directions about how to get to the hospital. In mere minutes, he was gone and I was left standing there sobbing, hoping against hope that I hadn't lost him this time.

TWENTY-FIVE

Nina

I sat alone in the bedroom Tristan and I shared, my hands shaking as I thought about what I must do in mere minutes. Muffled voices from outside the door signaled it was nearly time. Inhaling deeply, I closed my eyes and tried to calm my nerves.

The door opened and Jordan peeked her head in. "It's time, sweetie."

I pressed my hands to my thighs and took another deep breath. "Okay. I'm ready."

She came to my side and held my hand as I stood from the bed on wobbly legs. "Just wait until you see the flowers. They're really beautiful."

"The flowers?"

Jordan smiled weakly. "That's what they say at times like this, don't they?"

I saw how hard she was trying to be mature at that moment and appreciated it. "I feel like I'm in an episode of some TV melodrama. I know you want to say something snarky or crude, so go for it."

Her shoulders relaxed, and she smiled broadly. "Thank God! I've been tiptoeing around for hours, unsure I should be myself. You've been so quiet since returning from Venice, so I wasn't sure you were up for the full version of me."

I smoothed the back of my dress and rolled my eyes. "You don't have to pretend ever, Jordan. Venice was tough, but I got through it. I'm tougher than I look."

She raised her eyebrows in faux surprise. "Tough, huh? Wait until you get out there and melt into a puddle of girliness when you see your soon-to-be husband."

Jordan wasn't wrong. On normal days, seeing Tristan in a suit he wore to work made my knees weak. Seeing him in a tux waiting for me at the altar might make me fall over. "Tell me. How's he look?"

"Totally badass with that eye patch. Leave it to him to get a black leather one."

"I meant in the tux, Jordan. How's he look in the tux?"

As she buzzed around me tugging and fixing my wedding gown, she chuckled. "Like he was born to wear one. The guy looks more comfortable in a tux than other guys do in jeans and a T-shirt."

Her words took me back to the first time I saw Tristan dressed in a tux and then to that night of the book signing at his hotel. She was right. He wore formality so well, but I knew who the man beneath the clothes was. I knew his passions and his fears, his darkness and his light.

I finally could say I knew Tristan Stone.

Jordan stood back from me and smiled at what she saw. "But when he sees you in this dress, oh, he is going to fall apart. You look stunning, honey."

I looked down at the gown I'd marry my dream man in and nodded. "I hope so. That's the point, right? It won't be much of a honeymoon if the groom doesn't like how the bride looks."

My gown felt more incredible than anything I'd ever worn. White satin that hung like it had been created just for me, it was classy and gorgeous and everything I'd always dreamed I'd be. Now, as I stood in the bedroom I shared with the only man I'd ever truly loved, I finally was that woman in my dreams.

After smoothing my veil over the back of my head, she pulled the ends out near my elbows and let them fall against my arms. One last tuck of a stray hair behind my ear and she was done. "All set. You ready to become Mrs. Tristan Stone?"

I didn't know why, but I began to tear up at those words. Mrs. Tristan Stone. They said the third time was a charm, didn't they? Looking away, I said, "I don't know what's wrong with me. I'm crying like a crazy woman."

"It's okay, Nina. This is a big deal. Just think of it this way, though. After all you and Tristan have been through, getting married is going to be like a walk in the park. Or more like a walk in the garden on a beautiful summer night."

Jordan laughed at her joke about where the wedding was to be held, and I rolled my eyes. "Funny. And by the way, not to make you nervous or anything, but you look pretty incredible yourself in that dress. Maybe tonight's the night Gage asks you out."

She smoothed her hands down over her hips and slinked toward the door. "Oh, by the way, I can report that those muscles are real and there's no sex with bugs."

I thought about what she just said and laughed. "You're terrible!"

Turning her head, she peered over her shoulder at me. "Nothing terrible about it."

"How? Jordan, did you…?"

She winked and then shook her head. "Not yet, but he stopped by my apartment one night last week. We had a nice time together."

"Take it easy on my bodyguard, okay? He saved my life."

Jordan dropped the sexy act and nodded. "I would never do anything to hurt him, sweetie. It's not everyday I have a chance with a hero."

"Okay. Then you have my blessing."

A knock at the door ended our serious moment, and she opened it to Gage standing there. With a smile, he asked, "Did someone order a hero?"

A blush raced up her cheeks, and Jordan turned to look at me with a silly grin. "Mental note to self. Hearing and skulking—expert level."

"Nina, it's time. You ready?" Gage asked, sneaking a look at Jordan.

"I am. Jordan, you ready?"

She nodded and held out her hand to take mine. Squeezing it, she whispered, "I love you, Nina. Now go marry that sexy man so we can have champagne and cake."

"And dancing," I added. Looking past her at Gage, I asked, "Do you dance?"

Flashing us a charming smile, he winked and said, "A little. Enough to get by."

I couldn't help myself and joked, "Saves damsels in distress, has superhero hearing, and he dances?"

Jordan shook her head and walked out mumbling, "Let's go, Cupid. Tristan's waiting."

Gage laughed as she passed, and when she was out of earshot, said, "She's a handful. I'm wondering what you've gotten me into."

"Nothing you can't handle."

From the back of the house the sound of the harpist playing the wedding march filtered through the open windows of the bedroom signaling it was time to go. Gage held out his hand for mine and gave me a gentle smile. "You're on. If we don't get out there, Tristan's going to think you're not showing up."

I took his hand and laughed. "We've had enough of that. I'm ready."

The stone pathway to the garden lay before me, the final walk to Tristan and our new life together. In my hand, I held my bouquet of pink and white roses straight from our garden. Tied with a baby pink ribbon, it was simple and just what I wanted for my big day. With Gage's arm linked in mine, I gazed down the pathway at Tristan as he waited for me stunning in his black tux, his expression a mix of anticipation and love.

We slowly made our way, passing boughs of baby's breath hanging by deep pink ribbons from shepherd's hooks above tea light lanterns to guide us on our way down the stone pathway. Jordan stood to the left of the minister in her gorgeous peacock blue gown holding her own bouquet of baby's breath she chose herself, and candles of all sizes stood flickering soft light behind the altar

Jensen, Maria, and Tristan's assistant Michelle and her husband sat watching Gage and me as we moved closer to the moment he'd give me away. His strong arm held me stable, even as my knees shook from nerves, and then I saw Daryl. Dressed in a black tux similar to Tristan's, he stood at his side as his best man, an odd but understandable choice. Still sporting his mountain man style, he looked like he'd gotten that bushy red hair of his cut and even taken an inch or two off his prized beard for the occasion. He smiled one of those rare Daryl smiles that lit up his features and made me want to giggle.

We were quite a group.

Finally, we reached the end of the pathway and Gage leaned down to kiss me on the cheek. With a simple smile, he handed me to Tristan, and he took my hand in his, giving it a small squeeze. In that moment, nothing else in the world mattered but us and the life we were about to embark on. I looked up at him and saw in his face everything would be all right.

We faced the minister in front of us and listened as he began the ceremony. "We're gathered here together to celebrate the joining of Tristan and Nina. We rejoice in the love of this man and this woman and wish them happiness. Marriage symbolizes the joining of two hearts, each person retaining their own individualism as both travel their path together."

Tristan squeezed my hand as the minister announced we'd written our own vows, and we turned to face each other. I pulled the sheet of paper I'd written mine on from the silk satchel around my wrist, and when I looked back at him, I saw he had nothing in his hand.

Searching his face, I tried to understand what was happening. Had he changed his mind? Fear tore through me, but he simply smiled at me and began speaking.

"Nina, I tried over and over to write my vows last night, but I never found the right words. I woke up this morning and tried again, but still nothing came. I decided I'd just say what was in my heart when it was time, so I hope this comes out right. All my life, I've had whatever my heart desired, and I thought I was happy. Then I lost everything and happiness became something I believed I'd never be lucky enough to have again. I lived like that until one day I was convinced I was meant to be alone. Then one night I met you, and from that moment I've been happier than any man could hope to be."

He stopped for a moment as I struggled to hold back the tears. This man who said so little most times was standing there in front of our friends confessing his love in a way only he could. My heart swelled at how tender and sweet his vows truly were. Straight from his heart, they were him.

"I promise to be the one who makes your days brighter. When the rest of the world can't or won't see who you are, I will. I can't promise I won't make mistakes, but I can promise that you'll never doubt I love you more than my clumsy words can ever say. I love you, Nina."

I covered my mouth with my hand, whispering, "Oh, Tristan" as the tears I'd held back finally began rolling down my cheeks. "That was beautiful."

He silently nodded and gave me a tender smile. I looked at my vows I'd written the night before and suddenly wanted to give him the honesty he'd given me. Stuffing the paper back into my satchel, I held his hand and said what was in my heart.

"Tristan, I love you. You've shown me a world more incredible than anything I'd ever dreamed of. And I'd give it all up as long as I had you by my side. If tomorrow all we had were the clothes on our backs and each other, I'd still be the happiest woman on Earth because I'd be with you. I wouldn't trade a moment we've shared for anything in the world. I promise no matter what you'll always be my knight in shining armor. And someday, when we're old and gray, I'll look back on our life together and know the night I met you was the luckiest night of my life."

With a small smile, Tristan showed me my words touched him like his had mine. We stood there silently, looking at one another like there was no one else in the world at that moment but the two us.

The minister looked at Daryl and Jordan and asked, "The rings?"

We turned and took the rings from them and the minister said, "Repeat after me. I pledge to you my love and my life."

Tristan and I said those words together and gave each other the rings that symbolized our union. All that remained were the minister's final words.

"May you keep the vows you made here today. May you comfort each other, share each other's joys, and support each other in times of trouble. By the power vested in me by the State of New York, I pronounce you Husband and Wife. Tristan, you may kiss your bride."

Cradling my face in his hands, Tristan pressed his lips to mine in a gentle kiss and whispered in my ear, "I love you, Mrs. Stone."

"It's about time. I thought you two would never get here," Daryl joked.

I leaned around my new husband and shot his best man a dirty look. "I'll take that as your congratulations."

Jordan piped up with a comment that put him in his place, and I saw Gage smile at her, probably wishing he had said it. As everyone around us hugged and kissed me and shook Tristan's hand, I thought for a moment how much I wished my father had been there to share this with us.

Performing her maid of honor duties perfectly, Jordan corralled the guests to the table in the garden where the reception was to be held. When they had all moved away, Tristan still stood there, looking down at me in that special way that told me he had something on his mind.

"What's wrong? I see that tiny pout you make when something's wrong."

"It's nothing. I was just thinking about my father and how much I wished he could have been here."

Tristan pulled me close in his arms, and I knew he felt the same. After all that had happened, our love had finally helped us put our families' pasts behind us.

"Somewhere, our mothers are smiling," he said with a wink. "You know how mothers are."

I reached up and gently ran my fingertip over the edge of his eye patch. "I guess I got my pirate after all."

"I guess you did, at least until the doctors say my eye's better. What do you say about letting this pirate escort you to the reception and maybe later I'll make you walk the plank."

"Was that a joke, Mr. Stone?" I asked with a smile, knowing he was working hard to make me forget my sadness over my father missing the biggest day of my life.

He shrugged and said, "It happens sometimes. I don't know what kind of pirate that makes me, though."

Holding his face in my hands, I kissed him long and deep. "It makes you my pirate, and that's the best kind there is."

"I have a surprise for you," he said quietly. "Close your eyes."

I shut them tight and let him lead me ten steps before we stopped. I heard our guests whispering and Tristan said, "You can open them now."

Slowly, I opened my eyes and saw everyone sitting around a long table lit with a line of lanterns and candles down the center. Jordan stood smiling and poked Tristan in the arm. "I wasn't ready yet." Turning to speak to me, she said, "Wait till you see this."

She flipped a switch in her hand and above us what looked like hundreds of little white lights lit up. Strung along grapevines that created a canopy above the table, they twinkled like the night sky. I gazed up at the incredible work Tristan had done to make our reception so beautiful and turned to see him smiling at me. "It's so gorgeous! Thank you."

"I can't take the credit. Jordan is the architect of all this."

I looked over at her and saw her nod. "Your husband here called me as soon as he got home from the hospital and asked for my help. I told him I knew exactly what you'd like. Remember that day we spent looking through all those wedding magazines? You saw that picture of the nighttime garden wedding and loved it. So I told him just leave it to me."

Looking around at all the beautiful decorations and lights, my eyes began to fill with tears at how wonderful the people in my life were. "It's perfect. Thank you. And thank you everyone for being here to celebrate this with us."

"No crying allowed," Jordan joked. "Tonight is a celebration. So let's get to eating and drinking. The best caterer in the city has made us a meal to put all other meals to shame."

Tristan and I sat down at the head of the table as uniformed waiters filled the table with baskets of sliced baguettes and tomato basic garlic crostini. As everyone talked and laughed, a gorgeous summer greens salad was served, and then we all enjoyed our meals of peppered beef and lemon herb chicken home style, sharing our meal together, like it should be.

I watched as the people closest to us enjoyed a night that had been a long time coming. Under the table, Tristan squeezed my hand, and I turned to see him looking at me. I squeezed his in return and whispered, "You did good here, Mr. Stone."

"You haven't had any cake yet."

"I'm not sure I can fit cake in after all of this," I joked. Of course I would eat a piece of our wedding cake.

His expression grew serious, and he lowered his voice to the merest of whispers. "Are you happy?"

"Crazy, blissfully, in love happy. What about you?"

"Happier than I ever thought I could be. I love you, Nina."

Before I could tell him I couldn't wait until everyone had left so I could show him exactly how much I loved him, a waiter wheeled a cart toward us with a towering pink icing wedding cake made from individual cupcakes decorated to look like pink roses. They were exactly like the picture I'd shown the caterer, even more perfect, if that was possible.

"I made them promise me they'd match your bouquet, Nina," Jordan said with a smile as the cart stopped next to me.

"They're gorgeous!" I said as I took one from the waiter and passed it to Tristan. Turning toward him, I said with a smile, "And if you try to push that cupcake into my face, we're going to have our first married fight, Mr. Stone."

"And ruin a piece of art like this? Never," he said with a chuckle.

"Gorgeous and intelligent. I love that in a husband."

Jordan stood and cleared her throat as the waiter poured champagne into everyone's glasses. When we all had ours, she began her wedding toast.

"Congratulations to Tristan and Nina on their marriage. This day has been a long time coming. I've known Nina for years and always told her that good things happen to good people. I believe that. These two people are the perfect example of that. So now, after all they've been through, this good thing has happened to these good people. Tristan and Nina, here's to great things in your future. You deserve them."

We all raised our glasses, and Tristan clanked ours together as we and our guests said in unison, "To great things!"

I slid my hand over Tristan's and weaved my fingers through his. He turned his head and looked at me with an expression that told me he wished we were alone. I knew how he felt. I did too.

"I think they're going to expect a dance from us at least before they let us sneak off to begin our honeymoon," I said quietly as music began playing behind us.

"Then let's give them what they want," he said with a sexy grin.

He lead me to the center of the garden as the harpist played a love song, and there, for the first time, we danced as husband and wife. Later, after all the guests had gone and we were alone in the house, he took my hand and led me to the sitting room where we'd sat together that first night. As I stood in the middle of the room, he turned on the music and we danced to our song as he whispered the words to Nothing Compares To U by Sinead O'Connor just like he had that summer night a year before.

The music ended and cradling my face in his hands, Tristan whispered, "I love you, Nina. You make happier than I likely deserve."

"You deserve everything good. Remember, good things happen to good people, and you're one of the best people I've ever met, Tristan Stone. So no more talk about not deserving things."

He kissed me and whispered in my ear, "Then let's get this honeymoon started."

EPILOGUE

TRISTAN

"Daddy, tell us the story about when you became a pirate!" Tressa squeals as she jumps onto the bed. "Dee wants to hear the princess story, but I want the pirate one."

Diana, her twin sister, struggles to lift her leg to pull herself up onto the bed, so I reach over and take her into my arms. My reward is one of her adorable smiles, a better payment than anything I could ask for.

With a pout, she says in her tiny voice, "Daddy, Tressa pushed me out of the way. I want to hear the princess story. Tell the princess story, pleeeeeease."

Two pairs of brown eyes stare up at me, begging for their favorite stories and making the word no an impossibility. Both girls bounce on their knees as they wait for my decision on which story would be the one for the night.

"Diana! Tressa! Where are you?" Nina calls from the hall. "Are you bothering your father? He just got home from work."

She appears in the doorway, her arms folded across her chest and her best "Mom" face on to let the girls know she isn't happy they've done exactly what she told them not to. I'm more to blame than they are, though, since they know I love to see them after a long day away.

"Girls, your father's tired and it's time for you to go to bed."

Diana turns to face her and quickly answers, "Daddy said he'd tell us a story. He's going to tell us about the princess."

Her sister isn't going to be beaten on this, though. "No, he's going to tell us about when he became a pirate. That's my favorite story ever."

"It's okay, Nina. I like this part of my day best, so I think I'll tell both stories tonight."

In unison, my daughters throw their arms up in the air and yell, "Yay!" They take their seats next to me and wait for me to begin. Which story to choose, though? I prefer the princess story, to be honest.

Nina walks over to the bed and sits down on the edge, taking Tressa's long brown hair in her hands to braid it. "You know what story I like."

I smile at her playful jab. She prefers the pirate story, like Tressa, so now we have a standoff. After pretending to consider my choices, I announce my verdict. "I think the pirate story is the one I'll tell first."

Diana's mouth turns down into an adorable pout much like the one her mother puts on when she's disappointed, so I pull her onto my lap and whisper near her cheek, "But I promise to tell the princess story just for you, honey."

Her pout turns into another of her gentle smiles, and she wraps her little arms around my neck. Kissing me on the cheek, she whispers, "Okay, Daddy."

"One night, your mother and I were at the hotel in the city and she told me that she wished I was a pirate. I told her that I didn't think saying 'Aarrgh' all day during meetings would work, but she insisted that she'd love me even more if I were a pirate."

Tressa reaches out and points at the patch covering my left eye. "And that's why you got an eye patch—because Mommy wanted you to be a pirate."

"Exactly. So now, Mommy gets to say she's married to a pirate."

"Daddy, do the pirate voice!" Tressa squeals. "Please?"

In my deepest voice, I do my best pirate imitation. "Aarrgh, matey! Shiver me timbers!"

The 'shiver me timbers' part always makes her giggle, and she bounces on the bed again, excited her story has been the first one told. Nina just smiles, like she always does when I tell the story to explain why I wear an eyepatch. It's far more interesting and less traumatic than saying I got beaten to a pulp when Karl tried to kill us. Five year old girls demand a far more romantic story than that.

"And that's why you have your pictures on your arms," Tressa says, motioning on her own body where my tattoos are.

"Yes," I say with a smile, amused by the way she refers to them.

Diana touches just above my heart and says, "The snakes are for you and your brother, right?"

I nod. "My brother and I were twins like you and Tressa, so I got the snake tattoo to show we were forever together, no matter what, just like you two."

"Let me see the one about us, Daddy," Tressa pleads as she tries to push up the sleeve on my right arm to show the tattoo I had done right after the girls' birth.

I unbutton my shirt at my wrist and slide the fabric up my arm to show the bottom of a tattoo that depicts an intricate pattern symbolizing both Diana and Tressa. Like the one on my left bicep, it's a tribal design but this extends from my right shoulder down my arm to just above my wrist.

As Tressa runs her fingers over my arm, tracing the tattoo from the crook of my elbow to my wrist bone, Diana whispers in my ear, "Now the princess story, Daddy. Tell the princess story."

"Once upon a time, there was a beautiful princess. She had long brown hair and the prettiest blue eyes. When the prince saw her for the first time, he saw nothing but those blue eyes staring at him. He took her for a ride in his carriage and got to talk to the princess, and he felt like he'd never felt before. She was sweet and gentle and just the kind of princess he wanted."

Nina rolls her eyes and smiles. Diana whispers near my cheek, "Say her name, Daddy."

"And then he found out the princess's name was Nina."

"The same as Mommy's name," Tressa says as she looks back at her mother.

"Yes, it was. So the prince asked the princess to come live with him and help him make his castle more beautiful. Thankfully, she said yes and she became the princess at his castle."

Diana whispers again, "And then she painted the prince a picture, right, Daddy?"

"She did. And she made the prince very happy. Then one day the prince and princess had two little princesses."

"Tressa and Diana!" Tressa screams, throwing her arms up in the air. "No fair, Daddy. That story's about you and Mommy. That's why the pirate story's better."

"Time for bed, girls. Say goodnight to your father."

Nina picks Tressa up and carries her out of the room to the bedroom she shares with her sister. "Goodnight, Daddy!"

Diana remains silent on my lap, staring up at me. Looking down into her soft brown eyes, I ask, "Ready for bed, sweetheart?" as I lift her off my lap and place her feet on the floor.

"Are we princesses, Daddy?" she asks in the cutest little voice.

I look down at her beautiful face and see so much of her mother in her, far more than I ever do when I look at her sister. Tressa is a true Stone—much stronger than Diana, who is gentle and kind, like her mother. She's also very much like Nina with her questions. Tweaking her on the tip of her nose, I nod. "Yes, you're my princesses."

"Will I be a pirate like you when I grow up?" she asks, her eyes wide with curiosity.

Picking her up, I hold her in my arms and kiss her cheek. "No, you won't be a pirate, honey."

She presses her forehead to mine and studies me before she says quietly, "That's because I'm a girl, right?"

I have to laugh at her logic. "No, it's just because there can only be one pirate in the family and I'm already one."

Diana tightens her hold on my neck as I begin walking toward her room. "I love your stories, Daddy. Do the prince and princess live happily ever after?"

We reach her room and I gently place her on the floor in the doorway. Her little face turned up toward me, she waits for the answer to the question she asks me every night. With a smile, I nod. "Yes, they live happily ever after, honey. Night, night."

I opened my eyes to see Nina next to me curled up like she always was in the morning. Rubbing the sleep away, I marveled at how real my dream had been. I almost wanted to walk down the hall to see if we were the parents of two little girls. As I struggled to remember the fine details that were already beginning to slip away, I shook my head as if to answer my own doubts.

Nina snuggled next to my side. I wrapped her in my arms and kissed the top of her head, still thinking about the children in my dream. Twins, just like my brother and me, they were as different as night and day.

"Hey, what's up? You've been tossing and turning all night," Nina said quietly. "You okay?"

Looking down, I saw her smiling up at me as she laid her head on my chest. "I'm fine. Just had a wild dream."

"What about?"

"Well, we had twin daughters named Diana and Tressa, for one thing."

Nina smiled a big grin. "Two little girls? I've always dreamed of having a little girl, but two would be even better. And twins? Wow!"

"Not feeling too rushed, are you? We're still on our honeymoon and I'm already talking about kids. Or at least my dreams are."

"Wait until I tell Jordan. Twins she can be an aunt to. She's going to love it."

"How do you feel about it? That's the important part."

She thought about it for a moment and smiled slyly. "I like it. I guess only time will tell."

Rolling her over, I slid over her body and kissed her on the lips. "Time may tell, but I think for now, we should see what we can do to help it along."

As she looked up at me with love in her eyes, she nodded. "I like the way you think, Mr. Stone."

For now, it was just the two of us, but maybe someday we'd be blessed with those little girls I dreamed about. Until then, Nina was my princess and I was her pirate.

And we'd finally found our happily ever after.

THE END

Be sure to visit K.M.'s Facebook page for all the latest on her books, along with giveaways and other goodies! And to hear about Advanced Review Copy opportunities and all the news on K.M. Scott books first, sign up for her **newsletter** today!

Other books by K.M. Scott:
Crash Into Me (Heart of Stone #1)
Fall Into Me (Heart of Stone #2)

Love sexy paranormal romance? K.M. writes under the name Gabrielle Bisset too. Visit Gabrielle's Facebook page and her website at **www.gabriellebisset.com** to find out about her books.

Books by Gabrielle Bisset:
Vampire Dreams Revamped (A Sons of Navarus Prequel)
Blood Avenged (Sons of Navarus #1)
Blood Betrayed (Sons of Navarus #2)
Longing (A Sons of Navarus Short Story)
Blood Spirit (Sons of Navarus #3)
The Deepest Cut (A Sons of Navarus Short Story)
Blood Prophecy (Sons of Navarus #4)
Blood & Dreams Sons of Navarus Box Set

Stolen Destiny
Destiny Redeemed

Love's Master
Masquerade
The Victorian Erotic Romance Trilogy

CPSIA information can be obtained at www.ICGtesting.com
Printed in the USA
LVOW08s1721060314

376323LV00006B/995/P